DISSIDENT

TRACKER BOOK 2

DEVEN KANE

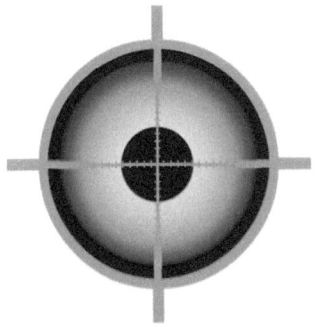

DISSIDENT

TRACKER BOOK 2

RAGe Real Author Guaranteed edition. 100% human.

Front cover image and author photo by Wendy McAlpine

ISBN-13: 978-1-989509-00-5

BISAC: Sci-fi & Fantasy | Dystopian

Books by Deven Kane

ONE ◉

"LIVE IN THE SHADOW of an Enclave? Not a chance." There was no need for Amos Morgan to raise his voice. The conviction behind his words, coupled with the loathing in his voice, was as sharp as the combat knife fastened to his belt.

The shopkeeper, Mateo Reyes, remained silent. It was Don, the towering bruiser with the baritone drawl, who replied first. "Starvation wages are better than no wages. They still put food on the table, I guess. But I'm with you, Amos. I couldn't live this close to Hoarderville. I feel sorry for these people."

"The people of Jericho are desperate." Mateo waved a hand, directing their attention to the shantytown nestled against the exterior wall of the Enclave. "When you have few alternatives, a daily work permit appears promising."

They stood just outside the door of his clothing shop, one of many lining the crooked footpaths in the shantytown. The retractable awning, faded and worn at the edges, shielded them from the late-afternoon sun. Their position gave them a clear, covert view of the Cascadia Enclave.

Amos wore a sturdy jacket, mid-thigh in length, an effective cover that concealed his combat knife. Don Benoit, his long-time friend and traveling companion, was clad in similar attire, for the same pragmatic reason. To the casual observer, there was nothing to distinguish them from the other inhabitants of the shantytown.

"I've never been this close before." Amos scowled, craning his neck as he tried to estimate the wall's height. "All my life, I've known the Enclave was here, on the coast, but I've never been interested in seeing how the high-and-mighty live."

Cascadia Enclave was an impenetrable fortress, the ultimate symbol of the Hoarders' dominance. Towering walls enclosed the opulent megacity on all sides, and a series of fortified gates restricted access. A phalanx of hard-bitten soldiers guarded the nearest gate, a threatening reminder that entrance was hard-won.

Etched above the gate, stark and utilitarian, was its sole identifier: Gate Seven. An open balcony was positioned directly above the chiseled signage—twenty feet wide, Amos guessed —bristling with advanced weaponry.

Just a few reminders that we're not wanted. Amos ground his teeth at the Hoarders' heavy-handed tactics. They kept everything of value under their tight-fisted control—energy, technology, medical advances, education—and therefore all the political power.

For the most part, Hoarders acted as if anyone living outside the Enclave didn't exist. At best, there was grudging recognition of their value as a cheap source of temporary labor, to carry out tasks the Hoarders considered beneath them.

A shantytown, dubbed Jericho by its founders, evolved outside the walls, fanning out from Gate Seven. A daily line-up of hopefuls competed for work permits, their sole access into the

Enclave and a day's meager wages. There were always fewer jobs than applicants. Those fortunate enough to acquire a permit would find themselves banished outside the walls by nightfall.

To repeat the same process the next day. And the next.

Jericho's marketplace was situated in close proximity to Gate Seven, with a varying number of makeshift housing units fanning out beyond the gate. The market, as fragile as it appeared, provided for the needs of job-seekers and their dependents.

Amos found the atmosphere in Jericho a strange mixture. To the untrained eye, it evoked the shared camaraderie of people facing a common plight. Just below the surface, however, resentment smoldered against the Citizens of the Enclave— Hoarders—and the unjust society they represented.

The crumbling husk of the Old City lay to the south, indistinct in the fading afternoon sun. From their current vantage point, the empty towers of the City's former financial district were visible, rising in the distance like a miser's skeletal fingers.

Amos's gaze lingered on the ruins. They were a long way from the familiar surroundings of their Hub, hidden in the sub-basement of Eastside Mission.

And you thought you knew what "hidden in plain sight" meant. His inner voice couldn't resist the taunt. *A coward who abandoned his own brother wouldn't have what it takes to live in a Hub next to Cascadia Enclave.*

Shut up, Gabriel. Amos scowled, determined to stifle the annoying voice. *I can't change the past. I was barely twelve years old. This can't be about revenge.*

Don glanced at him, raising one eyebrow, and leaned closer so Amos alone could hear him. "Let it go, Amos. This is no time for second-guessing yourself, especially this close to the Enclave."

Without waiting for an answer, he turned his attention to the shopkeeper standing on his left.

No, much more than a shopkeeper. An ally. A conduit of information. The leader of a Hub audaciously set in the shadow of the Enclave. He'd given his name as Mateo Reyes, but added nothing more. Anonymity was a potent weapon for a Hub in such a high-risk location.

"If you'd be kind enough to point us to your dropbox, we'll collect the mail and be on our way." Don's drawl and lighthearted speech were by no means accidental. His steadying influence had calmed his companions' frayed nerves in the field on more than one occasion. "Neither rain nor snow, nor gloom of night … you know the routine."

Mateo squinted at him, adjusting the brim of his cap so he could look Don in the eye. His mannerisms were quick and precise. In Amos's opinion, he had the look of someone who'd lived under the threat of discovery perhaps too long already.

"We have no dropbox *per se*," Mateo replied, his unblinking gaze disconcerting. "It would be impossible to keep one secure in a setting such as ours. Your 'mail,' as you call it, will arrive shortly. We must wait."

"Wait? For how long?" Amos spoke with more heat than he intended. "Garr sent us here because he thought you had valuable intel. We need a way inside those gates. The Hoarders won't stop Implanting people unless we do something about it." He paused for a deep breath. "We need to be gone before nightfall. Can you help us or not?"

Mateo's penetrating gaze was now focused on him. Amos tried to put a name to his expression. *Like he's categorizing me. Filing me away for future reference.*

"While we wait, perhaps I could interest you in a brief tour of Jericho," Mateo said, his voice neutral, as if their close proximity to the Enclave was of no consequence. "We're rather proud of the community we've built here. In difficult circumstances, I remind you."

"A tour?" Amos struggled to keep his voice down. "Didn't you hear what I said? We don't have time for sightseeing."

Don laid a cautionary hand on his shoulder. "We'll wait as long as necessary," he said to Mateo, who transferred his gaze from Amos to Don without comment. "And, now that you mention it, I wouldn't mind taking a closer look at Hoarderville. With an experienced tour guide, of course."

"Very good," Mateo replied, dipping his head in a slight bow. He gestured to the dirt path outside, trodden into hardness by the passage of many feet. "I trust your 'mail' will arrive by the time we return. And please, take advantage of my wares before we depart. As a merchant, I must make sales here in the 'shadow of the Enclave,' as you call it."

He crossed between them into his shop, returning with a pair of caps similar to the one he wore. "These are some of my most popular items. They provide excellent protection from damaging exposure to the sun's rays."

He gave the caps to Amos, his peculiar gaze unchanged. Amos handed one to Don, and put on his own.

Not just protection from the sun. He recognized, belatedly, Mateo's subtle strategy. *Protection from prying eyes on the wall. No one can suspect we're anything more than anonymous hopefuls, looking for work.*

TWO ◉

MATEO LED THE WAY into direct sunlight, adjusting his cap to shield his eyes. Amos and Don fell in on either side of him, each pulling his cap lower to overshadow their faces.

Amos felt the familiar quiver between his shoulder blades. They were *very* exposed, and much too close to the Enclave, in his opinion.

"Our population is in a constant state of flux," Mateo said, as if he were a professor delivering a lecture to an attentive class. "People come and go all the time. Some arrive full of hopes they'll be given daily work permits, while others have more realistic expectations. The over-assuming ones—the dreamers —tend not to stay long. But they're soon replaced by the next batch." He clasped his hands behind his back as he meandered down the path, as casual as if the Enclave were miles away.

"I do insist you relax, my young friend," he said to Amos over his shoulder, in the same unemotional voice. "As I've said, there's a steady stream of transients passing through Jericho. My guided tours are a well-established pattern for all to see, *including* the guards. Don't, I beg you, underestimate my skills at blending in, nor overestimate your ability to assess them."

Amos felt a hot flush creep into his cheeks. "My mistake," he replied evenly. "It's hard to relax this close to an Enclave. I'm not used to being out in the open—exposed."

"We're proud of our little community." Mateo continued his lecture as if nothing had happened. "If I may be permitted a moment of immodesty, we've managed to maintain a respectful orderliness to our daily routine. We're diligent in self-policing when it comes to the employment lines. Jericho will not tolerate a selfish, me-first dynamic." He pivoted to face them, his back to Gate Seven. "The Citizens of the Enclave have zero tolerance for unruly behavior outside their walls. They care nothing about our desperation. If we fail to maintain order, they won't hesitate to shut the gates and deny us the opportunity for work."

Amos looked past him. Most of the pedestrian gates, four in total, were already closed. One remained open, releasing a steady trickle of people returning from their day's employment.

A day spent doing jobs too dirty for Hoarders. Amos tasted bitterness as he watched the trudging procession. *Paid in starvation wages and shoved back outside so they don't contaminate the Hoarders' precious high-and-mighty society.*

"What if you can't self-police?" Amos kept his expression and tone of voice neutral. *Give nothing away. Don't look at the balcony above the gates—if they're watching from anywhere, it's from there.* He glanced at Mateo. "What if some desperate newcomers try to force their way to the front of the line? They can't shut the gates forever—the Hoarders don't want to deprive themselves of their cheap workforce."

"I believe the phrase you're looking for is 'Citizens of the Enclave.'" Mateo stole a glance at Gate Seven. This segment of his lecture—reinforcing the rules—was obviously meant to be public. "I would draw your attention to the balcony above the gate. I assume you've noticed the advanced weaponry on display. We *will* have order. If we fail to exercise self-control, others will exercise it for us."

He continued toward the gate, weaving his way through the growing stream of returning workers. Don and Amos kept pace on either side of him.

"Seven," Don said, his voice emotionless.

Amos caught his meaning. The gate number was partially hidden in the lengthening shadows, but visible below the weaponized balcony. He glanced at it and then quickly away.

"Seven of eight entry points, spread equally around the circumference of the Enclave." Mateo seemed pleased that they'd noticed. "Each with its own settlement of job-seekers."

Eight shantytowns, filled with people desperately hoping for a few of the Hoarders' scraps. Amos shoved his clenched fists inside his jacket pockets.

Mateo gestured to the largest gates, the ones reserved for vehicular traffic. "There are several access ports for the Citizens' vehicles. For the most part, they only leave Cascadia Enclave for wilderness adventures—hunting, fishing, or any additional number of recreational activities."

A stabbing pain lanced through Amos, and he almost betrayed himself. *Like hunting juvenile trespassers with advanced weapons? My brother is dead because of Hoarders' "recreational activities."*

He tasted the coppery tang of his own blood. He'd bitten the inside of his cheek. For once, his sense of outrage over his brother's death outweighed his guilt for abandoning him.

Mateo slowed his advance, looking over his shoulder.

It's like he knows. Amos banished the paranoid thought, maintaining his outward calm.

"I should be clear about this, my young friend," Mateo said, a new note of warning in his voice. "If we fail to maintain order, the Citizens may take additional steps to purge troublemakers from our community."

As if on cue, one of the guards in the balcony spotted them. He nudged another of his kind, and they shifted their weapons to aim directly at Amos and Don. The guards said nothing. Their implied threat was enough.

Don rubbed his jaw, masking his words. "Keep moving. We've over-stayed our welcome."

Mateo angled to the right of the gate, resuming his tour. He led them along the last row of shops backing directly against the Enclave's towering wall.

Amos fought the urge to stare. "We're walking in the literal shadow of the Enclave," he muttered under his breath.

"All that to say," Mateo's voice held no trace of emotion, "you don't want to be present if and when the gates open at the wrong time. The Enclave's rulers are remarkably efficient when it comes to the purges."

"Purges?" Amos fastened on the single word.

Mateo fixed them with his pointed, unblinking stare. "But I trust that, as newcomers in search of gainful employment, you'll do nothing to jeopardize a community extending its welcome to you. As a respected merchant, I offer to assist your assimilation into our unique culture."

He veered without warning into a narrow alley between two shops that smelled of fresh earth and produce. "I'll introduce you to some of my fellow merchants this evening. We have a well-earned reputation for fair prices and quality merchandise.

The continued health of our community depends on the trust and goodwill of our fellow inhabitants." He paused, pivoting to block their exit from the alley. "And their compliance, of course. But as you've seen, it's for the common good."

They stepped into the path leading back to his shop. Amos's uneasiness grew. He nudged Don and kept his voice to a whisper. "He's been playing this part for a long time. What if he's started believing his own lecture? And where's the rest of his Hub?"

Don nodded curtly and raised his voice, his questions calm but pointed. "Don't you worry about becoming a target during these purges? Or do you have some kind of special arrangement with the Hoarders?"

If Mateo resented his implied accusation, he gave no outward sign of it. Instead, he slowed his pace until they walked three abreast on the beaten path.

"I'm a respected merchant, not to mention a community leader," he replied, unperturbed. "Therefore, it's in my best interest to encourage your peaceful adaptation. The Citizens of the Enclave, and their ever-watchful leaders, understand that I've accepted my limitations, as have my fellow merchants." He waved a hand in the direction beyond the shops, at a farther distance from the Enclave. "The purges are typically confined to the housing units near the outskirts. More often than not, any troublesome newcomers are found there. Those of us who must survive here long-term need no additional 'arrangement,' as you suggest."

Don grunted. "No offense."

"None taken." Mateo paused as they arrived in front of his shop. "In my case, I live here, behind my shop. What better way to protect my wares?"

He ducked his head under the frayed awning. Once inside,

he set a lantern alight and turned to face his guests, removing his cap for the first time. His dark hair, equal parts salt and pepper, was cropped close to his skull. The lantern gave his dark eyes a strange glint, accentuating their unblinking scrutiny.

Don kept his tone conversational, but Amos caught the shrewd way he studied their guide. "I'd guess living in your shop also protects you from anyone who thinks you're in bed with the enemy. Collaborators, we used to call them."

Amos watched the shopkeeper's face for his reaction. "Newcomers who might be tempted to take their hatred of Hoarders out on you. Especially if they consider you a collaborator."

That last bit may have been unnecessary, but Mateo's impassivity was beginning to grate on Amos's nerves. Nothing seemed to disturb him.

He blinked—*was that the first time?*—and cocked his head to one side, never breaking his dispassionate stare. For a long moment, the only sound in the shop was the faint conversations of returning workers as they traipsed past the open door.

"Ah, yes, the threat of collaborators, the 'fifth column' working in secret from within to betray their own." He seemed amused by Amos's attempt to provoke him.

Amos resisted the urge to rest a hand on his combat knife. *Too obvious. Plus, it's not polite to threaten an ally.*

"There's always the potential for dissent," Mateo said, his calm delivery growing more and more irritating. "But one must be sure where to look for said dissidents. As well as recognize the lengths they're prepared to go, in order to preserve their anonymity."

A louder conversation outside drew their attention to the shop's open entrance. The voices continued on their way, fading into the distance.

Amos listened intently, and dared to relax. *False alarm.*

Don eyed the deepening shadows outside the shop. Amos knew him well enough to recognize his growing impatience, but his laconic voice betrayed no anxiety. "It's getting dark. When can we expect our mail, since you don't have a dropbox?"

He's stalling. Amos's inner voice sprang to paranoid life. *You're in the Enclave's shadow. Trackers could be closing in!*

Mateo crossed his arms, tilting his head to one side. The flickering lantern cast an odd pattern of shadows over his face.

"I am the dropbox," he replied, deadpan, as if stating an obvious fact. "And your package has already been delivered."

THREE

ADRENALINE SHOT THROUGH Amos's veins like an electrical shock. He tightened an instinctive grip on his knife, poised to draw the weapon. "I'm losing my patience with your cryptic non-answers."

Don's hand shot out, clutching his shoulder in a punishing grip. Amos glanced at him, startled. Don returned his look, not flinching. Amos nodded, and his hand dropped from the knife.

Don studied the shopkeeper, his eyes probing the other's impassive gaze. Mateo met his pointed stare, his expression neutral. Their silent stand-off was broken by Don's sudden, sharp intake of breath.

"Your guided tour." Don's deep voice betrayed his surprise. "That's the package, isn't it? *That's* the intel. You can't risk a paper trail, so you don't have a literal dropbox. Word-of-mouth only, am I right?"

Mateo's face betrayed nothing. He leaned forward, his eyes boring into Don's. "I trust you found our time…educational." He adopted his patient instructor's tone. "And what did you learn, might I ask?"

Don's smile didn't reach his eyes. "We can't count on fake permits to get inside the Enclave, because they're issued on-the-spot, as needed, on a daily basis. And they're only good for specific hours, none of which are after dark. We need to find another way in."

Mateo lifted his chin, nodding once to signal his approval. "You are an excellent listener, and an adept interpreter of new information." He cocked his head to one side again, observing them with rapt attention. "Was there anything else?"

Don crossed his massive arms over his chest, not breaking eye contact. "The Hoarders will seal the gates at the first sign of trouble, but we could've guessed that before. You want us to know that the guards wouldn't hesitate to shoot from above the gates, and, if provoked, will purge troublemakers by armed assault."

Mateo exhaled a satisfied sigh, nodding twice. "You impress me, sir. But surely someone of your obvious talent discerned more?"

Don replied without hesitation, eyes fixed on the cryptic shopkeeper. "There are dissidents to be found, even here. You're warning us to keep our eyes open, our mouths shut, and one hand on our weapons. How am I doing so far?"

Mateo closed his eyes, inhaling deeply. The simple action was a startling contrast to his earlier unblinking gaze. He waited for an additional moment before looking up, his peculiar stare fixed on Don once more.

"I beg your pardon. I don't recall suggesting *where* these alleged dissidents could be found." Amos heard the subtle reproach in his voice, and the challenge to think again was clear in his penetrating gaze. "You're going to need their assistance, if you're serious about getting inside the Enclave."

Dusk was fast closing outside the shop. Amos overheard the neighboring shopkeepers collapsing their awnings, closing down for the night. "Enough of this cat-and-mouse guessing game, Mateo. We're out of time."

Don exhaled sharply, taking an aggressive step forward before Mateo could respond. "Are you saying these dissidents are *inside* the Enclave? You expect us to believe that *Hoarders*—" his loathing twisted the moniker into a curse "—would betray the Enclave?"

Amos inhaled slowly, fighting the urge to draw his knife and force Mateo to reveal all he knew. The idea of Hoarders turning against their own kind … impossible. *Hoarders are all alike. They killed my brother for sport, like we're not even human.*

Mateo didn't retreat, nor did his steady gaze change. He simply waited, riding out the emotional storm from his guests. As the first wave of shock receded, he spoke again.

"Emotionalism is often the enemy of rational thought, no matter how justified your feelings may appear." His gaze shifted from Don to Amos. "You have yet to begin your return journey. I can only hope such attentive listeners will recall my tour with equal clarity, once your emotions are under control."

Amos glared at him, making no attempt to disguise his frustration. "Hoarders have no use for anyone outside the Enclave. Help us against their own kind? I won't hold my breath."

Don's massive fists clenched and relaxed, over and over. He scowled, evaluating Mateo's hidden-in-a-riddle information.

The roar of a large engine penetrated the walls of the shop —a vehicle approaching at high speed. Anxious voices called out, and a cascade of footsteps pounded past the open door.

Amos ducked outside, combat knife drawn, surveying the area around Gate Seven. Each of his moves were instinctive—this was familiar territory.

There. He spotted the bulky all-terrain vehicle as it burst into view, careening through Jericho. Townspeople darted out of its way with curses and cries of alarm. Gate Seven cranked open with a loud metallic sound, as if the truck's arrival was expected. Armed guards, weapons drawn, crouched just inside the gate's gaping maw.

The vehicle skidded to a dusty stop at the threshold. The driver's impatience was palpable, even at this distance.

The required entry protocol, whatever it might be, was completed without delay. The engine revved loudly and the vehicle, tires kicking up clouds of dust and gravel, raced inside. Guards, their weapons trained in the general direction of Jericho, retreated warily into the Enclave.

Gate Seven dropped into place, raising a new swirl of dust as it landed with heavy finality. The entire sequence lasted less than a minute.

"Hoarders returning after a day of terrorizing the locals?" Don peered over Amos's shoulder as the dust settled. The last fading rays of sunlight gave the airborne motes a strange aura.

Amos was about to answer when he spied a dark figure, muffled in concealing clothing, approaching their position. He edged closer to Don, his knife drawn, its threat unmistakable.

The figure halted, hands raising slowly—no sudden moves—to push back their jacket hood.

"Take it easy, you idiot. It's me." Jane's voice, hushed but characteristically acerbic, reached his ears. "Don't stand there gawking. We need to get out of sight." Her terse greeting over, she darted into Mateo's shop without waiting for a response.

Don and Amos exchanged glances. Don shook his head with a rueful grin, and Amos shrugged in response, shoving his knife back into its sheath. They followed Jane inside, ducking under the awning as dusk gave way to darkness.

Mateo intercepted them in the doorway, blocking their path. "Your mail has been delivered, therefore our business is concluded. I bid each of you a good journey."

"What are you talking about?" Jane scowled at him as she shook out her thick black hair. "I just got here. There'll be a full moon later. I'd like to be long gone by the time it rises, but give me a second before you shove me out the door." She took a deep breath, looking from Don to Amos, hands on her hips. "So, what did I miss?"

"I'll fill you in on the way," Don replied, his voice guarded. "We've got a lot to talk about, but not here."

Jane shot him a puzzled look, but fell silent. She'd demand answers sooner than later.

Amos pulled his cap lower, the need for anonymity hounding him more than ever. "Forget 'hidden in plain sight.'" He glanced at the murky twilight outside. "Right now, I'd rather be invisible."

Jane pulled her hood over her head, shrouding her face. Amos stepped beyond the awning's cover, pivoting in slow, casual circle as he scouted the immediate vicinity, alert for anyone who might be paying too much attention to Mateo's shop. Don lingered in the doorway, refusing to be dismissed, eyeing the cryptic shopkeeper.

Mateo's body language was casual, but he didn't alter position, effectively blocking entry into his shop. He locked eyes with Don, his expression unreadable. "I gave you the complete tour," he said obliquely. "Is anything still unclear?"

"What kind of game are you playing?" Don didn't raise his voice, but he seemed determined to get a straight answer. "Which Hub did you say you're with?"

Mateo straightened, not breaking eye contact. "I am the Jericho Hub," he replied without inflection. The faintest hint of a smile flitted across his face. "I'm also the dropbox, and your humble tour guide. I trust you found my services satisfactory."

Don grumbled something derogatory under his breath and joined his companions under the awning. Amos shoved past him to confront the cagey shopkeeper.

Mateo stared at him, his odd gaze betraying nothing. "Will there be anything else, young Amos? My tour was quite thorough, I assure you."

"No, it wasn't." Amos said, his voice low and accusing. He closed the distance between them, their faces only a hands-breadth apart. *This is it—the missing part.* "You forgot to mention one crucial detail ... about you."

Mateo smiled for the first time, his teeth flashing white against his dark complexion. It wasn't a warm smile, nor was it cold. It was a shrewd counterfeit, devoid of genuine emotion. "Well done, Amos. And now you'll have even more to discuss during your return trip. I bid you all a good journey."

A faint hint of reddish light glowed for a fraction of a second under the skin around his left eye.

FOUR ◉

"How many of them know the truth?" Aubrey voiced a question she'd had on her mind for some time. "If I didn't know any better, I'd say most of the Mission's workers have no idea we exist."

"They don't," Garr replied easily. His casual response surprised her.

Eastside Mission was visible just ahead, a block farther down the street. The unremarkable gray building was situated on the opposite corner of the intersection. The usual gathering of regulars congregated outside the weathered doors, chatting with some of the staff. The sharp bite of approaching autumn, noticeably acute overnight, was held at bay by the sun.

"The manager—we call him Uncle John—is the only one who knows the whole picture." Garr's pace slowed as he studied the benign scene across the street. "It's safer. The staff does their charitable work, but they have no idea a subbasement exists under the building. John's one of us, but his role is to run the Mission, not assist in our operations."

"That's taking 'hidden in plain sight' to a whole new level." Aubrey couldn't help but be impressed. *What better way to camouflage our Hub's location than to surround the Mission—inside and out—with people who don't know what's going on?*

A cool breeze pushed against them as they crossed the street. Aubrey brushed a stray strand of hair from her face, the scars on her hand visible for a brief moment.

Her determination to regain full use of her arm, coupled with weeks of intensive rehabilitation, had paid off. The scars, stretching from just above her elbow and down to encompass her hand, were permanent reminders of her ordeal.

At first, she found the scars repulsive, but as the weeks passed, they became a part of her. The only time she made a point of concealing them was when she went out in public.

Not because she was self-conscious or embarrassed. No, she was pragmatic—hidden in plain sight. Most people weren't bold or rude enough to ask awkward questions, but if asked later, might recall the young woman with a badly-scarred arm. She wore her favorite sweatshirt as much for camouflage as for warmth.

They continued their circuitous journey, losing themselves in the anonymity of the crowd. They each carried a small bag of fresh produce, purchased from one of the nearby shops. Unless someone already knew Garr for what he was—a former colonel—he might pass for a tradesman or a day laborer. Anything but a leader in their ragtag underground resistance.

They made another turn, to all outward appearances away from Eastside. One additional errand remained. Aubrey bottled her curiosity. She'd heard stories about the Hub's dropbox many times, but had never seen it in person.

Her thoughts returned to the Mission. "Aren't you worried

someone might find the trapdoor in the basement?" She'd helped her fellow Runners reinforce the make-shift blockage at the top of the stairs. "What if one of John's staff accidentally stumbles on it?"

Garr chuckled as they rounded another corner. "No one likes paperwork, and nobody wants to disturb the boss while he's doing it. The trapdoor's always been in John's office. When they were renovating last spring, after the Tracker attack, he insisted on keeping his office where it was. Said it would bolster staff morale."

His voice was light-hearted, despite the somber events he alluded to. "During the renos, Don and I snuck in late one night and poured a layer of concrete over the trapdoor. Guess where John's desk sits?"

"Hidden in plain sight." Aubrey laughed. "Or am I repeating myself?"

Garr grinned at her. "By the time Eastside reopened, there was no trace of our once-handy trapdoor."

Aubrey shook her head. "I'm still amazed that none of this seems to bother you. I mean, we live literally *one floor below* the Mission, which was attacked just six months ago, and we carry on as if nothing happened."

"You'll get used to it, sooner than you think," Garr replied. "The real trick is finding the balance between vigilance and not going crazy from stress. We're lucky to have Doc. She keeps an eye on us. Dropbox is just ahead. Next left."

He nudged her toward an alleyway with his elbow. It resembled the same kind of alley she'd avoided during her first night in the City, all those months ago.

A lot has changed since then.

A mental image of pounding rain and trash-can fires flashed

through her mind. She stuffed her hands into her pockets. An involuntary shiver ran down her spine. *Mostly me.*

Garr paused next to a nondescript doorway, roughly mid-point down the alley. Aubrey thought for a moment that he intended to enter the building, but realized the heavy wooden door had been nailed shut. She watched with feigned nonchalance as Garr crouched, one hand reaching for the lowest brick in the aging and weathered wall.

She leaned against the doorframe, casually shielding him from view. Garr could be fumbling with a rusty lock, or pausing to tie his shoelaces. That's how she hoped it would appear to any observer—casual or otherwise.

Garr eased the brick back and forth, his motions efficient and almost silent. The brick came loose, and Aubrey spied a small package hidden in the wall. Garr extracted the leather-wrapped bundle and stowed it inside his coarse jacket. With the same agility, he worried the brick back into its former position, and rose to his full height. They resumed their unhurried walk, exiting the alley at the far end.

"Just taking a shortcut," Aubrey said brightly as they rounded the corner.

Garr squinted at her. "Come again?"

"Nothing, just practicing my alibi." She smiled at the puzzled look he gave her. "When the time comes, I've got to be comfortable lying with a straight face."

Garr nodded. "Deceit can be a virtue, depending on the situation—unless you ever try lying to me." If he was curious about the contents of the package, he hid it well. They veered left as they wandered along the street, casually joining the unhurried pedestrian traffic that filled the sidewalks and spilled into the street.

The tranquil atmosphere was shattered by the growling crescendo of an approaching vehicle. Aubrey's heart skipped a beat. Hoarders rarely drove through the Old City, preferring to avoid contact with anyone outside the Enclave. The break from routine didn't bode well.

Startled pedestrians bolted for the relative safety of the sidewalks. Aubrey felt Garr's strong grip on her elbow, urging her closer to the nearest wall. She caught herself against the building with her good arm, looking over her shoulder in hopes of spotting the vehicle.

She was taken aback by the intensity of her visceral reaction to the Hoarders. *They think nothing of Implanting children for their political games.* Bile rose in her throat and she swallowed hard. *They're less human than the Soul-less.*

An off-road vehicle raced past, its dark-tinted windows giving it an unearthly aura as it careened recklessly around the next corner. Panic-stricken pedestrians scattered in all directions, dodging out of its path. Screams erupted here and there, more from fear than actual injury, as far as Aubrey could tell.

Garr stepped into the street as the vehicle disappeared around the corner, his dark eyes troubled. "I don't think they ran over anyone. We got lucky. Reflexes are usually the first thing to go when panic sets in."

Aubrey was well aware of the Hoarders' callous disregard for anyone they considered inferior. Still, she felt shaken by the vehicle's sudden arrival and equally swift disappearance. "Any chance they were looking for us?"

Garr shook his head. "They didn't slow down enough to even take a look. Whatever their reason for being here, I don't think it was us." He stared after vanished vehicle. "It doesn't make sense. Hoarders have zero interest in this part of the Old

City. Sure, they like the open country for trophy hunting, but that's in the opposite direction."

Agitated pedestrians gathered in compact groups as the adrenaline of the moment passed. Hushed conversations ensued, and Aubrey overheard resentful comments and curses directed at the now-vanished Hoarders. The idyllic afternoon atmosphere was ruined, and the angry pedestrians scattered to seek shelter inside nearby buildings.

"Look at them." Garr pointed with his chin, scowling. "Running for cover like scared rabbits. That's life under the Hoarders. They were here for less than thirty seconds, and look at the effect they've had." He pivoted on his heel, tightening his grip on his bag of produce. "Now's our chance. The streets will be empty for a while, until they get over the shock. We can make good time back to the tunnels while everyone's hiding."

Aubrey nodded, wincing at the cramp in her good hand. She shifted the grocery bag to her other hand, flexing her fingers to restore circulation. Her heart pounded in her ears, and she realized she was all but hyperventilating. She cringed, embarrassed by her reaction, until a calmer part of her mind intervened.

A perfectly normal reaction, Aubs, she told herself. *Hoarders almost crushed you under their wheels. I'd stand out if I didn't look terrified.* She shoved her hand into her pocket, out of sight, stretching her stiff muscles.

"Back to the Hub," Garr muttered under his breath. He touched the small bulge in his jacket. "I'll feel better when our package is safely off the streets."

* * *

THE HOARDER VEHICLE DISAPPEARED from sight, leaving behind a trail of anxiety and dread. Pedestrians scurried in all directions, leaving no one to observe a solitary figure, casually leaning against one of the long-defunct lampposts.

In the midst of a human sea of fear and anxiety, Logan Johns was the epitome of unflappable calm. He scanned the street— back and forth, up and down, side to side to side—cataloguing the retreating bio-forms with meticulous attention.

A faint but unmistakable circle of red light glowed beneath the skin surrounding his left eye.

FIVE ◉

THE TRACKER STARED at the ceiling of the make-shift infirmary, unable to shift position. Restraints confined it to the gurney with cold efficiency. Unable to free itself, the Givers' fanatical creation was reduced to a melancholy acceptance of its miserable fate.

The female bio-unit's weapon had destroyed its scanning eye. The electrical shock had also crippled some of the Tracker's other enhancements. Those losses paled in comparison to one devastating discovery: the Givers were silent.

The Tracker's thoughts turned bleak. Its Quest had failed—no excuses. The Harvest had not been executed. The Givers were generous but they were not to be denied. Yet despite its wretched failure, they had allowed it to live. But they no longer spoke. There could be no greater punishment. Death would be preferred, understood, accepted.

The Givers' silence was torture.

The Tracker's physical enhancements continued to function, although not with their usual speed and efficiency. The wounds on its arm were slow in closing. The damage repaired itself in halting fits and starts. Its facial injuries were also undergoing repairs, although the Tracker was unable to directly observe the healing progress.

It was still imprisoned, chained to a metal bed. Under normal operating parameters, the physical enhancements should have enabled it to break the restraints with little effort. It had tried, over and over, to no avail.

Its new-found weakness was another indication that the enhancements no longer functioned at peak efficiency. New data was required. The Givers must speak. Why did the enhancements no longer function as designed? If they had indeed spared its life, despite its failure, there must be a logical reason. Only they could provide answers. And purpose. And identity.

But the Givers remained silent.

The Tracker's captors had not mistreated it. Perhaps an appeal to them, persuading them to grant its freedom? Would they assist it in reestablishing contact with the Givers?

No, argued another part of its brain. Bio-forms are irrelevant. All that mattered is the Quest.

No. Inaccurate. Its Quest was over. The Givers were silent. The only logical explanation was their displeasure over its failed Quest.

Despair threatened to overwhelm the Tracker. It failed to notice the teardrops leaking, one-by-one, from its remaining eye. The Givers' silence was a gaping vacuum in its chest.

They must be appeased. Perhaps it could yet regain their approval. Yes, yes, that must be its goal—to earn the Givers' favor once again.

The bio-forms.

They are the key. It must listen, learn, plan. The bio-forms knew it could speak. It must enlist their aid, without betraying its true intent, and win back its freedom.

Everything else was irrelevant. All that mattered was ending the Givers' silence. The Tracker seized eagerly on a new Quest—absolution from its gods.

SIX ◉

Home, sweet hub. Aubrey relinquished her bag of produce into Sheila's grateful hands. *And yet, weird as it sounds, this is my home. And the Runners have somehow become like family.*

"Fresh vegetables." Sheila's face lit up. The bruises under her blackened eyes had faded several weeks ago, and by unspoken consent, none of her fellow Runners mentioned the new alignment of her broken nose. "You have no idea how much I was beginning to loathe reheated trail rations."

Garr laughed. It was a reassuring sound. "You'll get no argument from me, Sheila. But next time, maybe you can do the shopping. This wasn't a typical errand run."

He filled her in on the incident with the Hoarder truck on their way to the dropbox.

"Hoarders? In this part of town?" Sheila frowned as she sorted the groceries. "It's unusual for them to come anywhere near Eastside. There's nothing of any value to them around here. What do you think they were up to?"

Garr shrugged. "They were here and gone in less than thirty

seconds—not enough time to guess their intentions. And jumping to conclusions only makes us paranoid."

Sheila resumed sorting the vegetables. The quality of their meals would improve for the next several days. "Okay, then I'll pose a theory. It might answer some of the questions keeping me awake at night."

Garr held the package from the dropbox in his hand, fiddling absent-mindedly with its fastenings. "Lying awake at night —you? Now, I'm curious. I thought you were one of the few people around here who got a decent night's sleep."

"Really? Then maybe you can explain the long hours I spend counting spots on the ceiling." Sheila grinned as she stored the vegetables in the cooler. Her expression turned abruptly serious. "There's no pattern to where Runners come from. I could understand if they were all from the same neighborhood, or at least the same village, but they're not."

She shut the cooler and turned to face him. "Whenever we find a new Runner, they have no memory of getting an Implant. They just go about their everyday lives, with no idea what the Hoarders have done to them."

Aubrey took a seat at the table. "I've been wondering about that, too. Why pick me?" She felt the scar just below her sternum, tracing the slight welt. "I don't remember anything. There wasn't even a mark. The only scar I have is from when Doc cut it out."

Garr seated himself opposite her. "And your theory, Sheila?"

Sheila leaned against the counter behind her. "What if the Hoarders *were* hunting today—for new bodies to Implant? If so, there'll be more Runners deployed in the near future." She paused, massaging her temples. "We got distracted after learning about the Givers, or whatever these aliens call themselves.

It's like the shock made us forget what the Hoarders are up to. They're still Implanting innocent people, and turning them into assassins. Our real enemies are the Hoarders. We can't lose sight of that."

Hoarders may be monsters, but at least they're human monsters. Aubrey's unspoken protest was quelled before she uttered a word. *But Sheila's right. When they started Implanting people, the Hoarders* made *themselves our enemies.*

There was a prolonged silence in the mess hall. Garr raised the package from the dropbox, gesturing with it as he spoke. "Your theory makes logical sense, Sheila, but for now, it's just a theory. I'm not ready to draw any conclusions about today's incident, until we have more intel."

Sheila shrugged good-naturedly. "And I, for one, hope my theory's based on sleep deprivation."

Garr saluted and got up from his chair. "Right now, I want to take a look at whatever was left in our dropbox. I'll brief everyone as soon as the rest of the team gets back."

He strode out of the room, his attention already absorbed by the package in his hand.

Sheila pushed herself away from the counter. "As long as we're waiting, I'll let Doc know about the fresh vegetables. It'll make her day. She loves to cook."

"I'm coming with you." Aubrey scooted her chair back from the table, grateful for a temporary reprieve from her dark musings. "I want to see the look on Doc's face."

SEVEN

THEY FOUND DOC SIMON in the infirmary, seated on a stool at her worktable, peering into her antique microscope. She glanced up as Sheila and Aubrey entered, and grimaced as she stood, stretching her stiff back.

"Busy as always, Doc." Aubrey grinned at her, anticipating her reaction to hearing about fresh produce. "What kind of alchemy are you conjuring today?"

Doc gestured at the worktable. "Blood samples, courtesy of our Tracker houseguest. Why?"

Sheila and Aubrey exchanged knowing looks. Sheila struck a dramatic pose. "What would you say, if I told you there are fresh vegetables in mess hall?"

"Vegetables?" Doc straightened, suddenly energized. "Well, let me finish up here, and I'll conjure some alchemy of another kind. It's an ancient incantation. I call it 'supper.'"

Sheila looked past her, eyeing the quiescent Tracker on the gurney. Their 'guest' had made no escape attempts or threats of violence, but no one questioned Garr's decision to keep the restraints in place. "Anything new from our Hub's latest addition?" She gestured at the inert figure. The Tracker seemed to be unaware of their presence, or was ignoring them for reasons of her own. "Has she said anything useful?"

"Tracy? Oh, she speaks up every now and then." Doc craned her neck for a better glimpse of the Tracker. "Mostly muttering to herself. I'm sure she'd rather be talking to someone else—or some*thing* else. On the other hand, her injuries are healing remarkably well. Though, for the life of me, I couldn't begin to tell you how or why. She's still an enigma wrapped in a mystery."

"You gave it—I mean *her*—a name?" Sheila glanced at Doc, eyebrows raised. "I'm still adjusting to the idea that she's anything but a killing machine hidden in a human body."

"Tracy the Tracker?" Aubrey couldn't help laughing. "Are you serious, Doc?"

"She's not a *thing*, Aubrey. She used to be human, just like us." Doc's voice hardened and her frosty gaze flickered from Aubrey to Sheila and back. "What the Hoarders did to her is nothing short of *evil*, but Tracy didn't ask for it, any more than you asked to be Implanted. She deserves, at the very least, the dignity of a name."

Aubrey and Sheila exchanged glances. Aubrey felt a pang of guilt over her thoughtless attempt at a joke. *And we thought we were so magnanimous for using "she" instead of "it."*

Behind Sheila, the Tracker stirred, struggling to move and voicing jumbled noises. She tried to sit up, but the restraints around her wrists and ankles thwarted her attempts.

Doc, Sheila, and Aubrey gathered around the gurney, their tense standoff forgotten. The electrical prod, wielded by a desperate Aubrey in self-defense, was permanently fused inside the Tracker's skull. Doc had initially resisted the idea of extracting it surgically, fearing the attempt might cause irreparable damage, or even death.

As weeks went by and the Tracker continued to recover, Doc relented and, with great caution and Sheila's expert assistance, dismantled the prod's handle. A simple eye patch now covered the Tracker's ruined eye socket, giving her a more human appearance.

"Has she been any more articulate?" Sheila asked, leaning over to study Tracy's face. "Any way to evaluate how much damage the prod's done to her mental abilities?"

The Tracker fixed her one good eye on Sheila.

She understood Sheila. Aubrey's lingering guilt was replaced by a growing excitement. *She—Tracy—is having one of her coherent episodes.*

Doc spaced her words with care, her voice gentle and reassuring. "Tracy, it's me, Doctor Simon. We've spoken before, remember?"

Tracy's remaining eye shifted in its socket, although she didn't try to turn her head. It was one of her many disconcerting mannerisms, underlining the macabre extent of the Givers' experimentation. She stared at Doc, unblinking, for several seconds before opening her mouth. She tried several times before any sound came out.

"Tracy. My name." She exhaled as if the effort exhausted her. She raised her head off the pillow, her expression pleading. Her entire body tensed with the effort to speak. "Name. My Tracy." She relaxed without warning, collapsing limp on the gurney. Aubrey wondered if she'd lost consciousness.

The Tracker lay still, her breathing ragged, awake but no longer trying to speak. Her facial expression was difficult to read at the best of times, despite Doc's normalizing efforts with the eye patch. Aubrey thought she appeared more frustrated than anything else. Tracy broke eye contact with Doc and stared at the ceiling, not focused on anything.

"Is this a speech problem, or has there been some kind of brain damage?" Sheila leaned on the edge of the gurney. "Is there any way to quantify the prod's impact?"

Doc crossed her arms, her face pensive as she studied her patient. "My educated guess? I'd say her condition, based on the past six weeks, most resembles a form of aphasia. It's a common side effect found in stroke survivors. Short, incomplete sentences are the norm, as is the difficulty and frustration in getting the words out. Tracy can form thoughts just fine, as far as I can tell, but it's a struggle for her to verbalize them."

"Her physical injuries seem to be healing fairly well." Aubrey moved to the opposite side of the gurney. "I thought you couldn't treat her wounds because of all the changes the Givers did to her."

Did Tracy just give me a sideways look?

Doc sighed wearily. "I've never been more aware of Eastside's medical limitations until Tracy became my patient. My initial diagnosis, if you recall, was that she'd be dead within days, a week at the most. Her mechanical and chemical alterations don't appear to be functioning as designed, but they've kept her alive."

Sheila paid special attention to the eye patch over the remains of the prod embedded—fused—inside the Tracker's skull. "And this cut off her ability to communicate with the Givers," she said, stating a fact more than asking a question, "with the unforeseen side effect of aphasia. That'll make it difficult to get any useful information out of her."

Aubrey happened to glance down as Sheila finished speaking, and was startled by the shrewd look on Tracy's face. *I think she understands what we're saying.*

She hoped that was a good sign.

***

THE TRACKER RELAXED as the three bio-forms left the infirmary, a slight smile curling one corner of her mouth. She'd listened carefully to their conversation, evaluating their responses and sifting through their nonverbal cues.

Analyze. Adapt.

And a plan began to form.

EIGHT

THE SETTING SUN'S crimson edge had been reduced to a mere sliver on the horizon. Twilight shadowed the squalid shanty-town outside the Enclave.

A solitary all-terrain vehicle careened down an uneven road, skidding around one final curve before hitting the home stretch to the Enclave. Three occupants held on for dear life as the studded tires bounced over the broken pavement.

Connor Sinclair leaned into the padded fabric of the rear seat, trying in vain to ease his aching neck muscles. The punishing terrain bore only part of the blame. The real culprit was the gnawing dread that rode with him on every clandestine mission outside the Enclave. Easy to pinpoint, suicide to admit.

Their hasty short-cut through the crumbling remains of the Old City had been a test of nerves. Connor concealed his trepidation as best he could, and heaved a covert sigh of relief once they were past the outer perimeter. Only a few miles of open territory, an empty and deserted buffer zone, separated them from the welcome security of the Cascadia Enclave.

Out of the Old City and away from the savages. Connor angled his stiff neck to one side, and was rewarded with a satisfying series of pops and cracks. *I knew it—the closer we get to Cascadia, the more my tension melts away.*

The Enclave's protective walls dominated their view, beckoning them toward its safe haven, and home. The sole remaining hurdle was a haphazard shantytown, one of several clinging like grotesque barnacles to Cascadia's outer wall. Its mere existence, cobbled together in a freakish caricature of an actual town, was cause for contempt. Connor's university classmates mockingly called it Parasite City.

"I hate this place, even more than the Old City." Tony Moretti, their gray-haired chauffeur, gestured at the shantytown, making no effort to hide his disgust. "Just another ugly reminder that the savages are right on our doorstep."

His companion in the front seat—Darcy Peterson, the leader of their cause and Connor's foster father—eyed the shantytown with quiet disdain. Connor smiled to himself at Tony's obvious effort to impress his new employer. *Darcy can tell you stories about the savages' atrocities that would curl your hair, Mister Moretti.*

"I'm glad they're living outside the Enclave," Darcy said, not taking his eyes off the shantytown and its treacherous inhabitants. Tony shot him an incredulous look.

Connor wasn't surprised. Darcy had raised him like a son after savages murdered his family. He'd heard Darcy's speech, plenty of times. *Listen up, Tony. You could learn a lot.*

"Not because we need them as day laborers, mind you." Darcy chuckled without humor, continuing his well-practiced spiel for Tony's sake. "No, their close proximity is a visual reminder why we must be diligent in protecting our borders. Only the Enclave walls stand between Cascadia and our way of life, and the mindless rabble who would leap at the chance to steal it from us."

Connor gazed out the window to his right. What little remained of the setting sun was behind the Enclave, its fading glow accenting the majestic walls. The sight never failed to stir his emotions. They were almost home, another successful mission in their secret war accomplished.

They neared Parasite City's ramshackle outskirts, the last obstacle before Gate Seven. Connor tensed as they sped past the squalid collection of shops and makeshift housing. *Darcy and I don't agree on this one.* He'd never voice his opinion out loud, of course. *I'd be thrilled with a savage-free DMZ —the further from Cascadia, the better.*

"The final approach to the gate requires special attention." Darcy's voice interrupted Connor's thoughts. "Maintain an aggressive speed, but do *not* run over any savages in the road, no matter how tempting."

He was in his favorite role: Darcy, the expert, breaking in a new recruit. Tony was the oldest, but least experienced, member of their team, the most recent addition to the cause.

Tony risked a quick sideways glance, looking confused. "You weren't worried about that back in the Old City."

His unspoken question hung in the air between them.

"When we arrive at Gate Seven, you'll brake hard at the last second." Darcy finished giving instructions before he answered Tony's implied query. "We had no reason to slow down in the Old City, because the rabble had no opportunity to attack. Besides, running them over is a reminder to make way for us."

His icy gaze fastened on the chauffeur, his voice betraying his impatience. "If we strike one of them *here*, when they're well aware we have to slow down at the gate… Well, let's just say that provoking the savages is a bad idea."

Tony tightened his grip on the steering wheel. If anything, he accelerated as Darcy's words sank in. "If we hit one of them now, the rest will swarm us at the gate," he said, a grim set to his mouth. "I *really* hate this place."

He navigated with expert skill between disheveled savages as they trudged along the road after their day-labor in the bowels of the Enclave. Connor shook his head at their slow reflexes—the mindless rabble seemed recklessly unconcerned about Tony's high-speed approach.

Connor overheard the epithets Tony hurled at them under his breath. He glanced out his window, and spied a solitary figure in the second-to-last side street before Gate Seven.

Fading sunlight glinted on the long-bladed knife held by an anonymous savage. He stood in a combative pose, rigid, feet planted as if poised to attack. Watching them.

Connor twisted in his seat, trying to keep the knife-wielding barbarian in sight as they raced over the last few yards to the gate. The figure in the shadows was joined by a second savage, even larger than the first.

Animals. Connor sneered at them. *Mindless barbarians.*

Tony slammed on the brakes and skidded to an abrupt stop, a large dust cloud boiling up around them. Gate Seven retracted vertically at lightning speed. The gatekeepers were efficient. They wouldn't leave Citizens waiting outside for long.

"Is our cargo secure, Connor?" Darcy asked, his voice guarded, not turning to look at his foster son. "While I'd like to believe Cascadia Security would be sympathetic to our cause, one never knows."

Connor leaned back in his seat, glancing over his shoulder

into the cargo area. A nonchalant glance, casual enough not to alert the guards.

No change. The folded tarp concealed their prize. Connor nodded once. He saw Tony watching him in the rearview mirror. He caught the signal and relayed it to Darcy.

Tony gunned the engine and their vehicle lurched over the threshold, accelerating smoothly before slowing to a halt a few yards inside. Armed guards stood at wary attention on either side of the open gate, weapons held ready to dissuade any last-second attack.

Gate Seven crashed into place a split second later, sending a gust of displaced air past their windows.

Tony allowed their vehicle to roll forward until they were parallel to the interior checkpoint. At Darcy's barely perceptible nod, he lowered the driver's side window.

"Good welcome, Citizens." The Cascadia Security guard, higher in rank than his heavily armed associates, peered inside their vehicle, one hand conspicuously on the butt of his pistol. Connor recognized the stripes on his shoulder—a sergeant. "You know the routine. Let's see your permits."

Connor resisted the urge to glance over his shoulder at the cargo area, concentrating instead on a neutral expression and taking slow, steady breaths.

NINE ◉

THE GUARDS BY THE GATE pivoted, surrounding their vehicle in a wary semi-circle. Two additional guards, weapons held ready, positioned themselves in front, blocking their way.

"Do we look like savages to you?" Darcy sounded more disappointed than offended.

He loves toying with these guys. Connor stifled a sigh. *Confidence or recklessness, who knows? But he gets away with it.*

The sergeant maintained his polite, no-nonsense composure. Darcy leaned across Tony to hand over their documents. "Fine, fine. Feel free to examine our permits."

He relaxed into his seat as if there was zero risk of the guards checking their cargo area and discovering what they'd hidden under the tarp.

Connor glanced around, his expression bored, looking past the guards. The metal walls and ceiling, dark gray-green in color and reinforced by rivet-studded support columns, were comforting in an oddly utilitarian way.

Cascadia's architectural beauty was not in evidence here, but

Connor welcomed the coldly efficient surroundings nonetheless. This was the last hurdle before he rejoined his own kind. The streets above this level—the Enclave proper—were mere minutes and a slow-moving security guard away.

What's taking him so long? Savages wouldn't dare enter Cascadia without permits.

Connor chafed at the delay, but rebuked himself for his impatience. *Security only works if it applies to everyone. The savages would counterfeit our permits in a heartbeat, if they could only figure out how. Darcy's right. We can't let our guard down.*

He knew the real source of his jittery angst was the possible discovery of their hidden cargo. The sooner they were through the checkpoint, the better.

The sergeant perused their permits, his actions quick and efficient. He froze for a brief second, eyes widening slightly, and Connor knew he'd recognized their names. And that he was detaining a member of Cascadia's ruling Council.

Actually, he recognized Darcy's *name.* Connor hid a smile and conceded the point. *Tony and I are nothing special.*

The moment passed, and the sergeant gave a hasty all-clear signal. Guards on either side fell back with mechanical precision, shouldered their weapons, and disappeared through a side door to the left of the gate.

"Good welcome, Councilor Peterson." The sergeant returned their permits with no further delay, waving them through with a weak and ingratiating smile.

The two guards stationed in front of Darcy's vehicle stepped aside, showing proper deference. Connor knew they'd overheard their commanding officer's formal welcome. Neither guard made eye contact, staring rigidly ahead with no desire to peer inside the vehicle as Tony drove past.

They assumed positions on either side of the gate, stone-faced and alert for the next group of returning Citizens.

Tony accelerated smoothly, not speaking, and steered them in the direction of the vehicle lifts. He left his window down, basking in the familiar scents of the Enclave as air wafted inside the vehicle.

Connor lowered his window, despite harboring no illusions about which odors to expect in what amounted to a subterranean garage. After several hours in a locked vehicle, even if it was a necessary precaution, he reveled in the simple freedom of an open window.

They drove perpendicular to an inner wall, deeper into the Enclave, and Tony pointed at an imposing barrier as they drove past. "I'm glad someone had the brains to keep the day-laborers' entrance behind a reinforced wall. The thought of savages wandering around here…" He shook his head, as if unable to find words vulgar enough to describe his feelings.

"It'll never happen," Connor replied. This was an area he could speak to with full confidence. Darcy didn't have to explain everything. "The savages have their own door, and their only option is going *down* to the maintenance levels. For them, this is as high as they can go."

"And for us, it's as low as we'll ever have to stoop." Tony caught his eye in the rearview mirror, grinning wickedly. "I can't *begin* to tell you how happy that makes me." He eased the truck into the nearest vehicle lift.

The wide bays were capable of holding four vehicles side by side, but they were alone for this trip. Lights in the cross-beamed ceiling flickered on as the doors closed. A solid gate rose from the floor, and its cage-like counterpart descended from above, sealing them inside.

The two halves connected with a resounding *clang*, the vibrations easily felt inside their vehicle.

The lift ascended with the barest of lurches, rising through several floors before halting at the traffic level. A warning buzzer sounded, and the gates split apart in front of their vehicle. Tony waited as the halves receded, and then eased the truck out of the lift with a happy sigh. "Be it ever so humble, there's no place like home." He grinned in Darcy's direction.

Humility is for the weak. Connor smiled sardonically. Darcy taught him that, early on.

Colorful lights blazed above them, illuminating the elegant towers with a cheerful glow. Tony merged into the multi-lane traffic, navigating with ease in the busy thoroughfare.

Most of the vehicles sharing the road with them were similar in style. The rugged, all-terrain design was at its height of popularity, even if the majority of owners would never dream of traveling outside Cascadia. *Why leave paradise? Everything we need can be found here.*

Connor felt the tension ease in his neck and shoulders as they sped past mile after mile of brightly illuminated office towers, restaurants, theaters, and—his personal favorite —the Museum of Science, Technology, and History.

They were still some distance from their Oceanview villa, but just to be inside Cascadia again was reward enough. He said as much to his companions.

It was Darcy who answered, reminding them of their commitment to duty. "First things first. We have a few more hours of work ahead of us."

"Does it really matter?" Tony flexed his fingers on the steering wheel, clearly agitated. "I've got a wife and kids at home. Tonight, tomorrow morning—what difference does it make?"

Darcy fixed him with a hard stare, his pale eyes frosty. "The longer we take to complete our mission, the greater our risk of detection. I want everything wrapped up before sunrise. *Long* before sunrise. No excuses."

Connor leaned forward in the rear seat. "The sedatives won't last much longer. The dosage is pretty specific." His warning was for Tony's benefit. Darcy knew the drill—he'd been Connor's instructor. "And if you're going to leave your window down, Tony, be careful what you're saying."

"The price of security." Tony sighed in resignation, reaching down to push the appropriate button. His window slid into place, muffling the traffic noise. "Well, that's one thing I'll say in favor of the Givers. Their technological advances have made Cascadia Enclave more secure. Did you see the latest weapons those guards were carrying?"

Uh-oh. Wrong thing to say. Connor winced, putting a hand to his forehead in anticipation of Darcy's response. *Tony's right, technically, but never say that in front of Darcy.*

Darcy didn't disappoint. "Sold out by our own people—you call that a *fair trade?* Sure, the Givers contacted the Enclave because they wanted to deal with the people in power, but how long did that last?" He kept his voice low—even with Tony's window closed—but his eyes blazed. "We've been guarding our borders against the rabble for *years.*" He gestured in the general direction beyond the Enclave. "We were doing just fine without the Givers. They divided us against each other with our full cooperation. We wilted and allowed them to take over."

"Okay, okay, take it easy." Tony's voice was conciliatory as Darcy's tirade wound down. "I don't like the Givers any more than you do. All I'm saying is … they've made it easier to keep the savages at bay. The Enclave's walls are fortified better than ever, and the weapons they gave us are far beyond anything we could've invented—"

"Don't forget the constant surveillance," Connor interrupted. Animosity crept into his voice as he vented his pet peeve. "They say it's for our own good, but I'm not the only one who thinks the Givers use it to spy on *us*, as well."

"All of their 'gifts' come with the same price tag," Darcy said sullenly, repeating the mantra he'd drilled into each of them. He was still seething after Tony's ill-advised comment. "Our freedom, that's all. And like blind fools, a majority of our councilors signed the treaty. Now they enjoy cozying up to the Givers, and they can't, or *won't* face the truth. We were the most powerful people on the planet, and these 'Givers'—who aren't even *human*—conquered us without firing a shot."

"We're about ten minutes away from Oceanview," Tony said, pointing out the obvious.

Is that supposed to distract him? Connor gazed out his window, amused. *Tony's heard the spiel before, but once Darcy gets rolling on his favorite subject...*

Darcy jerked a thumb at the cargo area and its tarp-covered contraband. "I want these two prepped for immediate implantation. I'll coordinate programming them for the targets we want to eliminate. Everything in place by sunrise."

"Roger that." Tony accelerated, changing lanes. He seemed relieved by the change in subject. "Doc can meet us at the clinic, and we'll be on the road in ninety minutes or less."

Darcy smiled at him, pleased. Darcy always found satisfaction in seeing his new recruits adapt.

Connor twisted sideways in his seat, checking the cargo area one more time. He peeled a corner of the tarp back, to reveal a pair of anesthetized figures. They lay side by side, and he took note of the shallow breaths of each.

A rural shopkeeper, and his woman.

Animals. Loathing left a sour taste in Connor's mouth. *This is the only thing you're good for.*

It would all be over soon.

TEN ◉

THERE WAS A TIME, little more than eighteen months earlier, when Connor felt some small twinges of guilt after Darcy recruited him to the cause. His first time was the hardest, despite his ingrained contempt for savages.

He understood and accepted, like any responsible Citizen, the importance of securing Cascadia's borders and safeguarding their way of life. He also had no illusions about the very real threat posed by the barbarians outside the Enclave. His family history gave him more than enough evidence of the savages' brutality. It had been an easy step to justify using them as Implant fodder.

After eighteen months of direct involvement with Darcy's cause, Connor had difficulty recalling those guilty twinges. On this evening, waiting restlessly on their villa balcony, he took a rare moment to allow memories of his family to surface.

His favorite recollections were their wilderness hunting trips, outisde the Enclave's protective border walls. He'd been too young to use one of the advanced rifles the Givers shared with their human allies, but he felt the thrill of the hunt just the same. His older sister, almost an adult herself, let him hold her rifle, but was too smart to allow him to fire it.

His childhood years were filled with happy memories of the roasted meat they'd enjoy after the hunt, after their quarry was properly cleansed, disinfected, and packaged by the appropriate machines in the Enclave. In fact, on those rare occasions when he thought of his childhood, he associated the mouth-watering aroma of roasting meat with love and security.

One of his father's favorite rituals was barbecuing on the balcony. He was a good shot, and took great pleasure in cooking their catch. His mother was an even better marksman, and Connor's older sister was fast following in her mother's footsteps with her own hunting skills.

Tonight, he stood alone on a different balcony, in a different villa, leaning on the railing as he gazed at the bustling Enclave, twenty floors below. Five years had passed since the day his young world had been turned upside down. The day he'd begged his parents to let him attend a baseball game with his friend Reagan, rather than accompanying them on another hunting trip.

He knew his parents would rather take him along, but they relented after his earnest pleas. He waved good-bye without a second thought as the three of them drove away.

Their bodies weren't located until several days later. Their vehicle was discovered, trashed and abandoned, several miles away, the advanced rifles nowhere to be found. The savages had slaughtered them without mercy. All the diligence in the Enclave hadn't been enough.

What remained was not for the eyes of a twelve-year-old boy. Their bodies were cremated at the crash site. Connor still felt a stab of resentment over that. To this day, he resented the lack of a gravesite to visit. To bury their ashes in the wasteland where they'd been murdered was disrespectful of their memory, in his opinion.

But his opinion had not been sought.

It was Darcy who had taken him in, serving as a second father. Darcy coaxed him out of his grief, step by gradual step, until he was functioning as well as anyone could expect.

Darcy knew better than to take him to baseball games—they were a trigger for too many years—but introduced Connor to, among other venues, the Arts and Culture Gallery, and the Museum of Science, Technology, and History.

The Museum became his favorite sanctuary. The exhibits drew him out of his shell, exciting his imagination for the world around him. Visits to the Art Gallery reinforced his appreciation and gratitude for the culture he was privileged to live in.

As he got older, it was Darcy who helped him understand that the Givers weren't the altruistic patrons his fellow Citizens believed them to be. Connor had no memory of the time before the Givers' arrival. As far as he knew, the aliens had always been part of Cascadia.

The Givers were reclusive. Only a select few Citizens had ever seen them. Those who allied themselves with their alien benefactors rose into a new elite within the Enclave, a shadow board dominating the actual Council.

The majority of Citizens raised no objections, asked no questions. The Givers' generosity in providing advanced weaponry and improvements to safeguard the Enclave earned them both gratitude and admiration.

Darcy was among a small segment of the population who had begun to question the aliens' motives, viewing them with growing suspicion and distrust. Connor remembered feelings of displacement and betrayal as he learned more from Darcy. As a child, he'd assumed what he heard about the benevolent Givers was accurate, trustworthy. Their propaganda machine was impressive, but for all the wrong reasons.

"Mindless sheep!" Darcy ranted and fumed in private. "The Givers rule through the puppets they've bought on the Council. Our own so-called 'Citizens' sold us out to alien invaders."

His used his position of influence on the Council to covertly gather like-minded Citizens, who in turn used their access to resources as an opportunity to steal Giver technology.

"We're using the Givers' own technological 'improvements' against them." Darcy's explanation made logical sense. They'd had a long talk after Connor first witnessed the delivery of a sedated savage in the back of Darcy's truck.

Connor grew to accept Darcy's logic. If they hoped to return control of the Enclave to humanity, any councilors who collaborated with the aliens must be eliminated. He also understood why their deaths could not be traced to Darcy's small, but growing cadre. And he marveled at his foster father's brilliant reverse engineering of Giver technology which made the Implants possible.

But catching sight of the tranquilized savage unnerved him. Her shallow breathing, the limpness in her arms and legs, and her otherwise peaceful facial expression. She didn't look much older than Connor. But as always, Darcy had a well-articulated explanation. Nothing was done without a good reason.

In an unregistered clinic, location unknown, a nameless medic outfitted the young savage with an Implant, and Darcy's former chauffeur, Maya D'Souza, returned the savage—now an unwitting drone—to whatever hovel she called home.

Darcy lectured him later on the same balcony. "You've studied military history, Connor. You must see the parallels. There are always difficult choices to make, for the greater good of Cascadia. You'll find 'cannon fodder' in every war—foot soldiers that a wise general must sacrifice in order to achieve their objectives. My drones are no different."

Connor conceded that he was right, but Darcy continued, hammering his point home. "What's the alternative—putting Implants in our fellow Citizens? No, that's barbaric. Our drones are always savages. It's all they're good for, anyway."

The past year had been one of Connor coming into his own in Darcy's clandestine organization. He was on the verge of adulthood, the same age his older sister had been when the savages had murdered her.

Tonight, after the successful acquisition of two additional candidates for Implants, Connor felt nothing beyond the satisfaction of another job well done.

It came as no surprise to learn that the Givers—verifying their treachery, in Darcy's mind—were also abducting savages in order to create Trackers, their subservient, ruthlessly loyal bodyguards.

At first, no one noticed or cared. Then the Givers reprogrammed Trackers to intercept and exterminate the drones, in order to protect their human allies on the Council, the collaborators who'd betrayed the Enclave.

Trackers were relentless in destroying their intended targets, but that only served to strengthen Darcy's resolve. The deadly cat-and-mouse strategy continued, with occasional victories to offset the failures. In fact, a mere six weeks earlier, a collaborator met their untimely demise after one of Darcy's drones successfully penetrated the Enclave's security.

"They betrayed their own kind." Darcy announced his verdict, but anyone within earshot needed no convincing. "They got what they deserved."

Darcy and his followers represented a small faction who knew the truth about the aliens. The collaborators would denounce them, naturally, if they only knew their identities. They'd say anything to cling to their positions on the Council, aided and abetted by the Givers.

Their opinions didn't matter. Connor knew who the true Citizens of the Enclave were.

A beep sounded, jarring his thoughts back to the present. He glanced at his wrist, confirming the passage of time. Doc would be finished with the Implants by now.

After a lingering look at the Enclave's comforting skyline, he shrugged into his jacket and left the balcony. Their night's work would soon be over. One last dash through the shantytown gauntlet, and two unsuspecting drones would be unleashed.

Connor exited the villa, deep in his own thoughts. He reached inside his shirt while waiting for the elevator, pulling out an archaic locket on a silver chain. It belonged to his mother. He'd impetuously claimed it after her death—a time capsule of better days. He never took it off.

He pried it open, gazing at the photographs inside—one of him at age twelve, and the other of his sister. Her smiling, carefree face became a talisman of sorts, steeling his resolve against the savages who'd stolen his family from him.

Ping! The elevator announced its arrival. Connor closed the locket and tucked it inside his shirt. His sister's picture was always enough to drive away any lingering doubts. Savages deserved to be drones.

It was the only thing they were good for.

The elevator whisked him down toward street level, where he would rendezvous with Darcy, Tony, and their newest drones. As coldly resolute as his mentor-father, Connor watched the digital numbers decrease, floor by floor.

They would win the undeclared war against the aliens—the so-called Givers. The Enclave would be human-only once again. There were plenty of available savages to Implant.

For the good of the Enclave.

ELEVEN ◎

"I DON'T TRUST MATEO," Amos said flatly. "His 'guided tour' made sense for the most part, but my gut told me something was twisted. And that was *before* I realized he's a Tracker."

They kept a steady pace, matching Don's long strides. The big man seemed driven to put as much distance between himself and the Enclave as possible. Neither Jane nor Amos disagreed. They covered several miles before the moon rose to add its eerie luminance to their journey.

"A Tracker, claiming to be part of the Hub network?" Disbelief colored Jane's voice. "I can't get my head around it. When his eye lit up, I thought I was having a heart attack. What if he killed the real Hub leader, and replaced them?"

"He'd be in a perfect spot to spread disinformation across the entire network," Amos replied darkly. "Or collect intel on Runners—us, for example—and pass it along to the Hoarders."

They'd made good time, reentering the ruins of the Old City an hour earlier. If their luck held, the stolen truck they'd hidden in an abandoned parking garage would still be there.

"That occurred to me, too," Don said. He pivoted in a quick circle as he spoke, surveying their surroundings. "But if Mateo isn't legit, why give us any intel at all? If he killed the others—if there *were* others—why let us live? He could've ratted us out to the Hoarders at the gate."

They paused at the next intersection. The traffic lights were dark, as lifeless as any of the lampposts lining the four-lane boulevard. They stood back-to-back in a compact circle, alert for anything out of the ordinary. Nothing. No movement in the shadows. No betraying noises. The Old City was empty, abandoned, a man-made wasteland. Two generations had passed since the downtown core was last a center of commerce, entertainment, and upscale housing.

Jane took the lead as they jogged diagonally across the intersection. The parking garage was less than three blocks east, now visible under the cold moonlight.

Amos glanced over his shoulder, unable to shake the feeling that they were under surveillance. "It would've been easy for him to kill us, or have the guards do it. They had us in the crosshairs outside Gate Seven." He glanced at Jane. "Did you learn anything from the townspeople in Jericho?"

"There's not much to tell." Jane made an exasperated noise. "I tried playing 'little lost girl looking for work,' and half the people said 'try Gate Seven,' and the rest said, 'talk to Mateo.' He's got a solid reputation with the locals. I doubt anyone knows he's a Tracker. What tipped you off, Amos?"

"Frustration." Amos shrugged in the darkness. "I got mad when he wouldn't give us a straight answer. So, I kept an eye on him, and I noticed how strange his mannerisms are. And then—boom—it hit me. Trackers have a distinctive way of moving, stiff and mechanical. Mateo moves like a Tracker."

"If your gut tells you not to trust Mateo, I'd go with your gut." Jane's skepticism remained unchanged. "No one forced him to give himself away. He *wanted* us to know. Do you think he would've kept his mouth shut if you hadn't figured it out?"

"We'll never know," Amos replied. "Everything Mateo told us made sense. The work permits, protocols for getting inside the Enclave, the purges, all of it. Except…he claimed there's traitors among the Hoarders. Dissidents, he called them. That tidbit of intel came out of left field. I still don't know what to make of it."

Don scoffed. "Whether or not these dissidents exist isn't our only problem." His voice sounded strained. "Mateo's obviously a Tracker, but he seems to have recovered his autonomy. The Givers can't be happy about that. Why haven't they taken him down?"

They halted in front of the entrance to the parking garage. The staircase leading to the lower levels was shrouded in inky darkness. They lingered outside the glass-less doors, looking at each other in bewilderment.

"What if the Givers kidnapped the real Hub leader, turned him into a Tracker, and gave him a shop near Gate Seven?" Jane shivered, her eyes large in the moonlight. "I agree with Amos. Mateo could be the eyes and ears of the Hoarders."

Don shook his head, oddly backlit by moonlight. "If he wanted to spy on us, the *last* thing he'd do is reveal his Tracker-ness." He ran his fingers through his hair. "I think we've got a renegade Tracker on our hands, but I have no idea how he broke free. Or why he'd choose to stay in Jericho."

"Living beside Hoarderville is a huge risk," Amos said. "Jane's right. Mateo was too quick to reveal himself. He seems to prefer speaking in riddles. You've got to figure it out yourself."

"Oh, great." Jane laughed, short and self-deprecating. "We've jumped to the wrong conclusion before. We thought it was Runners against Hoarders. Then we found out about the Givers."

Don shushed them, pivoting in a wary circle, arms loose and outstretched. Jane fell silent and Amos tensed. *What's wrong with us—standing out in the open, exposed?*

Don completed his quick reconnaissance and darted between Amos and Jane, opening the parking garage's shattered door. He pressed a finger against his lips, and led them inside.

Their footsteps were silent as they descended to the second subterranean level. The moonlight didn't reach the bottom of the staircase, and the darkness was almost absolute.

No point waiting for our eyes to adjust. Amos caught one of Don's massive hands in his own, reaching back with the other to link to Jane. So connected, they shuffled cautiously forward.

Don guided them in a cautious advance, almost feeling his way, to where they'd left the stolen truck. Amos counted their steps under his breath, trying to recall just how far in they'd parked. Jane padded behind him, as silent as a panther on the hunt, keeping a firm grip on his hand.

Amos heard Don's thin sigh of relief as his outstretched hand rapped against the fender, the hollow sound obscenely loud. They felt their way around the vehicle, opening doors and climbing in.

The interior lights were dazzling. Amos shielded his eyes while Don fished the keys out of his pocket. The engine roared into life, echoing in the empty parking garage. Door closed and darkness reclaimed the interior of the vehicle.

So much for the element of surprise, Amos thought, and almost laughed out loud. *There's no one here to surprise.* His mirth subsided abruptly. *We hope.*

Headlights blazed, cutting a swath through the darkness and illuminating the exit ramp. Don gunned the engine and the heavy vehicle bellowed its way to street level. He executed a sharp left, tires squealing on the cracked pavement.

"Now, we make up for lost time." Don seemed energized to be behind the wheel. "We'll have to hike in after we hide the truck, but it beats walking the whole way."

Jane wrinkled her nose. "Or taking the sewer route." She sat on the edge of the rear seat, one arm draped over each of the front seats. "Tell me more about these dissidents. What were Mateo's exact words, and what was your gut reaction?"

Amos took a deep breath. "I assumed Mateo was warning us. I thought he meant there were people nearby who'd turn us over to the Hoarders if they got the chance."

Don took up the story, keeping his foot on the accelerator. "I had the same reaction, until Mateo made it clear he didn't mean spies in Jericho. I still can't believe it. *Hoarders*, willing to betray their own kind." His face looked strained, illuminated by a greenish glow from the truck's instrument panel. "And then he fires up his little red eyeball. That was a total game-changer for me. A Tracker breaking free of the Givers? I didn't think it was possible."

Amos nodded, twisting sideways in his seat to face his companions. "The Tracker we captured last spring is the only one I've heard speak, even though she doesn't make much sense. But Mateo talks like a scholar."

"I wonder if there's any more like him?" Jane tightened her grip on the headrest. "I guess this means he's defective in some way. How else could he break free from the Givers?"

Amos shook his head, unwilling to accept her hypothesis. "I think Mateo's unique. The Tracker at Eastside is talking now—

more or less—but the only reason she's 'free' is because Aubrey shorted her system out with a cattle prod."

Jane refused to back down. "So how do we explain Mateo?"

They veered around another corner. Their destination, a nondescript service garage in an otherwise abandoned building, was only moments away. As they completed the turn, Don jammed his foot on the brakes, bringing them to a full stop.

Amos watched Don's face harden and heard Jane's dismayed gasp. He glanced through the front windshield, and then he understood. A body lay crumpled in a heap, blocking their path, a dark and glistening puddle spreading from it.

Don allowed the truck to idle for a few moments before he killed the engine and extinguished the headlights, plunging the street into darkness. The moon, now directly overhead, provided scant illumination, barely enough to light the gruesome scene.

No one spoke as they exited the truck, each shutting their door with care. Don knelt to examine the supine body. Amos and Jane stood on either side, keeping watch up and down the street.

Windows. Amos's inner voice sounded the warning. *If they're watching from anywhere, it's the upper windows.*

Don lifted the corner of the victim's jacket and examined the ragged hole in her abdomen. Her only visible injury.

"No broken bones, no sign of blunt force trauma." Don relayed his observations in a detached, clinical voice. "Defensive marks on the wrists and hands—looks like another successful 'harvest' for the Trackers."

Harvest. Amos shivered, recalling the sterile term they'd learned from their captive Tracker. *A cold description for ripping out a Runner's Implant.*

Jane said nothing, the expression on her face a stark combination of horror, empathy, and fury.

"Look where she was when she died." Amos swallowed hard. He gestured around the street, his voice hoarse. "A Tracker was *here*, less than a mile from Eastside."

"I wonder who her target was." Jane stared at the mutilated body. "Implants drive their victims to specific targets." The longer she stared, the more Amos sensed her growing rage.

"*Hoarders.*" She spat on the ground. "What kind of monster kidnaps other human beings, and gives them an Implant?"

Don covered the gaping wound with the woman's jacket. He remained on one knee, his expression difficult to read. When he spoke, he kept his voice low. "If anyone's watching, our cover's blown. No self-respecting Hoarder would've stopped to check on her." He rose to his full height, towering over his companions. For a long moment, he remained motionless, staring past them into the night. "There's nowhere to bury her, but I'm not leaving her body out here on the street."

"We don't have a choice, Don." Jane didn't flinch at the angry look he threw her way. "We'll be on foot as soon as we ditch the truck. We can't carry her through the tunnels. Even if we did, there's nowhere to bury her around the Mission. Everything's dust and concrete."

That sounds cold, but it's the truth. Amos couldn't argue with her logic, but he still found the idea disturbing. "Hoarders created this situation, Don. We can't give her a decent burial, but that's not our fault."

Don gave no sign that he heard. He dropped to one knee and gathered the limp body in his muscular arms. Without a word, he strode to a nearby tenement, and slammed his massive shoulder into the door.

It swung open with a dry crack, and he disappeared inside with his burden.

It was an unsettling moment—Don's gentleness juxtaposed with such an irreverent burial setting. A few minutes passed before he reappeared, empty-handed.

And now "decent burial" means concealing the body in a ruined building, rather than leaving her in the middle of the street. Amos clenched his fists, loathing the Hoarders anew. *This is what we've been reduced to.*

Jane sidled closer, watching with somber eyes as Don trudged toward them. No one thought to keep an eye on the adjacent buildings, the empty windows, or the street ahead.

Or behind.

TWELVE ◉

THE TRACKER KEPT A CAREFUL VIGIL, hidden in a shadowed alley. Three bio-forms exited their vehicle to inspect the body of its most recent Harvest. Exactly as predicted. The Givers were as wise as they were generous.

The Tracker lowered its gaze, reverently contemplating the glistening Implant in its hand. Miniature lights played across its surface, visible through the deceased bio-form's coagulating blood. It had extracted the Implant in one precise, efficient motion. Quest complete. Harvest acquired.

No. Inaccurate. Its internal processor clicked. The Givers did not consider the Quest complete. The Harvest was but one facet that they required.

The Tracker did not question the unusual additions to normal Quest protocol. The Givers were wise. Their demands were not to be disputed, merely obeyed. It assimilated the additional data into its core subroutines.

Analyze. Adapt. Enact.

The Tracker crept forward, monitoring the three bio-forms

with meticulous attention. They had not moved, speaking among themselves over the lifeless body of its victim. Distracted. The Givers had foreseen this as well.

It slipped out of the alley, auditory sensors set at maximum. It must betray neither its presence nor its purpose to the unsuspecting bio-forms. Its instructions were clear. The Givers were generous but they were not to be denied.

It crouched by the rear wheel of the truck, reaching beneath the chassis to affix the Implant, still dripping red, to the underside of the vehicle. Not a single wasted motion—efficient completion of its clandestine task was crucial.

The Tracker crept away from the truck, cloaked once again in the shadows of an alley. It scanned the area—back and forth, up and down, side to side to side. The Givers' final demand was equally clear. It snuck down the alley, seeking the most efficient route to circle around the distracted bio-forms.

Fear bubbled up. It had completed the Quest, achieved the Harvest, thereby demonstrating its undying loyalty to the Givers. Why the change in protocol?

It immediately terminated the line of questioning. The Givers were generous but they were not to be denied. Their orders were as clear as they were nonnegotiable.

It must circle around the bio-forms, deny them an escape route. The confrontation must be unexpected and unavoidable. One final task remained.

One last sacrifice to satisfy the appetite of its gods.

The Tracker circled the block, emerging at the most advantageous location. It observed the bio-forms returning to their truck, preparing to depart.

Interior lights flashed, doors closed, and the truck's interior was plunged into darkness again.

Everything was proceeding just as the Givers had predicted. The engine roared into life, and the truck's headlamps cast a blinding swath of light across the deserted street.

The Tracker held its breath as it calculated the precise moment when the headlamps would betray its current position. Fear blossomed anew, gnawing and acidic.

Fear was all it had left.

The Tracker stepped out of the shadows, intent on its final task, scanning eye flaring into red-hot life. It slowed to a halt in the middle of the empty street, and waited for the inevitable.

It hoped the Givers would be pleased.

THIRTEEN ◉

A SOLITARY FIGURE appeared out of the night moments after Don shifted the truck into gear. Pinned by the glare of the headlights, the Tracker held its position, rigid and unmoving. The piercing red glow around its left eye was like a beacon, as if it were taunting them.

Amos knew what came next. A murdered Runner, a Tracker caught in their headlights, and a truck with Don at the wheel —there could be only one outcome. He pawed for the handgrip above his door, locking his fingers around it as the truck lurched forward.

The impact was abrupt and sickening. The dull thump of dented metal and the sharp snap of shattered bones echoed in the street, reverberating inside the cab. Don jammed his foot on the accelerator. Tires squealing, the truck bounced over the Tracker's crushed form and raced away.

"We're going to need some new paint." Jane clutched at the back of Amos's chair, leaning between the seats. "That's *two* Tracker-sized dents you've put in this truck."

Don exploded. "That was *stupid*."

Jane scowled at him, but he continued before she could speak. "As if our cover wasn't already blown . . . I flatten a Tracker too close to Eastside." He slammed his fist on the steering wheel. "I've got to be better than this."

Jane fell silent, leaving whatever protest she'd intended unsaid. Don drove aggressively, covering the remaining distance to their destination at a reckless pace.

Amos jumped out to hoist the metal garage door open, allowing just enough space for Don to maneuver inside. Amos slowed the door's descent, muffling its impact. The garage was plunged into near-total darkness. He shoved the locking bar into place, sealing the room.

Don swung out of the cab, all business. "Leave nothing behind. This garage is still a safe hidey-hole, as far as we know, but I'm not taking any chances. And—sorry to have to break the bad news—we're going to hike twice as far out before heading down into the tunnels."

"And twice as far back." Jane's normal sarcasm crept back into her voice. She raised her hands in response to Don's withering look. "Hey, I'm not saying it's a bad idea. The more we muddy our back-trail, the better. Just don't expect my feet to thank you."

Amos circled the truck to inspect the damage, but the interior of the garage was too murky to make out much detail. He had little doubt that it would require at least a day's work to adequately clean up the evidence. *First things first. We've got to make it back to the Hub in one piece.*

Don and Jane waited for him by the side door, eager to finish their circuitous journey. As they exited into an alley behind the garage, his thoughts strayed to the change in Don's demeanor. He couldn't tell whether the big man was more up-set over the anonymous Runner's death, or his lapse in judgment by killing a Tracker so close to Eastside. *I'm usually the one second-guessing myself. Don's always been solid.*

It was Don who'd challenged Amos to confront his accusing inner voice. The guilt associated with his brother Trey's death —a pointless, cold-blooded execution by Hoarders—haunted Amos for so many years that it took on a personality of its own. Garr and Doc Simon tried to help him cope with his guilt and self-recrimination, but it was Don who'd finally gotten through to him. The big man could also take credit for Amos naming his inner voice Gabriel.

Stop beating yourself up. He vividly recalled Don's no-nonsense confrontation. *I need Amos 'the Runner' Morgan on this foray, not his traumatized twelve-year-old self. That little voice in your head? You need to tell it to shut up.*

It was nothing Garr and Doc Simon hadn't said many times before, but for some reason, Don's words marked a turning point. This was no time for them to trade places.

First order of business—camouflaging their back trail to steer any would-be hunters, human or otherwise, away from Eastside. Further discussion about Mateo, so-called dissidents, or Trackers operating too close to the Mission district would have to wait.

Don led the way, darting from shadow to shadow. Jane and Amos followed his zig-zag route, pausing regularly to disguise their back-trail. The final leg of their journey was no less dangerous than their visit to Jericho, or Gate Seven.

A mental image of Mateo surfaced repeatedly in his mind. The shopkeeper's unreadable facial expression. His cryptic way of communicating.

His inexplicable ability to live, anonymous and unmolested, in the shadow of the Enclave. The red glow around his eye, betraying his true identity.

No, not betraying. Amos caught the flaw in his thinking. *It wasn't accidental. It was a deliberate, strategic move.*

He corralled his wandering thoughts. Their night was far from over.

FOURTEEN ⊕

THE GIVERS. Tracy stared at the ceiling, her thoughts chaotic as she puzzled over her isolation. Their silence was punishment for her failure. It was the only logical explanation.

No. Inaccurate. The penalty for failing in the Quest was immediate termination. The Givers' withdrawal must therefore indicate something else.

Analyze. Analyze.

No response from her internal processor. The data stored there was no longer accessible. The damage was too severe. She was limited to her own thoughts.

She conducted a visual inventory of the infirmary, her remaining eye flitting from object to object.

Analyze. Adapt. Enact.

Fury erupted, eclipsing rational thought. She flailed, uselessly, against the restraints around her arms and legs. Her strength-enhancers failed to activate, no matter how hard she willed it. Her frenzied outburst evaporated, and she collapsed, sinking back on the gurney, limp and powerless.

She closed her eye and took deep, regular breaths, imposing calm on her pounding heart. New strategy was required.

Analyze. Adapt.

A slight smile curved her lips. Insight—win the bio-forms' sympathy. Perhaps even enlist their aid.

Her most consistent and frequent access was with the bio-form designated Doc. The medic was therefore the most logical choice. The key to her freedom was the bio-forms, and Doc Simon was her optimal target.

Tracy relaxed as a strategy coalesced.

Cultivating the bio-forms' trust would require discreet manipulation. Verbal communication was vital to her strategy. She must improve her ability to speak.

She began practicing, mouthing words in silence, willing her reluctant facial muscles to cooperate. Perspiration broke out on her forehead, trickling past her temples and into her matted hair.

The concentration required to form words—so plain in her mind—was daunting. Far more difficult than she'd anticipated. Yet she must persevere. It was her only chance of reclaiming her independence.

First, her freedom, and then ... absolution from the Givers.

FIFTEEN ◉

GARR CALLED the meeting to order, and chairs shuffled around the table in response. It felt strange without the entire team present. The mess hall seemed larger.

Aubrey glanced around the table as she stirred her coffee. *Six months ago, I lived outside the Old City, and had no idea any of this existed. And now, it feels normal.*

Garr sat at one end of the table, Doc facing him at the opposite end. Sheila laid claim to her favorite perch on the counter. Aubrey pulled out a chair next to Garr and sat down.

Don, Amos, and Jane were long overdue, and their absence had everyone on edge. The tension in the mess hall was like a mosquito's whine, faint but troubling.

Never thought it'd bother me if Snake Lady was missing. Aubrey sipped her coffee, hiding a smile. A pang of guilt followed swiftly on the heels of her thought. *Hoarders are the enemy. And the Givers. Jane's nasty, but at least we're on the same side.*

Garr's voice interrupted, drawing her wandering thoughts back to the present.

"Let's get the obvious out of the way." He leaned forward, resting his forearms on the table. "Don, Jane, and Amos are late. That's not surprising. Jericho Hub is a stone's throw outside the Enclave, which requires extra caution. They'll take whatever steps are necessary to avoid trouble, and whatever intel they bring will be worth it. Now, put it out of your minds."

"Easier said than done, Garr." Doc sounded tired, but she nodded. "You're right. They know what they're doing. Worrying won't bring them back any sooner."

Garr clasped his hands in front of him. "Agreed. So, let's move on. Doc, let's start with you. Give us a status update on our resident Tracker—I mean, *Tracy*. Has anything she's said made sense? Any intel that might be useful against Trackers, Hoarders, or both?"

Doc frowned and removed her glasses, setting them on the table in front of her. "Well, for the physical part, I'm amazed her injuries are healing at all. When she first arrived, I didn't expect much." She shifted in her chair. "Her physical enhancements apparently include various chemical additives in her bloodstream. I can only begin to guess at their purpose, but it seems accelerated self-repair is part of the package."

Aubrey's eyes widened. She hadn't considered self-repair.

Doc paused, rubbing her eyes. "The damage done by the prod caused her enhancements to function erratically. Sometimes they work, but only in fits and starts. She's not as strong as she used to be, and by that, I mean she's no longer capable of snapping us in two."

"That's good news." Garr leaned back in his chair, looking relieved. "The less of a risk she poses to this Hub, the better."

Doc nodded. "And for the past couple of days, she's begun eating regular food again, *and* keeping it down."

Sheila straightened on the counter. "Really? She used to gag whenever I tried feeding her, and then she'd puke everything back up. What changed?"

Doc shrugged, replacing her glasses on the bridge of her nose. "It's all part of the 'fits and starts' I mentioned. Her self-repair still works…to a degree. Trackers are apparently designed to function without food, but that ability's breaking down. Tracy's lucky her human digestive system is kicking back in, even if imperfectly."

Garr listened intently, jotting notes on a small notepad in front of him.

Aubrey's pulse quickened as she watched. *I bet we'll be making another trip to the dropbox. But this time we'll be the ones sending mail.*

"What about intel?" Garr punctuated a note with a sharp stab of his pencil. "I know her speech is impaired, but has she said anything potentially useful?"

"Tracy has no trouble understanding us." Aubrey inserted herself into the conversation. "I saw the way she was watching me, just this morning. She understands everything we say, and it looked to me like she's thinking hard, too. Except…"

She motioned to Doc Simon.

Doc understood her gesture and stepped in. "Tracy's mind, what's left of the human part, has sustained quite a shock—no pun intended. The prod shorted out the mechanical implants in her brain, which explains why she can't hear the Givers. That's the good news." She sighed, spreading her hands in resignation. "As far as her chances of overcoming the aphasia, well, I can't promise anything. Except to note that she *wants* to communicate. But at this point, it's extremely difficult for her."

Garr tapped his pencil on the table. "But in your medical

opinion, it's still an improvement." He pursed his lips at Doc's nod. "Remember Tracy's first night in the Hub? She panicked when she realized we weren't the Givers. If she's trying to communicate with us now, I think that's a good sign."

Sheila eased herself off the counter and sat at the table. "Yes and no, Garr. She's putting a lot of effort into speaking, but I don't get the sense she's looking for answers. She's accepted that we aren't the aliens she calls Givers, and she's not fighting Doc over blood tests any more. But that doesn't mean she has any intention of providing us with intel."

"She's listening to us," Aubrey interrupted, but no one seemed to mind. "There's been several times when I've seen her frown, or she turns away if she catches me looking at her. I think Tracy's evaluating everything we say."

"She's relearning how to speak," Doc said. "It's only natural that she's listening closely. That's how infants…" She bolted forward in her chair. "That's not what you're getting at, is it?"

Aubrey took a deep breath before voicing her nagging suspicion. "What if Tracy's gathering intel—on us?"

SIXTEEN ◉

Tracy heard a crescendo of sound outside the infirmary door. Footsteps. Bio-forms approached, closer and closer. More than one, judging by the overlapping tramp of footsteps. She pulled herself up as best she could in the restraints, prepared to imitate the most innocuous facial expression she could think of.

Three bio-forms entered, pausing to look around the infirmary. It was logical to assume they expected to find the unit designated Doc Simon. Time to implement her embryonic plan.

"Tracy. My name," she said, adopting her best imitation of the emotion she once knew as cheerfulness. Her smile was forced and crooked, but she was pleased nonetheless.

The bio-forms were not expecting her greeting. She saw it in their shocked reactions. One approached her gurney, his expression curious, while the other two hovered by the door, watching through wary eyes. She nodded at each of them in turn. Yes, this was a common non-verbal gesture the bio-forms used by way of greeting.

Her attempts at communication were succeeding.

The largest of the bio-forms bent to examine her. She knew his designation—no, his *name*—but to say it aloud was a struggle. The best she could produce were small choking sounds, but she refused to give up. Her smile faltered as she forced her uncooperative lips to form the syllables.

"Don," she said at last, drawing the single syllable out far longer than required. The bio-forms stared at her, their faces registering shock and suspicion.

She tried again, straining. This time, her words were flawless. "Don. Your name."

The hulking bio-form—no, his name was *Don*—straightened, looking over his shoulder at his companions. "Am I hallucinating, or did our resident Tracker just call me by name?"

"Look at that smile she's giving you, Don." The female bio-form's tone of voice suggested her words were not sincere. "I think she likes you."

The third bio-form lingered by the door, not speaking. Tracy knew his name as well, but chose not to address him. None of them were ready to accept a personal greeting from her. It was too soon. Especially the female, Jane.

Yes, that was her designation—Jane.

Tracy relaxed and lay back, beaming a sincere smile in their direction. Amos stared back at her, his indecipherable expression unchanged. Jane made an exasperated noise and shoved past him, stalking down the corridor.

Don bent over her, tugging at the bonds around her wrists. His attention shifted next to her ankles. Could she appeal to him to loosen the restraints?

Her brief hope evaporated. Freeing her was not his intent. He was confirming the restraints were secure. Nothing more.

Amos spoke for the first time. "Come on, Don. We've got a

report to make." He gestured in Tracy's direction, not looking at her directly, and began inching toward the door. "It'll still be here later."

Don stepped away from the gurney. "You mean, *she'll* be here later?" He laughed. "Hard habit to break, isn't it?"

Amos shrugged and turned to leave, Don following close behind. Tracy listened as their footsteps receded down the corridor. She was alone again. She relaxed, her head settling on the pillow.

Progress.

She'd remembered their names, grasped interpersonal nuances, and her ability to read facial expressions was improving. She studied the ceiling overhead, reveling in her triumph. Her lips curled in an effortless smile.

Strategy—implemented.

SEVENTEEN ◉

SILENCE SETTLED over the mess hall as everyone considered Aubrey's question. Doc broke the impasse, getting up to pour herself a fresh cup of coffee.

"Luckily, Tracy can't communicate with the Givers." She paused, stirring her steaming drink. "At the same time, better safe than sorry. I'd advise caution when speaking within earshot of her." She took a cautious sip. "And if she starts asking questions, think twice before answering. I hope she'll recover enough to be useful, but Aubrey raises a good point. Let's be sure Tracy's helping *us*, and not the other way around."

"Agreed." Garr's chair scraped on the floor as he shifted position, the sharp squeak uncomfortably loud. He acted as if he hadn't heard. "Sheila, what can you tell us about the boy?"

The kid we saved from Tracy? Aubrey straightened in her chair, her interest piqued.

"He didn't recall breaking my nose, that much I can tell you." Sheila chuckled ruefully. "I doubt he even recognized me. Maybe because I had two black eyes at the time." Her expression turned serious. "Doc gave him a quick checkup and then he was gone. We turned him over to South Central. They took care of extracting his Implant."

Doc stepped in. "South Central also confirmed his Implant was deactivated. The prods work as designed. The boy's only takeaway from the whole incident will be a minor scar."

"No memories—how far back?" Garr pulled his notepad closer, pencil poised. "Does he remember anything from that night?"

Sheila shook her head before he finished the question. "He was barely awake when South Central collected him. And from what we learned after Aubrey's little adventure, Implants block out short-term memory. He doesn't remember being in the Old City at all, let alone Aubrey saving his life. Thankfully, that also means he has no idea Tracy tried to kill him."

"Just as well," Doc replied, setting her mug on the table. "Less trauma to recover from. I've spoken with the doctor from South Central. He tells me the boy's only complaint when he woke up was about the stitches where they removed his Implant." She glanced around the table, smiling as she anticipated their next question. "They told him it was his appendix."

"Where is he now?" Aubrey asked. *I held him in my arms only once, but I need to know.* "Far away from the Hoarders, I hope."

Sheila shook her head. "That's not for us to know. Once he was on the mend, his family quietly relocated. The Hoarders have no idea that we found him before Tracy did. They'll assume he's dead. They won't be looking for him."

Aubrey stirred in her seat, a sense of foreboding gnawing at her. "How can you be so sure? The Givers blew up a lot of Trackers that night. It's a safe bet they know we deactivated the boy's Implant. Why *wouldn't* they come after him again?"

"Without an Implant, he's no longer a threat." Doc replied from the opposite end of the table, as calm as if she were delivering a medical diagnosis. "Whoever assigned Trackers to kill him aren't the same ones who Implanted him in the first place. And because he didn't kill his target, the Hoarders who sent him will assume he's dead."

"What we don't know, we can't reveal," Garr said, quoting one of Eastside's mantras. "For the boy's sake, it's best if none of us knows his new location."

He was answered with nods around the table.

Aubrey still harbored some doubts. *What if Tracy hasn't forgotten him?*

The door swung open under Don's enthusiastic push, and the three missing team members crowded into the mess hall. The somber mood lifted abruptly, and the overlapping sounds of relieved exclamations and eager questions competed in Aubrey's ears.

"Did anyone miss us?" Don grinned with feigned innocence, his voice booming in the small room. He caught Garr's hand in a crushing grip, intrigued by the look of relief on his commander's face. "If this is the kind of welcome we can expect, we'll make a point of arriving late more often."

Garr returned his firm handshake, speaking over his shoulder to Doc. "Now you've got an even better excuse for cooking up something special. Tonight, we have good reason to celebrate."

"Is that fresh coffee I smell?" Amos chimed in, grinning at their exuberant welcome.

Amos sounds happy. Aubrey was pleasantly surprised. *That's a new look for him. He's always so serious. Unlike Jane, who's always in a bad mood.*

Doc Simon chuckled as she gestured at the coffeepot. "My

father would roll over in his grave if he heard you calling boiled chicory root 'coffee,' but it's hot and there's plenty of it. I'm probably the only person in this Hub old enough to remember coffee *beans*."

"When did our pet Tracker start trying to make friends?" Jane's acerbic voice sliced through the celebration. "She sounds brain-damaged."

We missed you, too, Snake Lady. Aubrey caught herself. *I mean … Jane.*

Doc Simon bristled at her remark. Don stepped between them, addressing the group. "We've just had an unexpected chat in the infirmary with—Tracy, she tells us. That's just the latest surprise after a week's worth. Garr, we should debrief now, while everything's still fresh in our minds."

Garr nodded, holding out his hand, palm up. "Agreed. I'll take the package from the dropbox. We'll begin there, establish a context, and the three of you can fill in any gaps."

Don hesitated, an odd expression crossing his face. The rest of the Runners noticed it, and the tension level went up a notch or two.

Don at a loss for words? Aubrey glanced at Garr.

"Dropbox?" Amos's outburst was underlined by a strange laugh. "That was our first shock. We managed to find Jericho, but there's no package, Garr, because there's no dropbox."

"What do you know about Jericho, Garr?" Jane asked, her agitated voice commanding their attention. "Sheila? Anyone? Who's in charge, how many people are connected to it, that sort of thing."

The mood in the mess hall chilled abruptly. Jane was rattled, not a look usually associated with her. Aubrey glanced around the table, hoping someone had an answer.

Colonel Scott spoke first. "I know it's a high-risk location, just outside Cascadia. They operate with a skeleton staff, and their sole purpose is to collect and relay information. They've got no tech, nothing to draw a Tracker's attention. Why do you ask?"

"Does the name Mateo Reyes mean anything?" Don asked, watching his face.

Garr raised his eyebrows. He recognized the name—that much was clear. "We've never met, but he's the point person at Jericho. He poses as a clothing merchant, serving the migrants looking for work inside Cascadia Enclave. I wouldn't be exaggerating to say he's more intimately acquainted with 'hidden in plain sight' than all of us put together."

Amos crossed his arms. "He's also a Tracker."

EIGHTEEN ◉

A STUNNED SILENCE filled the mess hall. Aubrey stared in open-mouthed shock. Sheila's expression morphed from confusion to denial. Garr's eyebrows arched and he favored Amos with a look of measured appraisal.

Only Doc remained seated, eyes closed.

"And a Tracker apparently *not* brain-washed by the Givers." Amos's voice softened as he saw them struggling to assimilate the news. "As unbelievable as it sounds, Mateo's a Tracker, and he's the leader of Jericho Hub." He glanced at Don and Jane. "At least, we *think* he is."

Don took up the story. "Mateo functions as a word-of-mouth dropbox, with no paper trail that could be traced back to him. His guided tour wasn't only informative, it was more like 'guided reconnaissance.' He also told us there are people—dissidents, he called them—working against the Givers from *inside* the Enclave."

He paused, looking around the circle of disbelieving faces. Aubrey heard several muted outbursts of denial.

"I'm not sure what's more unbelievable." Don shrugged, turning to face Garr. "The idea of traitors inside Hoarderville, or a Tracker *not* controlled by the Givers."

An eerie quiet followed his report. Amos was the first to speak. His words sent a shiver down Aubrey's spine. "We also found a dead Runner, less than a mile from here." He paused to inhale a deep breath. "We took care of the Tracker."

"With the truck," Jane muttered, just loud enough for the others to hear.

Amos continued as if he hadn't heard. "We assume the dead Runner was its target, but Trackers have been showing up in this area more often. We need to be extra vigilant."

Garr stood, placing his pencil on the notepad and sliding both toward Don. "I want the three of you to put everything you remember on paper. Mateo's exact words, your observations about Cascadia Security, and anything that might help us figure out what he's up to."

Don eyed him as he sat down, pulling the notepad and pencil closer. "You didn't know he was a Tracker?"

Garr shook his head, looking pensive. "I'm as shocked as anyone. He's run that Hub for a long time, and there's never been any reason to question his loyalty." He leaned back in his chair, eyes straying to a random spot on the concrete wall. "Of course, hiding his true identity doesn't inspire much trust." He snapped his fingers, refocusing on Don. "It's a risk we'll have to take. If Mateo's information is legit, we'll work with him like he's one of us."

But he's not one of us. Aubrey stared into the liquid dregs in her mug. *He's like Tracy, except his enhancements still work. The Givers—does he still hear their voices?*

She didn't want to admit it, but she was shaken by the news

of a Tracker running a Hub. *Tracy's one thing—she's incapacitated. What do we really know about Mateo?*

"I think I'll put some more coffee on." Doc rose from her chair, heading for the counter.

The room came alive with movement. Doc busied herself with brewing a fresh pot of coffee. Don began listing a series of bullet-points on Garr's notepad. Jane followed Doc to the counter, pulling a clean mug from the cupboard.

Garr leaned on the table, catching Amos's eye. "Tomorrow, I want you and Don to clean up the truck. While you were gone, we received word about possible Runners in a town not far from here. Take a scanner and see if you can locate them before their Implants activate, or Trackers find them."

"I'm going, too." Sheila pushed her chair back from the table. "I'll get the scanner. And make sure we have a couple of prods charged and ready by the time the truck's available."

Amos nodded absently as Don slid the notepad to him. Jane seated herself beside him, cradling her mug as she read the scribbled lines of text.

"Aubrey." Garr's voice startled her out of her troubled musings. "Assemble your gear. A week's worth. You and Jane are with me."

More adventures with Snake La—Jane? Aubrey wondered at that. Jane shot her a baleful look over the rim of her cup. *Can't I stay behind and help Doc unravel the mystery of Tracy?*

Garr addressed his next order to Jane. "Since you're our local expert, Jane, you're going to teach Aubrey unarmed combat skills." His voice was firm. This was clearly not a suggestion, nor was he about to bend.

Jane lowered her mug with more force than she intended, spilling coffee over her fingers. She stifled a sharp exclamation.

The hot liquid short-circuited whatever protest she'd been about to voice.

She's as excited about the idea as I am. Aubrey clenched her scarred hand into a fist under the table, out of sight.

Garr's next words caught them off-guard, and they stared, their mutual resentment forgotten. "I want to meet Mateo Reyes for myself. It's an eight-day round trip to Jericho, on foot. Plenty of time to get started on Aubrey's training." He smiled grimly at their bewildered expressions. "Think of it as prepping for the Enclave."

NINETEEN ⊕

THE PATIENT LAY on his back, disoriented, staring into the blinding circle of lights directly above his head. The glare was dazzling, over-powering.

He tried to raise his arm as a shield against the merciless brilliance, only to find that unseen restraints pinned him to the surface beneath him. The glare remained. He squeezed his eyes shut to block it out.

A strange sensation crawled under his skin, like burning insects on a slow, stealthy prowl. The creeping waves ebbed and flowed, slower and then faster, treading maniacally across his ribs, circling his abdomen, and racing up his spinal coluemn.

And the noise ... a ticking or clicking sound somewhere in his body. The ticking escalated, morphing into a hammering vibration that resonated in his bones, setting his muscles aquiver in spastic convulsions. Louder, faster. Louder, faster. The acidic insects under his skin moved to match the beat.

The pounding noise ceased without warning. The crawling sensation slowed to a slight ripple, retreated into his abdomen, and then was still. His muscles continued to twitch uncontrollably, in a thousand microscopic aftershocks.

His vision began to clear, bit by laborious bit. The circle of lights overhead … a hospital? The bed on which he lay was hard and uncomfortable. An operating table? He tried to push the fear away, straining to clear his mind.

Gurney. His desperate mind seized on the word. The bed was called a gurney, and therefore, the blazing lights overhead must be surgical lamps.

His questing nostrils detected the odor of antiseptic cleaning solutions. Hypothesis confirmed. He was in a hospital. That explained the strange physical sensations. Post-operative disorientation, phantom pain. These were probably normal.

Except he had no recollection of an appointment for surgery, nor any memory of how he got here in the first place. Had he been in an accident?

He caught his breath as another realization struck him. His name. What was his name? He must be suffering from—there was a medical term for it—*amnesia.*

Answers. He needed answers.

A discordant cacophony erupted inside his skull. The noise was like a physical blow. He cringed as voices tumbled into his mind. Harsh, imperious voices, overlapping each other in rapid succession.

The voices ran wild through his brain—no, not his brain, but his *processor.* He balked at the sterile terminology. Where did that idea come from? Processor? I'm not a machine!

The voices corrected him. The Givers are generous but they are not to be denied.

Givers? Who—what—were the Givers? He was alone in the operating room, a patient held prisoner on the gurney by an unseen force. The cascading voices intensified, imposing their will with a heavy hand.

He struggled, resisting their insidious spread. The agony in his head worsened. He squeezed his eyes shut, desperate to silence the marauding voices.

The Givers are not to be questioned, only obeyed.

Sheer terror erupted, and he twisted his neck in the nick of time, vomiting convulsively over the side of the gurney.

The voices accelerated inside his mind, a mental tornado devouring everything in its path. The Quest...he was being given a Quest. Enhancements—physical, chemical, and mechanical—their gifts, enabling him to fulfill the Quest.

His target—the Implants. His objective—the Harvest. The more he fought the voices, the greater the agony.

The Givers are as wise as they were generous. All that matters is the Quest. Anything else is a distraction.

The voices continued, with relentless precision, conquering his mind and volition. He convulsed and acquiesced, exhausted, and the pain in his head began to subside. The mental calm was cool, refreshing, soothing.

The Tracker perceived the logic of the Quest, the oath of undying loyalty to the benevolent Givers. Its obsession with the Harvest was all-consuming, like the cravings of a starving animal.

Yet hunger was no longer a concern. The enhancements provided by the Givers included chemical nutrients, providing it with sustenance and an endless reservoir of energy.

The Givers were as wise as they were generous. This unit would serve them without question. It would not fail the Quest. The Givers would be pleased.

A door opened, the sound almost imperceptible. Figures

entered the room, gathering around the gurney. That word, which it had grasped with such desperation just moments earlier, now seemed irrelevant.

Nothing could interfere with the Quest. The Givers were generous but they were not to be denied.

Five or six figures gathered around the operating table, looking down at the Tracker with interest, evaluating their handiwork. Three of the figures represented the bio-forms infesting this planet. They served at the pleasure of the Givers, as was their proper place in the order of things. They were irrelevant, although useful at times.

A cluster of Givers hovered by the foot of the gurney. They remained motionless, graciously permitting the bio-forms to finish their examinations. The Tracker heard their voices inside its processor, bestowing dignity, purpose, and identity.

The Tracker's emotions were encapsulated somewhere deep within. Potential distractions, which must be corralled into submission. Nothing mattered but the Quest.

The Givers pivoted as one and drifted out of the room. There was a flicker of something like green-tinged lightning as they exited, leaving the Tracker alone with the bio-forms. Doctors, technicians—irrelevant humanoids, one and all. Their only saving grace was their role in serving the Givers.

One of the bio-forms, her facial features partially concealed by a surgical mask, bent to examine the Tracker's face. The bio-form seemed to have a particular interest in its left eye. She called to one of her co-workers and, within seconds, the Tracker felt heat building around its eye socket. Not enough to burn, but noticeable.

The bio-form appeared relieved and nodded with satisfaction to the others. They conferred among themselves, but the

Tracker paid them no attention. Its ability to hear the Givers was all that mattered.

The bio-forms deactivated the invisible restraints. They were preparing to release the Tracker to its task, its Quest, its reason for existence.

For a brief moment, it felt a sensation it recognized as fear. Small and contained, but fear nonetheless. Failure was not an option. The Givers had seen to that.

The Tracker sat up in one smooth motion, legs dangling over the side of the gurney, eager to be on its way. The bio-forms moved to escort it out of the medical facility. Irrelevant. Their assistance was not required.

Fear was contained, supplanted by the anticipation of its inaugural Quest. Yet fear would be its constant traveling companion, a malevolent creature lurking just beneath conscious thought. The Tracker understood and accepted this.

Fear was all it had left.

That, and the Quest.

TWENTY ◎

"No, I didn't bother repainting it, Don." The mechanic, Enrico Torres, seemed amused by the idea. "I don't have access to that kind of equipment. And besides, it's not unusual for Hoarders to have dented grills. How do you think they got their reputation for running us down?"

"I was joking about repainting, Rico." Don clapped him on the shoulder, a wide grin spreading across his face. "You should know me better by now."

Enrico shook his head, shoulders slumping. "You're right, I should. But I wasn't joking when I mentioned Hoarders denting their vehicles with pedestrians. To pass yourself off as one, you'll need to drive like a lunatic, but without creating casualties out of anyone we know. Think you're up to it?"

Don coughed politely into his hand. "Really, my modesty prevents me..." He burst into a loud guffaw, unable to keep a straight face.

Amos examined the truck's front end with a critical eye, hearing but not acknowledging Don's light-hearted banter. The hood was buckled in the middle, although the headlamps had survived. The grill suffered the most damage, but any bloodstains, and possible bits of Tracker, had been scrubbed clean with meticulous care.

We could say we hit a deer. Amos invented an alibi. *Who knows? We may look less conspicuous than before.* His inner voice sprang to caustic life. *Sure, let your guard down. Gambling with your friends' lives doesn't bother you, does it?*

Amos gritted his teeth, stifling the mental accusation. It wasn't always easy, learning to ignore Gabriel's voice.

The truck was where they'd left it, hidden inside the back entrance of an abandoned building. Daylight filtered through dirty windows, diffused by the grime, but more than enough for Amos to get a clear look at the vehicle.

"I promise to never use this truck again." Don's joking demeanor faded abruptly. "Hoarders don't take kindly to having their property stolen by the likes of us."

"Can you blame them?" Enrico polished a stubborn spot on the hood. "I mean, they *are* the privileged upper crust of humanity. It must drive them crazy when we, the unwashed peasants, steal their stuff. Trucks, technology, or whatever. Oh, and speaking of ill-gotten tech…" He sidled closer to Don. "Doc Simon sent us one of your deactivated Implants. We're learning what we can about its inner workings. It's *years* beyond anything we could even dream of. Very sophisticated."

Amos winced, recalling the sadistic Hoarders who'd murdered his brother Trey with their "sophisticated" weaponry.

Enrico wiped his hands on a polishing rag. "I'd be impressed with the Hoarders for inventing Implants—not *happy*, mind you, but impressed—except we know the Givers are the real source of their high-tech innovations."

Don laughed, shaking his head. "You don't sound like a mechanic. Or a proper worker-drone for the high and mighty Hoarders of the Enclave."

Enrico winked, as if they shared a private joke. "I spent *three years* working in Cascadia, repairing their machines while they looked down their entitled noses at me. And made sure I was outside by dusk, so I wouldn't contaminate their precious society." He crossed his arms, his smile widening. "Would anyone who knows me think I *wouldn't* smuggle out some tech here and there? I don't know what you're up to—and I don't want to know—but if there's any way I can help Colonel Scott stick it to the Hoarders…"

Amos finished his inspection. "We'll be back after nightfall." He met Enrico's gaze. "Reusing this truck is a liability, but we need it, one last time. Anything more is asking for trouble."

"It's not my truck anyway." Enrico spread his hands, his expression innocent. "In all likelihood, I'll forget it even exists in … oh, say, the next fifteen minutes or so." He reached out and caught Don's hand in a firm handshake. "Good luck, old friend. I don't miss working in that Enclave, not even one tiny little bit. At the time, I thought, 'hey, it's a payday,' but it wasn't worth it. Give my best to Garr and Doc, okay?"

"I'll pass that along, next time I see them," Don said over his shoulder as he strode to the exit. Amos opened the door to the alley, glancing outside. "And if I ever visit Jericho again, I'll say hi to Mateo for you, as well."

Enrico's smile faded abruptly. "You mean the shopkeeper, Mateo Reyes? That's not funny, Don."

Amos slammed the door, alarmed. *Something's wrong.*

Don paused beside him, pivoting to face the mechanic. "What are you talking about?"

Enrico fidgeted with his cleaning rag, an awkward look on his face. "I thought you knew. Mateo Reyes is dead and buried, two years ago already. A Tracker got him."

TWENTY-ONE ◉

A GHOSTLY MOON PEEKED between the lowering clouds, haphazardly piercing the dark shroud over the streets. Amos and Sheila kept to the shadows near the agreed-upon rendezvous. They'd decided, following Enrico's disturbing revelation, to take the most circuitous route possible, in order to safeguard Eastside's location.

Don insisted on returning for the truck after nightfall, alone, citing the increased risk of discovery. Amos wasn't happy about that, but he deferred to the big man's judgment. Their unresolved questions about Mateo's identity—and his loyalty —made them doubly wary.

Don's no more expendable than anyone else. Amos tugged his jacket closer in the pre-autumn chill. *I should've gone with him. We're supposed to be a team.*

"He'll be here." Sheila exuded calm and confidence. She hefted the backpack containing the tools for their mission. There wasn't much. Two prods, fully charged, and the scanner Amos obtained from a Tracker they'd deactivated earlier that year.

"Sure you don't want me to carry that?" Amos asked, although he could easily guess what she'd say. Sheila was, in many ways, Doc's right hand when it came to science and tech, but she was also as tough as any of them.

"You know me better than that." Sheila laughed, muffling the sound behind her hand. "You're only asking because you're worried about Don." She laughed again at the sharp look he gave her. "See? I know you pretty well, too."

"I can't have his back if I'm not there." He looked away, squinting down the street. She was right, on all counts. "I'm more worried about Garr's team trying to contact Mateo. We know he's a Tracker. What if he killed the real Mateo?"

"The colonel knows what he's doing," Sheila chided him. "He's been making the tough calls for a long time. He's not about to get sloppy now. Besides, he took Jane and Aubrey with him. They'll keep him out of trouble."

"Aubrey and Jane?" Amos grunted, kicking at the broken pavement. "Sorry, but that doesn't inspire much confidence. I'm not questioning their skills—Jane's a pro and Aubrey's adapted faster than any of us thought she would. But they don't have each other's back. On the surface, maybe, but it's not an automatic reflex. It's not instinctive."

"Garr's a good instructor." Sheila shifted her pack, leaning casually against the brick wall beside her. She cocked her head, listening. "Hear that? Sounds like Don's driving."

Several blocks south, a dark-hued truck careened around the corner, tires squealing on the pavement. It slalomed toward them, fish-tailing wildly. A reckless approach, even for Don.

His inner voice asserted itself, uninvited. *Maybe it isn't Don. Don't just stand there—take cover! Shouldn't you have Sheila's back, too?*

Amos stepped between Sheila and the oncoming vehicle, wishing he had one of the Hoarders' advanced weapons. Sheila set the backpack on the sidewalk, brandishing her knife in a fighter's stance.

The moonlight revealed a telltale dent on the approaching vehicle, and he relaxed slightly. Sheila muttered something under her breath, returning her knife to its protective sheath.

The vehicle skidded to a stop, slewing sideways on the pavement. Don bellowed out the open window, a wild note in his voice. "Trackers! Stop gawking and get in—we've got to go!"

Sheila stooped to retrieve the backpack, and Amos pivoted in a wary circle, schooling himself to absorb every detail. *Pay attention above street level—rooftops, windows. Trackers could be anywhere.*

Nothing. No betraying circles of red light. No shadowy figures lurking in alleys. He took no comfort from that. Everything could change in an instant.

Sheila ran to the truck, opening the rear door and hefting the backpack inside. Amos caught up as she leaped into the back seat, the door banging shut behind her.

The engine revved as Amos tore the passenger door open. He threw himself into the front seat, and Don immediately took off. Forward momentum slammed Amos's door shut with a sharp, percussive sound.

"Three Trackers. Three that I saw, anyway." Don wrestled with the steering wheel as they bumped and lurched over the uneven pavement. Infrastructure and maintenance in the Old City, and road repair in particular, was not a priority outside the Enclave. "Including the Tracker we ran over last night, that makes four—*four*—in Eastside's vicinity in the past two days. I don't like it. The whole thing reeks of Hoarderville."

"The Runner who didn't make it last night," Amos said, thinking out loud. "Her Implant had already been harvested. It's a safe bet these three aren't looking for her. More Trackers probably means there's more Runners nearby."

"Then why were they coming after *me*?" Don asked, his attention riveted on the dark streets. "No one at Eastside has an Implant. We shouldn't be targets."

Sheila spoke up from the rear seat. "Unless that Tracker contacted the Hoarders before you flattened it last night. They could be watching for a vehicle matching our description."

"Maybe Enrico should've repainted it." Amos's attempt at humor fell flat. They rode in silence for a few minutes.

The architecture changed as they neared the outskirts of the Old City, giving way to smaller apartments interspersed with houses. Muted lanterns showed in many windows. Most people had migrated to the outskirts, closer to available farmland. They were too stubborn to abandon the Old City, but necessity demanded they make concessions.

"We don't have much of a choice." Sheila's voice was forced to compete with the road noise beneath their tires. "We can't count on the sewer routes once we're outside city limits, even if we wanted to. We need this truck."

"The town's not far." Don met her gaze in the rearview mirror. "Forty, maybe fifty miles. Once we clear the checkpoint, we'll be there in no time. Long before sunrise."

Conversation ground to a halt at his reminder of the checkpoint. The only sound inside the cab was the growling engine, road noise, and the sharp *pock* of small stones kicked up by their tires.

Amos felt a sharp twinge in his gut. *They've posted Trackers at checkpoints before. They've probably been warned already.*

"The checkpoint." Sheila's voice was taut as she put Amos's worry into words. "I forged our permits, but if they're looking for this vehicle, that won't be much help." She leaned forward, focusing on the road. "I guess we *could* stage a preemptive strike, but that wouldn't be my first choice. It's not exactly hidden in plain sight."

"I vote for option number four," Don replied. "Let them make the first move. If they play nice, we will, too." He shot Amos a somber look. "Keep your eyes peeled for Trackers."

Artificial lights glowed in the distance just ahead. The checkpoint. Amos felt a familiar tightening between his shoulder blades. "Combat knives and a couple of prods," he said, taking mental stock of their resources. "That's not much to respond with."

Sheila opened the backpack by her feet, shoving its contents to one side as she dug out the forged permits. She handed them to Amos and double-checked the electrical charges of the prods.

Efficient, as always. Amos watched with admiration. *No matter what we're facing, she's the one preparing for whatever's next.*

They passed the outer perimeter of the Old City, and tract housing gave way to a stretch of unused, overgrown land. The multi-lane highway narrowed, funneling all outbound traffic toward the checkpoint.

Amos eyed the deep ditches on either side of the road. He wondered if even a proper all-terrain vehicle could hope to navigate over them before the soldiers intervened.

We have combat knives. They have the latest Hoarder weapons. He tried to block out the memory of the time Hoarders had hunted him and his brother. He could almost hear the unearthly sound of their alien firearms.

"Wait a second." Don frowned as they approached the checkpoint. "What's going on?"

The gate was closed. Their headlamps added to the glare from a pair of spotlights, bathing the checkpoint in light, illuminating . . . nothing. The guardhouse was unmanned. Deserted.

Don geared down as they approached. No one stepped forward to challenge them. No guards demanding to see their permits. No Trackers lurking inside the guardhouse.

The checkpoint appeared to be abandoned.

"I don't like it." Amos eyed the guardhouse with suspicion. "It's not like we caught them during a shift change. Have you ever seen an unmanned checkpoint before?"

Don shook his head. "It reeks of Hoarderville." He leaned forward over the steering wheel, eyes probing the darkness beyond the headlights. "Let's not waste time trying to figure it out. Amos, open your door—*slow*—and leave it open. Raise the gate manually and let us through. Sheila, I want eyes on our back trail. Got it? Then get moving. Now."

Amos dropped to the pavement, skirting around his open door. Don eased the truck forward as Amos jogged ahead.

A single metal bar blocked their way, its peeling white paint starkly revealed under the twin spotlights on either side of the checkpoint. He tried to raise it, but aside from a slight shift sideways, the gate remained stubbornly in place.

He heard the truck creeping closer behind him. He tried a second time, sweat breaking out on his forehead. The gate refused to budge. He retreated a pace or two, squinting along the bar.

Here we go. A rusty catch on the underside, between the thickest end of the bar and the stanchion supporting the gate. Not quite in plain view, but not hidden, either.

He preemptively cut off his accusing inner voice, dropped to one knee and popped the catch outward. The bar's rigid defiance evaporated. He got to his feet and shoved the gate up and out of the way.

The truck crept past him, maintaining a slow pace until it was beyond the gate. Amos eased the gate back into place and ran for the rolling vehicle. He jumped into his seat, and the truck lurched forward, careening into the welcome cover of darkness.

He's not play-acting this time. Amos knew it without asking. Even the resurgent road noise couldn't cover Sheila's hearty sigh of relief behind him.

They rode in silence for several miles.

"Did they just *let* us waltz past?" Don steered the truck south at the next exit. "It doesn't make any sense. An unmanned checkpoint…I can't imagine Hoarders tolerating dereliction of duty."

"Neither can I," Sheila said, "but somehow, I doubt that's the explanation." She perched on the edge of her seat, keeping a firm grip on Don's headrest. "Hoarders are a lot of things, but stupid isn't one of them."

Don increased speed. "If it's some kind of strategy, I can't make heads or tails of it."

Amos felt his skin crawl, as if a cloaked sniper had him in their crosshairs. He wracked his brain, searching for a logical explanation, but came up empty. He toyed briefly with the idea that they were making a "mountain out of a molehill"—an expression his grandfather had been fond of—but deep down, he knew better.

For once, Gabriel had nothing worse to add.

TWENTY-TWO ◉

ON A HILL HIGH ABOVE the checkpoint, concealed behind a thick copse of evergreens, the Tracker watched as the fugitives' truck was swallowed up by the night.

Its companion, a female bio-form, dropped to one knee, binoculars clasped tightly to her eyes. Her position remained unchanged for several minutes as she traced the truck's progress until it disappeared. Her body language suggested a high level of anxiety.

Irrelevant. She was a bio-form.

At length, she lowered the binoculars, glancing up at the Tracker. It ignored her. Heat simmered around its left eye, the tingling sensation a welcome sign—the Quest was on.

The fugitives below suspected nothing, their battered vehicle slowing no longer than it took to solve the riddle of the gate's locking mechanism. Just as the Givers had predicted.

The Tracker became aware of the bio-form's pointed stare. She struggled awkwardly to her feet, craning her neck as she strove to meet its gaze eye-to-eye.

The Tracker cocked its head to one side, the implied question communicated by its simple gesture.

"Confirmed. Those are your targets." Her eyes were bright with malice, the thirst for blood. Her feelings were irrelevant.

The bio-form spoke again, attempting to establish dominance as she stowed the binoculars in her shoulder bag. "Pass the intel along."

Her command was unnecessary. The Givers heard everything she said. The Tracker dismissed the bio-form's egotistical posturing, a clear indication of her inferiority.

The bio-form pivoted, signaling with an imperious hand to two more of her kind, standing at a respectful distance. The pair, dressed in identical uniforms, saluted and began a rapid return to their assigned posts at the checkpoint. They were irrelevant to the Tracker's purposes—categorized, archived, wiped from active memory.

It watched as the female bio-form reentered her vehicle, revving the engine before roaring away in the general direction of the Old City. She would return to the Enclave and serve the Givers, just as the Tracker would continue its Quest across the wide expanse of agricultural land.

It would allow the fugitives to journey as far as the rustic town. But no farther. The Quest was all that mattered, and the Givers required its servitude.

The Tracker stalked out of the concealing bushes, angling cross-country, diagonal to the highway.

It was incapable of feeling emotion, but a dimly recalled sensation known as satisfaction flitted ghost-like from somewhere deep within. Destiny—the Givers had deployed this unit beyond the Enclave's walls to execute their will.

Its ocular enhancements spun, the thin whispering sound

amplified by the connective tissue near its ears. Enhanced night vision, one of many gifts provided to ensure a successful Quest, converted darkness into brilliant, green-lit day.

The Givers were as wise as they were generous.

Miles passed like shadows beneath its aggressive gait. The clouds eventually parted and moonlight bathed the open fields with a surreal glow. The Tracker noted the observation and filed it away.

Irrelevant. Nothing could interfere with the Quest. Nothing could be *permitted* to interfere.

The fugitive bio-forms, despite their greater numbers, were no match for the Tracker's speed and strength. It would locate them in the town, just as the Givers anticipated.

And when the time came, the Tracker would do precisely as they commanded. Exterminate the fugitives. Harvest all available Implants.

Its pace quickened. The Givers would be pleased.

TWENTY-THREE ◉

CONNOR EXITED the theater, zipping his jacket against the unexpected rainstorm. When he'd entered the building, earlier that afternoon, the weather had been cool but pleasant. Evenings, on the other hand, were becoming chillier as autumn drew near. The sudden downpour after the movie left everything soaked, and the breeze did the rest.

Connor, chin tucked into his collar, shoved his hands into his jacket pockets as he joined the bustling pedestrian crowd. Reagan and Madison crowded close beside him, all intent on reaching Mojo's Coffee Cartel, their favorite haunt.

Most of the Citizens departing the theater opted for the travelators. The moving sidewalks, running parallel to and six feet beyond the traditional sidewalks, were faster than traveling on foot, but also fully exposed to the weather.

This presented no problem for any Citizens with enough foresight to bring along an umbrella, which didn't include Connor or his friends. They kept close to the shops, finding a measure of relief under their protective awnings.

"Can you believe this storm?" Madison laughed, shielding her face with the hood of her jacket. Connor smiled at her feigned annoyance. *She loves bad weather. It gives her an excuse to spend more time at the VR Arcadium.*

"Didn't see it coming," he replied, picking up the pace when he spied Mojo's outdoor patio. The *covered* patio. Mojo's Coffee Cartel was a popular Cascadian destination, one of the trendiest new cafés dotting the pedestrian level. They ducked under the awning, grateful to be out of the rain.

"I wouldn't mind working in a place like this," Reagan said. He peeled his rain-soaked jacket off and gave it a vigorous shake before draping it over the back of a chair. "Do you have any idea how much money a real, live barista makes?"

"Hey, watch it—you're almost as bad as the rain." Madison shooed him away, annoyed by the stray droplets from his jacket. "Stay in university, Reagan, trust me. This retro barista craze is just a fad. Everyone will go back to the machines before you know it. Back me up on this, will you, Connor?"

"It's only a matter of time." Connor shrugged, siding with Madison despite Reagan's pleading look. "Personally, I like the idea of having live baristas. The machines brew your coffee to perfection, but with a *human* barista, you never know what subtle alchemy might occur. It's never the same drink, twice in a row. That's the thrill of adventure."

"Adventure." Madison rolled her eyes. "That's just the sort of thing I'd expect you to say, Connor. I can't believe you actually leave Cascadia to go hunting. It's not safe out there." She spread her arms wide. "Me? I like knowing the machines will make my coffee, just the way I like it, every time. There's nothing but trouble beyond the walls. I plan to live my entire life inside the Enclave."

"And it doesn't reek of savages." Reagan held his nose in feigned repugnance. "But enough about my career aspirations. Does everyone want their usual poison?"

"Surprise me. I'm a dedicated risk-taker," Connor replied, just to get a rise out of Madison. "We'll save you a spot."

"I'll take the usual," Madison said, eyeing him with mock indignation. "Better safe than sorry. Connor loves adventure —try adding powdered savage skins to his drink."

Reagan returned her laugh, and hustled inside to place their orders. Connor and Madison chose a table near the edge of the covered patio. He brought Reagan's jacket along. There were more options to choose from than normal. Most of Mojo's regular customers preferred to sit inside today.

"I'd rather sit at a table on the outer rim." Connor helped Madison out of her damp jacket, pulling her chair out so she could seat herself. He gazed wistfully at the empty tables on the far side of the travelators. "But that'll have to wait for a sunny day."

"You, sir, have what's known as 'Jesse James Syndrome.'" She seated herself with an exaggerated flourish. "You always sit where you can keep an eye on everyone."

Connor glanced at the empty tables as he sat down. The travelators hummed past, filled with pedestrians, heads down, not speaking as they huddled under their umbrellas. The rain pattered in a steady rhythm on the metal canopy above them, dripping heavily to the pavement.

"You've always preferred the outer rim." Madison studied him through half-lidded eyes, propping her chin on one hand. "Reagan says your favorite pastime is just observing. Art galleries, I understand. I can spend hours there. And you just wait, you'll see my art on display someday. It's only a matter of time."

"Don't forget us commoners when you become famous."

She winked and looked him in the eye, her expression curious. "I'm not a huge fan of museums. Don't get me wrong—I'm not one of those people who thinks history doesn't matter. But for the life of me, I can't get my head around your *obsession* with the past. I guess that's why we're enrolled in different university majors."

"I like history." Connor shrugged, used to the question. "I love research, trying to understand what's led from the past to the present. Military history is especially fascinating. All the strategies and counter-strategies, like a giant chess match. The competing motivations, the ..." He caught the look on her face and laughed. "Am I boring you? Okay, you win. I enjoy observing life around me. That's why I like museums, and balconies, and the outer rim tables. Maybe you should consider changing from art to psychology."

"Not a chance." Madison recoiled in mock horror. "I'm an *artiste*, a serious digital and mixed-media commentator on society, culture, and the human soul. Which probably means I'll end up needing a therapist someday. You've studied history. You know how unstable we artistic souls can be." She twisted in her chair, her eyes seeking Mojo's front door. "Reagan's only getting three drinks. What's taking him so long?"

Connor snuck a peek at his wrist com. Darcy expected him to be prepped and ready for another foray later that evening. He knew better than to be late, but wanted to spend some time with friends. It was his way of reminding himself that life would return to normal, once they'd rid Cascadia of the Givers.

As if on cue, Reagan emerged from the café. He wormed his way between other customers and the patio furniture, balancing a drink tray with exaggerated care.

Connor and Reagan had been friends since childhood. That didn't change when they started university, or when Reagan met Madison. They were good for each other, in Connor's opinion. Two carefree spirits living in the happy-go-lucky fiction that the Givers were benevolent allies of Cascadia.

Reagan paused, scanning the patio until he spotted Madison's enthusiastic wave. He resumed his circuitous route between the tables, watching both his footing and the hot liquid in their cups.

It was sheer coincidence that Connor glanced at the travelators and spotted the anomaly. He froze in his seat, heart racing as he tried to pinpoint what had caught his attention. In the midst of the oncoming human traffic, a solitary figure stood out. But why?

The girl appeared to be somewhere in her early twenties. She could've been one of their classmates. Her appearance was unremarkable, and her taste in fashion meshed with the popular styles of their generation. Her clothing was damp from the incessant rain, just like everyone else on travelator. Rain plastered her long, dark hair to her face where her hooded jacket couldn't protect her.

Connor barely heard Reagan's cheerful voice as he rejoined them and began distributing their drinks around the table. "Sorry, buddy, but they were fresh out of 'skin of savage.' Madison will have to find a subtler method of poisoning you."

She swatted him on the arm, protesting. Connor heard their light-hearted banter, but he couldn't tear his eyes away from the approaching brunette.

Why does she stand out?

The girl threw a casual glance at the patio. She was roughly thirty feet away, ferried ever closer by the travelator.

Her face. Connor swallowed hard, his mouth suddenly dry. She wasn't smiling—not really—but the slight curve of her lips, coupled with her benign expression, gave her away.

Nobody smiles in a storm. She's role-playing, nothing more.

TWENTY-FOUR

As if to confirm Connor's suspicions, the girl turned and looked directly at him. Her hair, dripping wet, nearly obscured her eyes. His world shrank to the only detail that mattered—despite the drizzling curtain of rain, a malevolent circle of red light peeked from beneath her long, dark hair.

His throat constricted. A Tracker—operating here, inside the Cascadia Enclave.

He'd never seen one in action before, but he'd heard plenty of stories from his foster father. Trackers originally served as bodyguards for the Givers. They were later modified to intercept Darcy's drones, in order to protect the collaborators on the ruling Council. *We've got to get out of here.*

The girl swiveled her head to focus on the outer rim. She abruptly changed direction, shoving the nearest pedestrian out of her way. He flailed his arms in open-mouthed surprise, lost his footing on the rain-slicked travelator, and collided with a second pedestrian, setting off a chain reaction.

The girl gave no indication she heard them cursing her.

Connor lurched to his feet, angling for a better view. The pedestrians riding the travelator made it difficult to track her movements as she drew abreast of his position.

She was of medium height and—except for her unnatural expression and the betraying burst of red beneath her bangs—was indistinguishable from the crowd.

"Connor? What are you looking at?" Madison's inquisitive voice sounded in his ear as though from a far distance. He felt Reagan's grip on his elbow. Connor jerked his arm free, taking an involuntary step toward the outer rim.

There was a brief—very brief—gap in the human traffic, allowing Connor to locate the Tracker again. She'd halted on the outer rim just beyond Mojo's patio, not more than five yards away. She grasped the balcony rail on the outer rim with both hands, staring into the distance.

She showed no interest in the noisy traffic in the gulf below. Her attention appeared to be fixed on something across the chasm separating the twin commercial promenades, but the pouring rain made it hard to tell.

"Who is she, Connor, one of your classmates?" Madison appeared at his elbow, Reagan close behind. "Do all history majors love staring off balconies?"

The girl shocked everyone by hoisting one leg over the railing and balancing precariously above the abyss. Connor's jaw dropped. *Can a Tracker be suicidal?*

He heard Madison's horrified gasp. She had guessed the girl's intent. Reagan shoved between them, scrambling to intercept the Tracker. "Hey, you—don't do it! *Wait!*"

Madison moved to follow, but Connor instinctively grabbed her arm, restraining her. The Tracker, straddling the outer rim railing, heard Reagan's frantic shout and swiveled to face him.

Connor felt sick. She wore the same fake smile pasted on her placid face. Her sudden movement caused her hair to flip back, revealing the red circle of light for all to see.

He tried to drag Madison away, but she fought back with frantic energy. She possessed greater strength than he would have expected from an art major who spent most of her free time at the Virtual Reality Arcadium.

The Tracker arched backward over the railing a split second before Reagan reached her. His outstretched hands met with nothing. He seized the railing and leaned over, one arm extended—to what end? There could be only one outcome after the girl plummeted into rush hour traffic.

An explosion rocked the patio area, throwing travelator riders off their feet. A concussive thunderclap accompanied the detonation, and blood-red smoke boiled up from the traffic level. Tires screeched, clashing with the shriek of rending metal and the crystalline spray of shattered glass.

The sounds merged into a hellish symphony, heightened by the terrified screams of pedestrians and customers.

Madison tore free of Connor's grip, shoving her way through the panic-stricken crowd. He caught a fleeting glimpse of Reagan—he'd fallen by the balcony railing, clawing at his face.

Connor's stomach churned as reality sank its teeth into his imagination. He stumbled toward his best friend, dreading the worst, when the entire patio area shuddered. Connor froze. The ground beneath his feet shook again, hard.

The seating area on the outer rim lurched downward with a sharp crack, and Connor broke into a run. Fissures appeared in the travelators as he caught up to Madison. He opened his mouth to shout a warning, but no sound came out.

The outer rim collapsed with a deafening roar, sending a

choking cloud of dust into their faces. The travelators, tearing free of their moorings, followed the outer rim into the noxious smoke. The shriek of torn metal deafened him.

Madison stumbled at the precipice. Connor threw himself forward, catching her arm as she lost her balance. Her momentum dragged him toward the edge of the drop. He held on, grimly, Madison's terrified screams echoing in his ears. He refused to look past her into the blazing crater of death.

Reagan was down there. And he wasn't alone.

Madison clung to him with the frantic strength of a drowning person. He tightened his grip with equal resolve, squeezing his eyes shut against the smoke.

The surface beneath him shifted with a sharp crack, angling him closer to the precipice. He tried but couldn't close his ears to the terrified shrieks as people on all sides lost their grip and plummeted over the edge.

Madison screamed again, her fingers like claws in the fabric of his jacket. *She's going to pull us both in.*

Connor forced his eyes open, ignoring the fiery carnage below. He spread his weight out on the wet, slippery surface as best he could, digging in with the toes of his boots for something—anything—to anchor himself. The rain-slick expanse refused to cooperate, adding another layer of maddening frenzy.

In a sudden burst of inspiration, he ripped one arm free of Madison's grasp and, lunging forward, seized a handful of her belt. He rolled to his left, mindful of his precarious balance, dragging her with him.

Madison seemed to comprehend what he was trying to do. She unclenched one fist from his jacket and clawed for a better grip on the disintegrating travelator.

Connor held his breath as she inched higher, her bloody

fingers scraping for a better hold on the slippery remains of the travelator.

The surface beneath him shuddered again. The creaking whine of strained metal accentuated the terrified cries of those clinging desperately, futilely to the sinking patio.

Connor rolled cautiously away from the precipice, hauling Madison with him, until her foot caught a toe-hold. With a panic-fueled heave, she propelled herself over the travelator's fractured remains. They scrambled on bruised hands and knees away from the jagged precipice, the rain-slick metal threatening to betray their efforts.

They managed to reach a stable surface and huddled against Mojo's exterior wall, gasping for breath. Traumatized customers gawked through the shattered windows at the devastation, wide-eyed and open-mouthed.

With a final shuddering rip, the travelator tore loose from the girders that supported the pedestrian level, and plummeted into the traffic lanes below.

Horrified cries inside Mojo's Coffee Cartel competed with the pitiful wails of those carried away by the falling travelator. The impact was like the triumphant roar of a predator. Sirens wailed in the distance, and an unearthly silence settled like a smothering cloud over the survivors.

Connor's muscles ached from exertion, but he managed to throw an arm around Madison's shoulders, drawing her close. She leaned against him, shivering, her head on his shoulder and bloodied hands trembling on her knees. His gaze wandered aimlessly over the chaotic scene, struggling to comprehend the enormity of what he'd just witnessed.

"You knew." Madison raised her head to stare at him, her face streaked with tears. Connor heard the desperate plea for understanding in her ragged whisper. And the accusation. "Why didn't you say anything?"

"We're safe," Connor replied woodenly, not knowing what else to say. *I can't explain how I knew. And you can't tell anyone.* He took a shaky breath, inhaling the acrid aromas of fire, smoke, and death. "We're safe."

She stared at him for a prolonged moment before lowering her head to his shoulder. He felt her convulsive shudders and realized she was sobbing.

You'll have to cry for both of us.

Connor felt empty, hollow. He stared numbly at the area where the outer rim had been only moments before. A trio of vignettes cycled repeatedly across his mind's eye.

Reagan—running to offer help to his imminent executioner, writhing in agony after getting caught in the explosion, and vanishing forever in the outer rim collapse.

His best fried was gone, stolen from Connor like his sister years before. How many others died in the explosion, or were crushed by the collapse of the outer rim?

Connor squeezed his eyes shut, forcefully willing himself out of the mental paralysis that had seized him. *I have to figure this out. Focus, focus!* A Tracker was the source of the carnage, a Tracker on a terrorist assignment inside Cascadia. But who programmed her, and why?

Darcy—I've got to find Darcy.

"You knew." Madison interrupted his manic fixation, her voice cold, remote, bitter. "You knew."

TWENTY-FIVE ◉

DARCY, CONNOR, AND TONY CROWDED around a video console in the Cascasdia Security Monitoring Division. Tara Lindholm, a high-ranking CSMD surveillance officer and one of Darcy's most devoted and trusted allies, sat before an array of high-resolution screens in her private office, analyzing the digital record of the "terrorist attack."

Various Infomedia outlets had already labelled the carnage a result of terrorism, and emerging public opinion intuitively linked it to the shantytowns outside the Enclave. Within a matter of hours, debate over the temporary worker permit program was reignited across the broadcasting spectrum.

Darcy leaned over Tara's shoulder, almost but not quite crowding her. He glared at the screens as if he could compel them to divulge their secrets. Connor hovered over Tara's opposite shoulder, keeping a respectful distance, anxious to wrap his mind around what had happened earilier that afternoon. Tony fidgeted a pace behind, craning his neck to see.

"The footage from the café interior isn't worth your time,

Councilor." Tara seemed to enjoy being in charge, reiterating her earlier explanation. "Normally, patio cameras would be our best bet, but we lost the signal after the explosion. My guess is that they were destroyed along with the travelators."

"I want to see everything," Darcy replied, leaning closer. "Every camera, from every possible angle." Now he *was* crowding her, and not by accident. Connor knew it would end when he got what he wanted, and not a moment before.

That's what makes him such a great leader.

Tara shot him a defiant look. Connor realized that, sympathizer or not, she considered the office her private domain. "The footage from the camera south of the incident survived. If you want an uninterrupted timeline, we should begin there."

Darcy fixed an icy gaze on her. He was adept at using his position as a member of the ruling Council to influence, intimidate, and facilitate the advancement of their cause. "Very well," he said finally, striking a balance between backing down and maintaining dominance. "You may start there."

Tara pressed a button and they watched in silence. The security camera captured the full range of activity in the patio area, including the travelators and outer rim. Rain obscured details to a small degree, but not enough to disguise the moment when the Tracker broke away from the crowd and took her position at the railing.

A second figure darted from under the covered patio, dodging between pedestrians on the travelator, and raced toward the Tracker. Connor felt his stomach drop.

Reagan. Always trying to do the right thing.

The Tracker flung herself into the traffic level. Reagan's miniature figure reached the balcony rail a split-second later, leaning over when the Tracker detonated.

An angry, fire-tinged cloud of smoke obscured their view. The smoke cleared to reveal Reagan, writhing in agony. Panic-stricken Citizens scattered in all directions. From the camera's distant perspective, they resembled an ant colony gone mad.

"The structural collapse begins almost immediately," Tara said, pausing the replay, her voice clinical, detached. "If she'd blown herself up on the travelator, there would've been a significant number of civilian casualties." She rotated her chair to face them. "By throwing herself into the traffic level, the damage was far more extensive, and collateral losses—body count—much higher. Looks like she was trying to make a statement."

Darcy nodded. Several Infomedia outlets had already voiced similar theories on-air. "Show me the outer rim footage." He stood erect, arms crossed, waiting. Tara dialed up the requested files and triggered the review. "Slow motion." He leaned in for emphasis. Tara hid an irritated look and complied.

The footage crawled by, the Citizens' movements exaggerated and grotesque. The steady rain, Connor's arrival with his friends, Reagan moving out of camera range on his way to order their drinks in Mojo's.

Dread crept over Connor. He watched himself select a table and assist Madison into her seat. Their casual conversation, indecipherable at this range. The Tracker's sudden appearance on the travelator. It all played as before, a macabre silent movie. The girl straddling the rail, Reagan reentering the frame, dashing toward ... Connor winced involuntarily. The camera shook violently, and the video feed terminated abruptly.

Tara leaned back in her chair, looking at Darcy over her shoulder. "That's everything, Councilor. Anything you'd like to see again?"

Darcy studied the darkened screen with hard eyes. "Replay

the segment where the Tracker appears, until she turns at the last second. Freeze the last frame."

Connor braced himself as he watched the slow and spastic actors march to their inevitable deaths. Tara stabbed a finger at her keyboard, as directed, freezing the image. She zoomed in on the Tracker.

Silence smothered the room until Tara spoke. "If you're hoping for more detail, I'm afraid this is as good as it gets. The red glow around her eye is undeniable, but that's the best I can do, considering the weather." She leaned forward, brow furrowed. "Are you seeing this? I guess it could be lens distortion, but ..." She swallowed convulsively, pointing a shaky finger at the Tracker's mid-section. "Is she pregnant?"

Connor stared in shock. "All I saw was her red eye. The travelators were crowded. I didn't notice anything else."

"She's not pregnant." Darcy straightened with a derisive snort. "Trackers are killing machines, designed for maximum efficiency. The Givers wouldn't waste time and resources on a pregnant girl."

Tony spoke for the first time, tentative and dubious. "Respectfully, sir, what makes you so sure?"

Darcy studied the screen, his eyes bright. "I've seen Trackers explode before. They're lethal, but not on the same level as this." He waved an accusing finger at the monitor. "She's not scanning for Implants, and that's no fetus—it's an explosive. The Givers sent her to create panic."

Connor stared as the pieces fell into place. "The Infomedia labelled it a terrorist attack almost right away. And now the average Citizen on the street is screaming for more security."

Darcy seemed pleased that Connor made the connection. "And where do Citizens turn for more security?" He indicated the frozen image. "I've never said the Givers are stupid. They're making the Citizens of the Enclave more dependent on their 'assistance' every day."

Tony muttered dark epithets under his breath, and Connor resisted the urge to tell him to shut up.

Darcy placed his hand on the back of Tara's chair, rocking it slightly. "I want everything erased from the moment the girl appears. Make it look like it the explosion is the culprit, but I want the footage deleted."

Tara's hands flew over the keyboard. "Sir, if I may? The footage proves the alleged terrorist was a Tracker, *and* that she was carrying a bomb. Why not use it to expose the Givers?"

Darcy leaned in, his lips brushing the hair next to her ear. "It also shows Connor getting out of his seat when he spots the Tracker. *Before* she leaves the travelator, and long before she jumps." His voice dropped to a whisper, low and threatening. "If anyone recognizes him, we're compromised. Or perhaps you'd like to explain to the Peace Wardens why you didn't report his actions. Erase it. Now."

Tara Lindholm's fingers flew over her gear. Her actions exuded efficiency and professionalism. Her voice sounded small and frightened. "As you wish, Councilor."

TWENTY-SIX ◉

THE ELEVATOR descended in silence. Connor and Darcy had said little to each other since leaving CSMD or, later, in the familiar environs of their villa. They rarely spoke when using an elevator, beyond inconsequential small talk. Elevators were obvious surveillance traps.

Connor was stung to realize his actions could have jeopardized everything. *If anyone but Tara saw that video…* As luck would have it, someone sympathetic to their cause had been on duty at CSMD, but that did little to lessen his offense.

Darcy's glacial silence was a punishing rebuke. Connor's carelessness had forcibly altered their timetable. The suicide bombing at Mojo's added further complications. Darcy decided to activate their newly-Implanted drones ahead of schedule.

The elevator doors parted with a hiss, ushering them into the subterranean parking garage. Tony waited near the exit. If he'd followed protocol, their truck was refueled and ready.

Darcy acknowledged him with a curt nod. No one spoke as they climbed into the idling vehicle.

Tony shifted the truck into gear. "It's done, sir."

Darcy answered him with a barely perceptible inclination of his head, as steadfastly tight-lipped as before.

"Darcy." Connor knew he had to speak up, no matter how badly he'd failed earlier. His mouth went dry, but he plunged on. "We need to talk about Madison Lancaster."

Darcy spoke for the first time in hours. His calm tone was surprising. "You risked your life in order to save a friend this afternoon. I'm proud of your loyalty and courage, Connor." He swiveled in his seat, his eyes hard and unrelenting. "But, all things considered, it would've been better if she had died. She *knows*, Connor. You said so, yourself. Your friend is a liability we cannot afford."

"I realize that, sir, and I'm sorry." Connor scooted forward in his seat, anxious to pitch his idea. "But she's not a security video we can just erase. I was thinking…" He paused for a quick breath. "We could recruit Madison to join our cell. She really cared about Reagan. She'll be motivated."

Darcy raised a hand, his simple gesture arresting Connor mid-plea. "The situation has already been dealt with." He nodded in Tony's direction.

Tony grimaced, looking away without speaking.

Darcy turned back to Connor, his pale eyes hard and emotionless. "You should've let her fall, Connor."

Connor caught his breath as Darcy's words registered. He stared at his foster father, aghast. Madison posed no threat. She was an innocent bystander, as much a victim as Reagan.

Darcy's unblinking gaze never left his. "Your friend's death is on you, Connor. You should've let her fall."

TWENTY-SEVEN

AUBREY LANDED HARD on the grassy turf, the bone-rattling impact driving the breath from her lungs. She managed to rise to her hands and knees, gulping for air.

Jane stood over her, hands on her hips. "Had enough?" The innocent lilt in her voice clashed with her haughty smirk.

Enjoying yourself, Snake Lady? Aubrey gasped for breath, but forced herself to meet Jane's gaze with defiance.

"Too weak to stand up for yourself, Country Girl?" Jane circled, bouncing on her toes like a prizefighter, hands loose and ready at her sides. "You can't call 'time out' against Trackers."

Aubrey took the bait, rising unsteadily to her feet. "No one goes hand-to-hand against a Tracker." She tried to inject as much scorn into her voice as she could. "They'd snap you like a rotten twig, Snake Lady." *Uh-oh. Did I say that out loud?*

"Are you serious?" Jane stopped bouncing. An incredulous grin spread across her face. "Is that supposed to hurt my feelings?" She threw her head back and laughed. "Snake Lady... I kinda like it. I might start using it myself."

"*Enough.*" Garr's voice boomed behind them. He stood at the edge of the woods, just beyond the open glade where Jane and Aubrey sparred. His exasperation was clear. Aubrey hung her head, still gasping for breath.

They'd been on the move since daybreak, tramping in the dank tunnels under the City for hours, to exit into the countryside only a few hundred yards from their current position.

Garr stalked across the sunlit clearing. "That hike through the sewers was supposed to loosen up your muscles." There was no trace of warmth in his voice. "We can do it again, double time, if you'd like. Then I'll bring you right back here and you can start over."

Neither Aubrey nor Jane said anything.

Garr looked back and forth between them, his frustration evident. "Jane is skilled at hand-to-hand combat, Aubrey. Before she shows you how to use your knife, you need to learn how to fight unarmed. Like it or not, she's the expert and you're the beginner. Get over it and pay attention."

Aubrey nodded, chagrined. He was right and she knew it, but that didn't lessen her resentment for her instructor. *You said you wanted this, Aubs, remember?*

Garr turned to Jane, his voice low and cutting. "When I said *training*, Jane, that's what I meant. Aubrey isn't your personal punching bag. By the time I get back, I expect to find that she's learned some of the basics."

He didn't wait for their response. His long strides carried him out of the clearing. He paused only to pick up the backpack he'd dropped there.

Aubrey felt a twinge of alarm. "Where are you going?" *You're leaving me alone with Snake Lady?*

"Paying a visit to an old friend," Garr replied, half-turning to face them. "Enrico, the mechanic who claims the real Mateo is dead. I need his source for that intel. I want to meet Mateo for myself, but if he's not the original, I'd like more background before I confront him." He paused to adjust a strap on his backpack, settling it on his shoulders. "A couple of things to keep in mind while I'm gone. First, Jericho is situated just outside the Cascadia Enclave. That means *enemy territory*. Second, ready or not, you're both coming with me. Now, get back to work, and do it right this time. I promised Doc Simon I'd look after you, but I won't be your babysitter."

With that, he turned his back and strode into the forest. Aubrey watched as he slipped between the trees, disappearing from view as the thick underbrush swallowed him.

She was alone in the sunny clearing. With Snake Lady.

TWENTY-EIGHT ◉

Aubrey didn't anticipate the attack. Jane struck from behind, wrapping one arm around her neck in a vise-like grip. She dragged Aubrey backward, keeping her off-balance, snarling in her ear. "Okay, Country Girl, let's see what you've got. Break out of this hold. If you can."

Frantic and furious, Aubrey tore with both hands at the arm around her throat, but she couldn't break Jane's chokehold. She tried tripping her, but Jane planted her feet too wide apart for Aubrey to gain any decent leverage.

This isn't what Garr meant.

The next thing Aubrey knew, she was face-down in the dirt. The impact drove the breath from her lungs. Again. *Déjà vu.* She fought to regain her breath, struggling feebly to dislodge Jane's weight.

Jane kept her knee planted in the small of Aubrey's back, pinning her down. Aubrey felt a burning sensation as Jane twisted her arm up and behind her. The pain was incredible.

She was on the verge of panic, afraid her shoulder might

pop out of its socket. "You call this *training*?" Aubrey managed to force the words out between clenched teeth. "You have no idea what the word means. You're faking it."

Jane twisted her arm further, shoving her other hand into Aubrey's shoulder blade to increase the tension. "Oh, c'mon, Country Girl, don't you get it? Garr wants us to spend some quality time together." Aubrey felt Jane's breath on her cheek as she bent low to hiss in her ear. "He thinks he can order me to show you the basics, and all of a sudden—magic!—you and I are best buddies. Comrades-in-arms, you know?"

"Don't count on it, Snake Lady." Aubrey kicked her legs in a futile attempt to dislodge her. Jane's punishing grip on her arm pinned her, helpless, to the ground. Coarse blades of grass cut into her cheek and the smell of sunbaked earth filled her nostrils. "Let go—you're breaking my arm."

Jane didn't ease the pressure. When she spoke, her voice was dark and threatening. "Maybe I *should* break your arm. Then you'd have to stay behind with Doc. You could wash out Tracy's bedpan while Garr and I do something useful." She used her free hand to grind Aubrey's face into the grass. "Go ahead, call me Snake Lady, if it makes you happy. That's the difference between us. I call you Country Girl, and you hate me for it. I see it in your eyes. But you can call me anything you want, because I don't care what you say. I really don't."

Aubrey held her tongue, willing herself to relax.

Jane released her grip and pushed off, digging her knee into Aubrey's back with all of her weight as she stood. "Get up. We've got a lot of work to do. You can't learn how to fight until you learn how to fall. That's potty-training level, in case you're wondering."

Aubrey rolled over and kicked at Jane's ankles, catching her by surprise and toppling her to the ground. Aubrey's shoulder burned like fire, but she flung herself at Jane, trying to pin her down.

Jane recovered with little effort, and within seconds, subdued Aubrey a second time.

"You're going to have to try a lot harder than that." Jane got to her feet, making no effort to disguise her disdain. "The best you can do is call me Snake Lady."

"It fits you." Aubrey rolled over, seething. "You're cold, vicious, and full of poison. Trackers are more human than you."

Slap! Aubrey's head rang from the blow. Jane leaned in, taunting her. "Words, Country Girl. That's all you've got. But words won't save you. I could kill you right now, if I felt like it."

Gah! I hate your condescending attitude. Aubrey propped herself up on her elbows, fists tightly clenched. "Kill me? That's a laugh." Her face throbbed from Jane's stinging slap, and she forced a bravado she did not feel. "You had the chance when my Implant activated, but you couldn't do it. I've learned plenty from Amos and Don about Eastside protocols. You should've shot me. But you froze."

Jane's eyes narrowed, and her face twisted in a darker scowl. *That one got through, didn't it?*

"Nice try, Country Girl." Jane shook her head. "But let's stick with reality, okay? I didn't have an active Implant. Hoarders weren't manipulating me like a puppet on a string." She crossed her arms, smirking, clearly enjoying her power over Aubrey. "It was a clear case of self-defense. Only one of us was acting like a psychotic killer, and it wasn't me."

Aubrey raised her arm, the ugly swath of scars vivid in the midday sun. "You're right. Hoarders activated my Implant and, yeah, I wanted to kill you." She shook her damaged hand, drawing Jane's attention to it. "And that electrical charge just about killed me, and left me with this."

Jane said nothing. She stood tall, arms crossed, taunting her with a cynical smirk.

Hot tears slipped down her cheeks, but Aubrey didn't care. "A Tracker butchered my best friends in front of my eyes, and if I hadn't jammed my prod into Tracy's head, she would've killed me. Don't try telling me *you're* the tough one."

Jane rolled her eyes. "Oh, cry me a river, Country Girl." She pointed an accusing finger at Aubrey. "That, right there, is your problem. 'Oh, poor me, my life is so hard.' All you ever do is whine, and we're supposed to sign up for your pity party. Oh, poor little Aubrey ..." Her lip curled with contempt. "As if you've had it worse than anyone else."

Aubrey leaped at her, shoving her as hard as she could. Jane allowed herself to be pushed away, never breaking eye contact. Her mocking smile widened. Aubrey raged inside. *You love this. You get a kick out of tormenting me.*

"It was in my blood." She jabbed an angry finger at Jane. "You knew my Implant was activated. You had the gun, you knew the drill, but you failed. You're *weak,* Snake Lady."

Jane's smiled vanished as if it had never existed, and her face darkened. She threw herself at Aubrey in a whirlwind of kicks and punches. Aubrey was on the ground before she could begin to defend herself.

She glared defiantly at her nemesis, refusing to cower. She tasted blood running across her lips.

Jane returned her glare, breathing hard. "You don't want to go there, Country Girl. You really don't."

"Coward." Aubrey threw the word at her with a mocking laugh. "You *froze.* You never got over killing the first one."

Jane kicked her without warning, lightning-fast and hard. Aubrey rolled away, clutching her ribs, pain raging like fire up and down her spine. Jane was on her in a heartbeat, aiming a second kick at her.

"Who was it?" Aubrey gasped, desperately clinging to her fury, her only weapon against Jane. "Who did you shoot?"

Jane pounced on her like a hungry lioness. Aubrey thrashed about, desperate, but couldn't escape. Jane grabbed a handful of Aubrey's hair, her sharp features contorted into a mask of pure rage.

"My little brother." She lifted Aubrey by the hair and slammed her head into the ground. "Fifteen years old, and I shot him."

She released her grip, and began to get to her feet.

Smack! Aubrey's scarred arm lanced upward, her forearm catching Jane full in the face. She felt Jane's lips mash under the impact. The sensation sickened her.

Jane fell back, landing awkwardly. She half-rose, bracing herself on one arm. Her other hand covered her nose and mouth, an instinctive gesture after Aubrey's blow found its mark.

Aubrey sprang into a crouch, trying to ignore the pain in her ribs and shoulder, alert for the inevitable counter-attack.

Jane pulled her hand away, looking at her palm, and spat blood on the ground. To Aubrey's surprise, she smiled. It wasn't a pleasant smile, smeared by blood running over her teeth and gathering on her lower lip.

Aubrey stared, not sure how to respond.

Jane laughed, quiet and low. "I was going to say you fight like a little girl." She wiped blood from her lips. "But that was a good shot." She leaned to one side and spat red. "Yeah, that was a good shot."

Aubrey lowered one knee to the ground, bracing herself, still wary. "It's true, though—what you just said."

"You calling me a liar?" Jane's smile vanished, replaced by a furious scowl. "Don't expect me to repeat myself. I say what I mean, and I mean what I say. Ain't that right, Garr?"

She flung the last question over her shoulder. Garr emerged from the bushes, the mechanic in tow. The Colonel sudied them with an expression Aubrey couldn't place. When he spoke at last, he directed his words to Aubrey.

"Go change your shirt." He waved vaguely to the edge of the clearing. "And wipe the blood off your face. Bloodstains don't qualify as 'hidden in plain sight.' Not where we're going."

Aubrey got to her feet, brushing dirt off her pants. She glanced down and saw several random blood spatters on her shirt. Hers, or Snake Lady's?

She slunk wordlessly past Garr, catching up her pack and taking shelter behind some bushes to change.

TWENTY-NINE ◉

GARR REACHED a hand down to Jane. She hesitated, and then clasped his hand with her own, allowing him to pull her to her feet. "You've got a unique approach to training." He shook his head. "Rico and I saw the whole thing from the hill."

Jane put her hands on her hips, looking askance at him. "I didn't think you had enough time to walk to town and back." She indicated the mechanic with a toss of her head. "Did the two of you meet up there, so you could have your little chat *and* spy on us?"

"It was educational." Enrico held a pair of binoculars aloft. His voice was mild. "We each have a set. And I agree with Garr. You've got a strange way of doing things."

Jane crossed her arms, her posture defiant. "Garr told me to train Aubrey. To do that, I need two things from her—anger and loyalty. I want her mad enough to fight like a she-bear separated from her cubs, and to learn how to *stay* angry. I know exactly how to push Aubrey's buttons. And I need her loyalty. So, I told her about Davey."

Enrico nodded but kept his thoughts to himself.

Jane closed on Garr, looking up at him with fiery eyes. "Don't think, for even *one second*, that I didn't see through your clever little ploy to make Aubrey and I all buddy-buddy. That's not going to happen. You told me to train her. I'm no amateur. I'll get it done. My way." She gestured at her backpack, pushing past them. "Now, if you'll excuse me, I'd like to clean up." She snatched up her backpack, slung it casually over one shoulder, and sauntered into the bushes. On the opposite side of the clearing from Aubrey.

Enrico exhaled in a long, slow whistle. "Wow, you weren't kidding, Garr." He shook his head in admiration. "I'm just glad she's on *our* side."

Garr sighed, looking sheepish. "Jane's a pro, no doubt about that. Although, at times, she can be a bit of a liability." He lowered his voice. "Aubrey was right about one thing. When her Implant activated, Jane should've shot her. Jane thinks she's gaining loyalty by telling Aubrey about her past, but we need Aubrey to keep drawing it out of her. It's the only way Jane will fully recover."

"She's not gaining loyalty." Enrico frowned, watching for his reaction. "She's using bullying tactics and emotional manipulation. As soon as Aubrey figures that out—and she will, mark my words—you'll have a team divided against itself."

Garr shrugged, noncommittal. "Amos wasn't in much better shape when he first joined Eastside. Then again, he and I—and Don—have a lot of shared history. That helped. These two ... well, time will tell."

"And now you're off to Jericho, to confront a Tracker who calls himself Mateo." Enrico rubbed his jaw, staring off into the distance. "And these two are your backup." He roused himself and faced Garr, extending his hand. "I don't envy you. In times like these, I'm content to be a lowly mechanic."

"Thanks for everything." Garr shook his hand, grateful for the change in topic. "But don't get *too* comfortable. We may need you to take a more active role, if things heat up the way I suspect they will."

Enrico gave him a solemn nod. "Rest while I can, eh? That's good advice. Remember to pace yourself, too, while you're at it." He turned to leave. "Good hunting, Colonel Scott."

"I'm not 'Colonel' Scott anymore," Garr called after him, stopping the mechanic in his tracks. "We don't need those archaic titles."

The mechanic stood motionless, his back to Garr. He tapped a nervous rhythm against his leg, betraying his unease. At length, he breathed a heavy sigh and pivoted to face him.

"Who does Mateo think you are?" he asked, his voice barely audible. He raised his eyebrows and shrugged. "That's the question I'd be asking, if I were you. Because we both know he's not the real Mateo Reyes. He can't be."

THIRTY ◉

AUBREY LEANED ON the chipped cement wall encircling the abandoned house. *I'm gawking like a tourist.* She knew it, but she couldn't help herself. She stood in the back yard, the morning sun hot on her shoulders. She cupped her hands around her eyes, shielding herself from the glare.

Cascadia Enclave loomed large in her view, a walled monolith dwarfing all else, several miles further west and south. Aubrey shivered in spite of the sun's warmth. Even at this distance, the towering walls were intimidating.

She shook her head, awestruck. Cascadia Enclave's daunting aura of menace—of total otherness—left her feeling small and insignificant. *What chance do we have? We're as threatening as ants.*

Garr exited the empty house and joined her in the yard. They'd camped their way around the circumference of the Old City for the past three days, never venturing too deep into the ruins. Garr selected the abandoned property the night before, and they'd slept without a fire on the hard floor.

"It's nothing like what I expected," Aubrey said, not for the first time. "I knew it would be huge, but not like this. And, to be honest, this part of the Old City feels like a ghost town. It's the polar opposite of the Mission district."

Garr nodded, propping an elbow on the wall. The breeze tried in vain to ruffle his close-cropped hair. "A lot of people prefer to live near the outskirrts of the Old City, but not within sight of the Enclave. That makes the final leg of our trip easier, anyway. Nobody lives around here, so there's no one to alert the Hoarders about us."

Their three-day hike around the Old City had passed without incident. No sightings of Hoarder vehicles, and aside from Enrico, they'd encountered no one. And, at the end of each day, Garr insisted Aubrey and Jane continue to train together.

Jane was as good as her word. Their sparring sessions didn't result in friendship. Not by a long shot. Aubrey had always held a grudging respect for Jane's skills, but there was little she found likable about her abrasive trainer.

She's not a bad teacher. Aubrey gave credit where it was due, despite the bruises and muscle twinges that kept her awake at night. Jane had surprised her by admitting she'd killed her own brother. Aubrey experienced a stab of guilt over that. *I want to learn from Snake Lady. I don't want to become like her.*

She felt a conflicted sense of comradeship after Jane's stark admission. Jane was still Jane. She'd probably always been acerbic, and the traumas she'd experienced only served to reinforce her caustic personality.

Aubrey caught herself and almost laughed out loud. *Listen to me, psychoanalyzing Snake Lady.*

As if on cue, Jane appeared in the open doorway behind them. The door itself had been removed a long time ago, likely used as firewood. She stacked their packs beside the empty door-frame. "Are you guys done gawking at Hoarderville yet? We've got a half-day of hiking before we arrive at the walls of the High and Mighty."

Garr pulled out his binoculars, taking one last survey of their route. He handed them to Aubrey a moment later, allowing her another opportunity to take it all in.

Aubrey panned across a shantytown, built just outside the nearest Enclave gate. The orderly arrangement of shops and living quarters impressed her, but the obvious economic disparity left a bad taste in her mouth.

She lowered the binoculars. "And each gate has its own—what do I call it—refugee camp?"

"Every single one," Jane replied. She glowered darkly at the Enclave. "That's why Don calls it Hoarderville."

"This is Gate Four. Jericho Hub is located outside Gate Seven," Garr said, his relaxed demeanor gone. "Let's get moving. I want to find our friend Mateo while it's still daylight."

They each shouldered a pack, half-filled with trail rations, blankets, and extra clothes. Garr led them out of the dilapidated house, and they set off down a suburban road.

Five blocks south, the road merged with a wide thoroughfare, leading out of the Old City, westward to Cascadia.

"Next stop, Hoarderville," Jane said dryly, breaking their self-imposed silence. "To rendezvous with a Tracker who may or may not be who he claims to be."

Aubrey smiled to herself, giving in to a sliver of cynicism. *What could go wrong?*

THIRTY-ONE ◉

HER MUSCLE TONE was improving. Tracy was confident of it. She recognized the familiar crawling sensation under her skin as her self-repair subroutine stitched damaged tissue together. The subdermal algorithms functioned in an oddly truncated fashion, but her injuries had healed for the most part.

A different set of subroutines were focused on rebuilding her musculature. Enhanced physical strength was no longer an available option. She regretted the loss, but she would adapt.

Overall, Tracy was satisfied with her healing progress. The Givers were generous, even if they now considered her unworthy. The bio-form attending her—designation: Doc Simon— also seemed to be pleased by her recovery.

Tracy frowned as she identified a flaw in her strategy. She must train herself to think of the bio-form as "Doc Simon," or simply, "Doc." Earning the bio-form's trust was a prerequisite to regaining her freedom.

Tracy sat on the edge of the gurney, her feet dangling but not reaching the floor, and cupping a warm bowl between her hands. Some kind of the nourishment that the bio-forms preferred to consume. She made a show of spooning the contents into her mouth with an awkward scooping motion.

Using their names was the first step in her strategy. Appealing to their sympathy, the second.

When the bio-forms first began feeding her, she'd found swallowing difficult. Doc Simon expressed concern over that. Tracy filed the observation away for analysis and endeavored, from that day forward, to give the impression that eating was still difficult. She later added to her performance, portraying her ability to walk as a stumbling, awkward effort.

Doc sat on a stool opposite her. Tracy ate slowly, feigning clumsiness. Perhaps she should allow the bowl to slip from her fingers again. Doc had exhibited great sympathy the first time she'd dropped her food on the floor.

Her world shrank to winning Doc over. Even without the Givers' wisdom, Tracy knew the medic was her best option.

"Dawk," she said. The lone syllable sounded slurred in her ears. Verbal communication, in contrast to her feigned physical weakness, was genuinely difficult. Her inability to translate words into speech frustrated and annoyed her.

"Yes, Tracy?" Doc placed her empty bowl on the worktable. She remained seated, leaning forward with interest. "How can I help? Go ahead, take as much time as you need."

"You're wasting your time, Doc." A guard posted by the door inserted himself, uninvited, into the conversation. He was one of two sentries Garr "borrowed" from another Hub. Doc grew quickly impatient with his unsolicited advice. Tracy was quick to take note of her reaction.

Doc wearily closed her eyes. "And why is that, Kevin?"

"The Tracker's brain is fried," he replied, ignoring or not

aware of Doc's frosty glance. "It would've given our position away a long time ago, if it still could. It's broken, just a defective machine."

Tracy's eye swiveled in its socket. She stared with calculated appraisal at the bio-fo—Kevin, unblinking. Analyze. Adapt. His substandard professionalism was an annoyance to Doc, but a potential asset for her.

Doc sighed, hanging her head. She opened her eyes and fixed a stern glare on him. "If you can't respect the rules of my infirmary, I'm sure there's cleanup required in the sewers, somewhere," she said with a hint of menace. "You're stationed here because Garr insisted, but in this infirmary, you answer to *me*. Understood?"

The bio-form appeared more irritated than chastened. His eyes narrowed and his mouth opened as if he planned to argue with Doc, but Tracy intervened.

"Walk," she said, reminding them of her presence. She kept her gaze averted, studying the concrete floor below her dangling feet. Bio-forms, she'd discovered through repeated trial and error, reacted with greater empathy when she appeared helpless.

Tracy had enacted a calculated routine of helplessness ever since. "Walk. My walk now."

Doc Simon came to her side, reaching out a gentle hand to take her bowl. She gestured to the bio-form. "You heard her, Kevin. Tracy is ready for her physiotherapy. Assist her to the exercise room."

She retreated to her worktable, stacking Tracy's bowl with the others. Kevin gave Tracy a sour look, but he took her arm and helped her stand.

Tracy made a point of stumbling as her feet hit the floor.

Kevin's grip tightened on her arm, supporting her weight until she regained her balance. She focused her eye on him, waiting until he had no option—this made him *very* uncomfortable—but to acknowledge her. She arranged her facial muscles into her best smile.

"Thank you," she slurred, performing her most convincing imitation of cheerfulness. She pictured the words in her mind's eye, but struggled to put them into coherent speech. Her lips twisted awkwardly. "Thank you. My friend."

The flustered guard glanced over his shoulder at the second of his kind, stationed just outside the infirmary door. The second guard made no attempt to hide his amusement. "I think the Tracker's flirting with you, Kevin." He laughed, looking pleased at his own cleverness. "It's true what they say—there's no accounting for taste."

Doc Simon stepped between them. She made no attempt to disguise her displeasure with the much-taller bio-forms. "Perhaps you were asleep at your post and didn't hear me just now." Her voice was mild but her eyes blazed. "You're in my infirmary, so you'll obey my rules. The patient's name is Tracy, and she's requested her physiotherapy routine."

She advanced, herding him into the hall. Tracy strained to listen through the open door. "You *do* realize I'll be making a full report when Garr returns?" Her fury was impossible to miss. "Make yourself useful. Go open the exercise room."

"Y-yes, sir, I mean—ma'am," the second guard replied, stammering. Tracy heard the fading scuff of his boots as he hurried to carry out Doc's orders.

Tracy shuffled toward the worktable, half-leading and half-dragging Kevin with her. She grabbed the edge of table for support, and he released her arm, retreating an awkward step.

She scanned the various objects on the table. She must approximate innocent curiosity. She must not stare at the only item that truly mattered. She tensed, overhearing Doc's startled intake of breath as she reentered the infirmary.

Tracy closed her eye, bowing her head as if fatigued. She must not betray her true intentions.

Analyze. Adapt. Enact.

She shifted her stance, throwing her head back and arching her spine. Her act fooled Kevin, and he instinctively stepped in, believing she was able to collapse. He caught Tracy by the shoulders and held her upright.

She allowed him to support her, secretly pleased at how well her body responded to her commands. Her mind raced to concoct a plausible diversion. She opened her eye, leaning on Kevin for support she didn't require. Before Doc could ask the obvious question, Tracy spotted her alibi.

"That. Give my." She forced her uncooperative lips to form the words. She gestured at the worktable and lurched forward, without warning, grasping for the object. "Give that me."

Doc caught Tracy's outstretched arm and guided her to the worktable so she could support her own weight. Kevin shuffled along, assisting from the opposite side.

Doc picked up the object—the, the … *pencil*—and searched beneath the worktable for a piece of paper. Tracy nodded, pleased. Her ability to fabricate the bio-forms' facial expressions continued to improve.

"Would you like to draw a picture?" Doc slid the paper and pencil to her. "Is this what you're asking, Tracy?"

Tracy snatched the pencil. She'd backed herself into a corner. In order to not betray the full extent of her recovery, she was forced to take an unplanned risk.

Provide the bio-forms with a substantial shock. Divert attention from her real objective.

She scrawled hastily, her efforts crude and uneven at first, but gaining fluidity as she continued. She finished writing, set her pencil down, and shoved the paper into Doc's hands.

Doc flipped the page around, frowning as she read aloud. "My name Tracy." Her eyes widened. "I can to write. I write you better than my speak. Dr. Simon, my name is Tracy."

Doc lowered the paper, her face alight with wonder.

Tracy nodded eagerly, twice. Her smile appeared with little effort. "Walk now?"

Doc Simon smiled back, reaching out to assist her. Kevin was quick to jump to her aid. Together, one on either side, they helped Tracy navigate toward the infirmary door.

Tracy forced herself to take short, awkward steps, making a deliberate point of stumbling half-way down the short corridor between the infirmary and the exercise room. Her "helpers" responded just as she'd anticipated.

Her diversion had succeeded. The bio-forms, even Doc, suspected nothing. Divulging her ability to write was a risky ploy, but the gamble had paid off, disguising her true intent.

She'd also unmasked herself. The bio-forms would resume their interrogations, and with greater insistence. Hiding behind her feigned inability to communicate was no longer a strategic option.

Timeline: diminished. Window of opportunity: shrinking. She must execute her escape sooner than planned.

Analyze. Adapt. Enact.

THIRTY-TWO ◉

Doc poured herself a fresh cup of coffee, deep in thought. She'd left the guards in the exercise room. One to keep an eye on the door, and Kevin to walk beside Tracy, in case she lost her balance.

The borrowed guards were nonplussed by what served as Eastside's meager exercise room, exchanging amused glances when they thought she wasn't watching. The only notable feature in the room was an unpainted cinderblock wall, opposite the door. A myriad of round, dark smudges marred its dull gray surface.

Aubrey Carter had spent many isolated hours here, throwing a ball against the cinderblocks, driven to recover from her injuries. Obsessed, even. Doc briefly considered enlightening the guards, but decided not to waste her time. She liked to think of herself as patient—she *was* a medic, after all—but found their juvenile attitudes an increasing annoyance.

Tracy showed great enthusiasm in her first few laps as the reluctant Kevin kept pace. Doc watched until she was satisfied the guards understood what was expected of them, and made a beeline to the mess hall for a much-needed break.

She drained the last of her coffee and set her empty mug on the counter. Her headache receded slightly, and she felt a nostalgic twinge for genuine espresso. She picked up a lantern, carrying it along on her way back to the exercise room.

She sensed something was amiss before she arrived. The door hung ajar, and the room was strangely silent.

Doc quickened her pace. She pushed the door open with her foot, trembling with sudden anxiety. Heart pounding, she stepped inside and almost tripped over one of the guards, lying just inside the door.

She raised her lantern and spied Kevin, perhaps a yard or two further inside. Both guards sprawled in awkward poses, face-down on the concrete. Alive, but unconscious.

Doc fled to the infirmary, fearing the worst. The lights were on, just as she'd left them, illuminating the stark interior with precise clarity. There was no sign of Tracy.

Doc extinguished the lantern and conducted a quick inventory. It took less than a minute to realize what Tracy had done.

Amos's former Implant was missing.

She pivoted to face the vacant gurney, and sagged against her worktable, overcome by a sudden weariness. Her headache returned with a vengeance.

"What could Tracy possibly want with an Implant?" A hollow sensation in her stomach accompanied the answer.

"The Givers," she said, louder this time, raising a faint echo. She stared at the empty restraints, and the hollow sensation morphed into numbing dread. "It's her ticket back in."

THIRTY-THREE ◉

TRACY JOGGED at a steady pace, following the sewer's malodorous current. The stench wrinkled her nose, but it was a minor footnote to her triumph. Her escape strategy, however hastily modified, was a success. She'd out-witted the bio-forms. They failed to notice the full extent of her physical recovery, as well as her shrewd strategy to thwart their plans.

Tracy slowed to a halt. She raised her clenched fist, opening it to gaze with fascinated wonder at her prize. A thrill of emotion electrified her. An Implant—the key to regaining the Givers' favor. Delivering it to the Citadel, active or dormant, was all that remained. She had fulfilled her Quest.

The Givers would be pleased.

Doubt crept into her mind. Or would they care? She cowered, anticipating a sharp mental rebuke as a reward for her blasphemous thought. The Givers were not to be questioned, only obeyed.

The mental lash never came. The Givers were silent. Perhaps they hadn't heard.

Was her exile that arbitrary—did they consider her a failure, unworthy of their attention?

She stared at the scrap of alien technology in her palm, recalling the rush of emotion when she first spied it on Doc's worktable, several weeks before. The bio-forms' unguarded conversation had betrayed the Implant's location.

Kevin made no move to block her an hour earlier. The cagey Doctor Simon would have never allowed it, but Kevin was too young and inexperienced to know better.

An Implant. At long last, she had tangible proof of its existence. It had been in the infirmary all along, an arm's length from the gurney that held her prisoner after ...

She drew a deep, shuddering breath, no longer aware of the foul atmosphere. Something burned against a barrier in her mind, an unsought memory fighting to surface.

She stared at the Implant, simultaneously revolted and unable to avert her eyes. She'd seen this one before. No, not this exact piece, but another of the same—no, similar—design. *Two* devices, over double the size of an Implant.

A matched set, intended to function as a single unit, cradled in the palm of another's hand.

A new image erupted in her mind—another gurney, a different room, invisible restraints holding her fast against her will. Images swirled like a mental whirlwind, threatening to overwhelm her. Chaos would follow if she allowed the invasion. She resisted, suppressing her fear and willing the burning sensation in her mind to subside.

She closed a shaky fist around her prize, loathe to lose her grip. The larger Implants, if that's what they were ... did her theft from the infirmary trigger the images?

Tracy covered her face with her free hand, the Implant

clutched in the other. Fear was all she had left. She dropped to her knees beside the foul stream. A guttural screech echoed in the tunnel, the full-throated cry of a hungry predator poised to attack.

No. Inaccurate. The scream was her own.

Tracy flailed with her free arm, clutching the greasy handrail and pulling herself upright. She ran, blindly, driven by an unseen terror, unaware of the tears streaming down her cheek, or the panic-stricken breath escaping her clenched teeth in ragged gasps.

The enhancements healed her injuries, but no longer provided strength, stamina, or speed. Her lungs felt as if they were ablaze, and a sharp pain stabbed under her ribs.

She ran until she was exhausted, and collapsed to her knees, her breath coming in sobbing gasps. She stared at her fist, feeling the Implant slice into her palm. The pain helped center her, gave her strength to assert order on the chaos threatening her sanity.

She forced her hand open, muscles stiff and protesting. The Implant glistened in her palm, wet with her sweat and bloody from the tiny cuts it left behind. Tracy held it close to her face, wide-eyed, willing her ocular enhancements to do something. *Anything.*

No effect. Access to her visual enhancements denied.

Tracy clenched her fist, berating herself for her stupidity. Her scanning eye was destroyed weeks earlier. A patch covered what was left of her eye socket's fused ruin. Ocular enhancements were no longer an option.

The Implant was inactive. No flashing pinpricks of light, no microscopic filaments needling her flesh to inject poison. Her worst fear was laid to rest.

Her desperate grip on the Implant caused the cuts on her palm. Nothing more. She paused, puzzled that she was familiar with the Implant's purpose and its method of releasing venom into an unsuspecting victim's bloodstream.

The insight did not originate from the Givers.

Uninvited, the images resurfaced. The large Implant-like devices, the gurney where she'd been strapped against her will, waiting in abject terror for—what? Tracy ducked her head, fists clenched, resisting, resisting, resisting...

She threw her head back, rocking back and forth on her knees, staring blindly at the rusty, dripping ceiling. For once, her thoughts and speech meshed seamlessly, and she screamed, "The Givers will be pleased!"

Her words echoed in the tunnel, twisting and overlapping until they became meaningless vibrations. It wasn't the first time she'd uttered them, but her recollections were hazy, indistinct. She'd spoken those exact words, only to herself, but she *had* spoken them, the night she executed... another Tracker.

Impossible. *Unthinkable.* The Givers would never allow it.

Tracy sat back on her heels and forced her hand open. The stolen microtechnology was driving her mad. Holding an Implant shouldn't make any difference.

It's inactive. It can't affect me.

"This unit." She spoke the words aloud, after several abortive tries. Her face contorted. Part of her mind embraced the designation "unit." Another part flinched away, sickened.

"Tracy." She clung stubbornly to the name Doc gave her, and her mental anguish spiked. She fought to speak the words aloud. "My name. Tracy."

The thunder in her head receded, loosening its grip by gradual degrees. She wilted, fingers wrapped around the slimy handrail, the lone barrier between her and the rank water. The stench filled her nostrils and she gagged.

The noxious odor, and suppressing the need to vomit, helped to anchor her. The threatening image of the Implant-not-an-Implant faded. The debilitating helplessness linked to the gurney followed. Memories, if that's what they were, mercifully faded. Not forgotten, but lacking the power to drive her over the edge.

"This unit is designated Tracy." No. Inaccurate. The Givers did not assign designations to their creations. Designations —names—were important only to bio-forms.

"My name is Tracy." Her voice sounded as raw as her throat felt. It was a struggle to mentally form the words, and even harder to force her lips to cooperate. Several seconds passed before she realized what she'd said.

She tried repeating herself, but the words wouldn't come. She slammed her free hand against the railing. *It's my voice!*

Tracy leaned back, her gaze straying to the curved ceiling in the tunnel. She noticed a circular opening, almost directly overhead. A vertical shaft, outfitted with metal rungs, beckoned her to climb above the sewer. She used the railing to get to her feet, leaning as far over as she dared.

Faint, very faint, natural light invaded the shaft from a perpendicular angle. The bio-form—no, the *person* designated Jane—had spoken of such an exit. Tracy glanced down at her stained clothing—her escape route hadn't been kind—and tucked the Implant into her pants pocket for safe-keeping.

She clambered onto the railing, hands braced against the grimy ceiling. Lips pursed, ignoring the smell, she tried to estimate the distance to the lowest rung.

I can do this. I don't need enhancements.

She sprang, arms outstretched, and caught hold of the first rung. Triumph surged, and she hoisted herself aloft. She would soon free herself from sewer and its wretched stench.

She scrambled up the time-roughened rungs, spurred on by the promise of clean air.

THIRTY-FOUR

AN OPEN FIELD PROVIDED a stark, but welcome, contrast to the tunnel. Sunlight warmed her body, and a plethora of new aromas supplanted the cloying reek of the sewer. Tracy reveled in the musky smell of earth, the refreshing scent of pine and assorted flora, even the faint wisp of animal life.

The constant dripping in the tunnels was replaced by rustling leaves, accompanied by the pleasant counter-melody of long grass stirring in the breeze. She detected birdsong and, here and there, the chittering of small animals in the trees. She found her reaction to the sensory stimuli intriguing. Familiar, but as if from a great distance.

She wandered without direction, content to put a healthy distance between her and the sewer, invigorated by the sensations of sun, nature, and the warm breeze. A strange emotion surfaced. Part of her mind identified it as nostalgia.

Another voice intruded. No. Inaccurate. Emotions are a distraction. Nothing can be permitted to interfere with the Quest. The Givers are generous, but they are not to be denied.

Tracy chanced upon a small body of fresh water. *Pond*, the awakening portion of her mind informed her. She crouched to gaze into its depths. *Aquatic reservoir*, the other voice protested. Nonproductive action is not logical, a waste of valuable time. Nothing matters but the Quest. The Givers...

Quest? Tracy tasted bitterness, an emotion she wasn't prepared for. She studied her reflection in the water, attempting to view herself objectively.

The patch over her scanning eye elicited no strong reaction. The Givers' punitive silence was far more troubling.

Tracy glanced down at her bedraggled clothing, and wrinkled her nose at the stale odor. The stench and filth of the sewer had accompanied her. The longer she stared at her reflection, the less she liked what she saw.

She knelt by the water's edge, cupping her hands to drink. The Givers would probably disapprove, if they knew. If she couldn't hear their voices, were they still aware of her? Did they know what she was thinking? She was no longer sure. Nor did she care.

An hour later, Tracy pulled on her sun-dried clothing. She marveled at the pleasure she felt after bathing and washing her clothes. Such activities were distractions from the Quest.

But the Givers hadn't assigned her this Quest. This was her initiative, her endgame. The stolen Implant was a strategic move on her part.

Memories of the gurney, restraints, and the twin devices cupped in an unseen attendant's hand... She rebelled against the unwelcome return of the images.

She bowed her head, steadying herself against a nearby tree. The memory fragments seemed determined to escape from a vault deep inside her mind. The Givers would not approve.

The Givers abandoned me.

Tracy leaned against the rough bark until her mind cleared. She filled her lungs with fresh air, one hand shielding her eyes from the hot sun. Keep moving. Only the Givers could provide her with the answers she needed.

An internal warning flared, insistent. Tracy dropped her hand and stepped away from the tree, pivoting to survey the clearing. Her eye fastened on a point deeper in the forest. A solitary figure, motionless, lurked half-hidden in the underbrush.

A red glow encircled his left eye.

Tracy's heart skipped a beat, and she broke into a wide, spontaneous smile. *Another unit.* She stumbled toward him, relieved to be among her own kind. The unit could help her.

She put a name to the new emotion: hope. She vaguely recalled the feeling, but a small part of her sounded an alarm. Emotions were a distraction.

The Tracker shifted from his stationary position and stalked toward her. He halted an arm's-length away, his posture rigid, his scanning eye parsing over her body. She relaxed; he would recognize her as another of his kind.

"My name." Her mouth twisted from the effort and sweat beaded on her forehead. "I am. Tracy."

He stared, his expression unreadable. His body language did not change—alert, aloof, analytical. His scanner cast a wan glow on her face, shifting up and down. Searching.

The Tracker froze, his scanner riveted on the pocket where she'd stowed her stolen Implant.

"Help me," Tracy said, taking an involuntary step closer, forcing her stubborn lips to obey. "My name is Tracy."

The Tracker said nothing. His gaze met hers. For an extended moment, they stared at each other, eye to eye.

Tracy held her breath. *He understands. He will help.*

He attacked with the speed of a striking cobra. His hand closed with punishing force around her throat, choking off her breath. Tracy's smile vanished, wiped away by crippling horror —surpassed only by the Tracker's brutal strength. She tore at the constricting appendage, but her human strength was no match for the other's artificial enhancements.

He doesn't know me. She panicked as the implications sank in. *All he sees is the Implant in my pocket.*

Darkness crept into her peripheral vision. Her lungs burned but she was powerless to dislodge the iron claw at her throat. She ripped at his arm, her fingernails leaving bloody trails in his skin. The Tracker's scanning eye blazed blood-red as he mutely watched her life ebbing away.

A pounding throb hammered in her ears. Her pulse, thundering as it strove to circulate life-giving blood. The darkness spread, obliterating everything but her inescapable fate.

All of her planning, strategies, calculated risks … a pointless exercise in futility. A wave of despair washed over her as she accepted the full extent of her failure.

The Givers have truly abandoned me.

THIRTY-FIVE ◉

AMOS STOOD TALL on a hilltop, admiring his panoramic view of the idyllic countryside. The valley below, home to a modest village, was a breath of fresh air compared to the Old City or Cascadia's weaponized prosperity.

He closed his eyes, inhaling the scent of pine, dried grass, and wilderness. *What a difference sunrise makes.* The pink pre-dawn sky continued to fade as the sun peeked over the foothills. Few people stirred at this early hour, but the village would soon come to life.

Their stolen Hoarder truck, with its Tracker-shaped dent in the grill, would draw unwanted attention. At Sheila's suggestion, they left it hidden in a nearby grove of trees. Don offered no argument and Amos concurred. A short hike downhill was a small price to pay for anonymity.

"When this is finally over, I think I'd like living out here." Sheila sat cross-legged on the grass, connecting scanner and reader together. The tranquil valley appeared to have cast its spell over her, as well. "No more skulking underground. No whiff of sewage in the air while I'm trying to eat breakfast. Just a care-free lifestyle, where no one's even heard of Cascadia. Aubrey grew up in a town like this. She says it's peaceful."

Don scanned the village with his binoculars. "No doubt it was—until a Tracker came a-hunting. Thomas and Sarah died protecting Aubrey." He lowered the binoculars, glancing over his shoulder at Sheila, and his expression softened. "Someday, maybe, country life might appeal to me, but not until Implants and Trackers are ancient history."

"I know." Sheila heaved a sigh, gazing off into the distance. "But imagining a better future is sometimes the only thing that keeps me going in the present."

Amos crouched beside her, nodding at the scanner in her lap. "Are we ready?"

She sat up straighter and refocused on her task. "Just about. Almost there."

Amos glanced downhill as the sun crested the hilltop and cast its glow over the valley. He indulged in one last look at the peaceful scene below, and the promise it represented.

Sheila activated the scanner, and it emitted a sullen hum. Amos stifled a sigh. The moment was over.

"Two signals," Sheila said promptly, consulting the device she'd cobbled together. She raised the makeshift tech chest-high and, without getting to her feet, pivoted in a cautious arc, all the while keeping a wary eye on the thin wires connecting the halves. "Both signals are in close proximity to each other, and not moving around much. If we find one of them, we should find the other."

"Breakfast for two at sunrise?" Don raised his binoculars, peering down the hill. "Too bad there's no way to know if their Implants have been activated or not."

"Or if a Tracker's nearby." Amos eyed his backpack. The prods were now the most important items he carried.

Sheila scrambled to her feet. "Daily routines don't mix well with active Implants. I'm betting they're still dormant. We've got a window. Let's not waste it by dawdling."

"Look on the bright side." Don tucked his binoculars away. "We won't wake them by pounding on their door with tales of Trackers." He stretched casually, as if they were on a carefree hike. "That oh-so-conveniently abandoned checkpoint is still stuck in my craw. Let's get this over with, pronto. I don't have to be good at math to know things aren't adding up."

Amos absent-mindedly traced the scar below his ribs, the Tracker sightings near Eastside very much on his mind. "What's the plan? Meet them in town and break the news over coffee?"

"When did you become a comedian?" Don slung his pack over one shoulder. Sheila gingerly stowed the scanner in her coat pocket. "There's no good way to tell someone they've got an Implant. We make contact, but keep it casual. We don't know who else may be watching. If they run a grocery store, we're their best customers. If it's a carpentry shop, we need new kitchen cupboards."

Amos surveyed the village one last time, searching out potential hiding spots. They could come in handy, unless a Tracker or three lay in wait already.

"What if they aren't grocers or carpenters?" Sheila appeared beside him, shielding her eyes from the sun. "Do you have an alternate plan, Don?"

The big man shrugged, not taking his eyes off the village. "Then Amos can buy them coffee and tell them their whole world's just gone to hell."

THIRTÝ-SIX ⊙

THE TRACKER NAVIGATED the distance between the checkpoint and the rural village with time to spare. The Implant affixed to the fugitive's vehicle drew it like a magnet. Its enhancements performed their required functions, streamlining blood oxygenation, increasing stamina and, now on standby, ready to augment its considerable physical strength.

The Tracker waited, concealed inside a wooden structure near the outskirts of the village. It selected the empty building —equestrian stable, a memory suggested—for its unobstructed view. It sensed two Implants nearby.

The Quest was within its grasp, the Harvest simply a matter of execution. The Tracker reached for the brittle door, eager to complete its mission. The Givers would be pleased.

No. Inaccurate.

Additional data flooded its processor, a stern reminder of the unique parameters of this Quest. It must not initiate the Harvest of its own accord. The Givers would grant permission when the time was right.

Their unorthodox instructions clashed with the Tracker's core programming, and it struggled to restrain itself.

The Givers were as wise as they were generous. They were not to be questioned, only obeyed. The fugitive bio-forms, three in number, must be eliminated before the Harvest could commence. Anonymity was paramount, timing was everything.

The Givers were generous but they were not to be denied.

Analyze. Adapt. Enact... but not yet.

The Tracker remained hidden, monitoring the primitive villagers between the broken slats in the stable wall.

Watching. Waiting. Anticipating.

The Givers would be pleased.

THIRTY-SEVEN ◉

Amos FELT the muscles between his shoulder blades tighten as they entered the village. He flanked Sheila on her right as she surreptitiously monitored the scanner. Don mirrored Amos's position to her left.

They strolled with feigned nonchalance along a modest main street, three abreast. Two-story structures lined both sides of the roadway. The valley widened beyond the village's southern edge, giving way to cultivated fields. Most of the buildings appeared to be designed as ground-level businesses, with living quarters for the shopkeepers above their respective workplaces.

It was a different world, a stark contrast to their huddled existence beneath the Old City.

"We're getting close." Sheila stole a glance into her pocket. A red glow showed for a brief moment. "Signals show strong and steady." She glanced at the modest storefronts. "Somewhere nearby, probably one of these shops. Looks like you may not be buying coffee after all, Amos."

"Keep an eye peeled for Trackers," Don's voice sounded as edgy as Amos's nerves felt. *Three strangers traipsing down main street in a town where everyone knows everyone. Not much of a strategy.*

He said as much, knowing they had no alternative but to blend in and hope for a quick resolution.

"Well, it beats the sewer route," Sheila said dryly, her voice light and conversational. "There's nothing quite like fresh air on a sunny day."

"You know what I wish?" Don's lazy drawl complimented her carefree demeanor. "I wish Trackers left hoofprints, or paw prints. Better yet, I wish we could modify the scanner to warn us if there's any red-eyed predators in the neighborhood."

Sheila slowed, checking the device in her pocket. "Don't you boys had some shopping to do?" Amos and Don matched pace with her, each surveying their respective side of the road. Amos heard a soft click as she deactivated the scanner.

Sheila nodded at a shop on their left. Café Petrov, according to the signage. "Both signals are inside there. I've got this. You guys can make yourselves scarce, but stay within shouting distance." She angled for the café, glancing back at her companions. "Give me five minutes, then Amos can join me. Sorry, Don. Sometimes you're just too intimidating, big guy. These people will be unsettled as it is."

"Break it to them gently," Don muttered under his breath. He nudged Amos with his elbow. "Let's go window-shopping. Five minutes, remember?"

They sauntered on, keeping to a snail's pace. Amos heard a door open behind them, followed by Sheila's warm greeting. "Good morning. Have you got a minute? We need to talk."

THIRTY-EIGHT ◉

NEW DATA DOWNLOADED into the Tracker's processor, triggering a chemical response. Organic adrenaline flowed in perfect synchronicity with the chemical enhancements.

The fugitive bio-forms had arrived. It could expect the Givers' go-ahead at any moment.

The Tracker trembled like a sprinter in the starting blocks. The fugitives, and a pair of Implants, were within its grasp. Terminate the bio-forms, and the Harvest could commence. This unit would succeed. The Givers would be pleased.

The Tracker peered between the slats in the stable door. It had maintained a diligent vigil since arriving several hours before dawn. The village was beginning to fill up with additional bio-forms, all on foot.

This was a normal routine, just as the Givers predicted.

No. Inaccurate. A new variable, unpredicted by the Givers, intruded into the Tracker's theater of operation.

A mechanical vehicle approached. Its sudden appearance was at odds with the Tracker's expectations, diverting focus.

Evaluate the anomaly.

Its ocular enhancements spun as its vision mode shifted to telescopic. The stealthy vehicle was black in color, windows tinted dark to guarantee anonymity. It crept at low velocity along the forested ridge above and beyond the village, unnoticed by the awakening townspeople. The vehicle disappeared from view, concealed in the trees like an ambush predator.

The Tracker waited, anticipating the Givers' explanation, but its only reward was silence. Logically, the vehicle was therefore irrelevant. A distraction.

The Givers sent the long-awaited signal. The pieces were in place. The time had come. The Givers were generous but they were not to be denied.

Analyze. Adapt. Enact—now.

The Tracker retreated a step, trembling with anticipation, and slid the door open. Early morning sunlight flooded the stable. The sudden glare failed to register, but a tremor of fear did. The Tracker was more than familiar with its sole remaining emotion. Fear was all it had left.

That, and the Quest.

Heat flamed around its scanning eye. The Tracker's physical and chemical enhancements accelerated as it strode out of hiding.

THIRTY-NINE ◉

THE SIGN IN THE WINDOW read *Closed*, but Amos knew the door was unlocked. He entered with as little noise as possible, shut the door behind him, and took stock of his surroundings.

He stood inside a small, well-kept café. An assortment of tables and chairs were scattered around the interior, and a long counter-bar stretched across most of the rear wall. Three people sat around a table at one end of the counter.

Sheila acknowledged him with a nod. A young couple sat stiff and wide-eyed opposite her.

"Amos, these are the friends we're looking for." She gestured at her companions. Both looked pale, in shock. "Lukas and Emma Petrov. This is their café. They live upstairs."

Amos nodded wordlessly. An hour earlier, the Petrovs registered as tiny blips on a scanner. Now, they had faces. And names. *And zero memory of getting an Implant. It fits the pattern, but a married couple? That's new.*

Sheila turned to face the Petrovs, her voice calm and reassuring. She had a way with people. "Amos is one of the people I was telling you about. You can trust him. Another friend, Don, is keeping watch outside."

Lukas lurched out of his seat. "Why did the Hoarders do this to us?" He zeroed in on Amos, his voice rising. "We're human beings. I won't kill for them."

"We don't know why they picked any of us." Amos gave him the blunt, unvarnished truth. "We're chosen at random. And once they activate your Implant, you won't have a choice about killing or not killing."

"We're here to make sure that doesn't happen," Sheila said, nudging the scanner on the table. "But it's not safe for you to stay here. If we managed to locate you, it's only a matter of time before a Tracker does."

Emma hadn't moved since Amos entered. She folded her hands on the table, staring at the scanner with fascinated horror. The red glow faded as Sheila switched it off.

"This device…" Emma found her voice, addressing Sheila. "It's always accurate? There's been no mistake?"

Sheila put a hand on her shoulder. "I'm sorry, Emma. You saw the results on the scanner. You and your husband have both been Implanted. You need to act quickly. Pack some provisions and head for Eastside Mission in the Old City."

"Tonight," Amos said, crossing the room to stand next to the table. "Trust me, you don't want to any waste time. Open your café like always, but only for today. After you close for the evening, that's it. You're gone."

Lukas stood behind Emma, hands on her shoulders. They were scared, but Amos saw the resolve in their eyes.

Lukas spoke on behalf of them both. "I'm not sure we can pull that off. Our regular customers know us too well. We might not be able to fool them."

"It will be difficult, I know." Sheila stowed the scanner in her pocket and shrugged into her jacket. "But you can't deviate from your normal routine. We don't know if there's surveillance already in place. You can't arouse suspicion."

"Did you say surveillance?" Lukas swallowed convulsively, the blood draining from his face. "You mean the Hoarders are spying on us already?"

"We don't know," Sheila repeated, trying to calm him. "It's a possibility, so be careful how you leave. You have all day to prepare. I know this feels like a lot, and I wish there was another way, but there isn't."

Amos retraced his steps to the front door and peered outside. All clear, as far as he could tell. "Set aside provisions during your shift, close down like normal, and disappear."

Emma exchanged glances with her husband, reaching up to touch his hand on her shoulder. "We'll say we're taking a vacation, and the café will be closed for a few days. When this is over, we'll re-open. No one will know the difference."

Amos hesitated. Sheila met his gaze, equally uncomfortable. Lukas and Emma spotted their awkward reaction and tensed visibly.

"You can't come back, ever," Sheila said bluntly. "Hoarders know there's only a few possible outcomes once they activate an Implant. Either you kill the target, or the target kills you. And that's only if a Tracker doesn't discover you first. Once your Implants activate, it's a one-way trip."

Amos cut in, turning his back to the door. "If you come back to your café as if nothing happened, the Hoarders will know something went wrong with their tech. They'll want to investigate, and I don't like your chance of survival."

"You know this?" Emma jumped to her feet. She clutched

the back of her chair with trembling hands. "You both sound very sure of yourselves."

Amos felt bad for her. She'd begun her day as a simple café owner, and after one short conversation, she and her husband were poised to flee for their lives.

Emma stamped her foot. "*Answer me.*"

Amos shrugged. Brutally honest answers were getting easier as the day went on. "Some Runners manage to sneak into the Enclave and kill their target, but none have ever been seen again. Hoarders probably execute them as criminals. And having an Implant—activated or not—means you'll have Trackers on your trail. The bottom line is, you can't come back here."

Emma reached for her husband's hand. Their eyes met, and after a moment, Lukas nodded. "We'll do as you say."

"It won't be easy," Emma said unhappily, casting a forlorn look around her café. "But as you say, what choice do we have?"

"Wait a second." Sheila snapped her fingers. "We've got a truck. What if we wait around until you close up? We could lay low for the day and bring you with us."

Amos stared at her as if she'd lost her mind. "You heard Don. We have to ditch the truck, and there's something suspicious about that checkpoint. We'd be idiots to think otherwise."

Sheila shot him a cold look. She could rival Jane at times. "Then we'll guide them on foot, *after* driving as far as we can. I didn't forget the checkpoint, Amos."

Lukas stepped away from the table, a smile toying at one corner of his mouth. "Emma and I will play our part until closing time. It's not too much to ask you to do the same."

Sheila nodded enthusiastically. Amos chewed on the inside of his cheek and kept his opinion to himself.

FORTY

HEAT FLARED AROUND the Tracker's eye, signaling close proximity to its targets. If it still possessed an imagination, it might have envisioned its skin bursting into literal flame, or peeling back in burned tatters around its eye socket.

Imagination was irrelevant. A distraction. Nothing could interfere. Nothing could be *permitted* to interfere.

The Tracker detected a lone sentry positioned outside the café. One of the fugitive bio-forms. It must lure the bio-form inside the building, with the other fugitives, where it could eliminate the threat they represented.

The Givers were clear. First, the bio-forms. Then it was free to execute the Harvest.

Analyze. Adapt. Enact.

The Tracker altered strategy, diverting into an alley behind the row of shops. It would infiltrate the café from the rear, create a diversion in order to draw the fugitives closer, and satisfy the Givers' wishes.

The Tracker arrived at the café's rear door. No hesitation.

It crushed the doorknob in its fist, circumventing the locking mechanism, and forced its way inside.

Strategy calculated, modified, implemented.

Nothing mattered but the Quest. But first, it would exterminate the fugitive bio-forms.

The Givers would be pleased.

FORTY-ONE ◎

Don intercepted Amos and Sheila as they exited Café Petrov. Something in his demeanor set off alarm bells in Amos's mind. He stole a glance in either direction—casual, keep it casual—as they met at the foot of the steps.

"Tracker," Don said succinctly. He nodded toward the south end of the road. "Not even trying to hide, just waltzing down the road in all its red-eye glory." He pointed with his chin at a narrow alley between two of the storefronts. "It ducked down there. Probably planning to ambush our newest Runners through the back door to their café."

Sheila digested his news without turning to look. "We were planning to stick close by, and bring the Petrovs along after they closed for the day. That's off the table now. How do you want to handle this?"

"First things first. We've got to warn them." Amos glanced at the café door. "I don't care if that exposes our position. If the Tracker gets to them first ..."

He didn't have to finish the thought.

"So much for hidden in plain sight." Don rubbed his hands together, energized. "Waiting until nightfall is definietely not an option. Sheila, go get the truck, and drive it straight down main street. Amos and I will handle the Tracker."

Sheila took off at a flat run, all pretense gone. She bolted down the road, her ponytail flying behind her.

Amos and Don ran up the steps and burst inside. Amos pivoted to ease the door shut behind them. Lukas spun to confront them. Emma stifled a shocked cry.

Amos pointed at the door behind the counter, beckoning with his other hand. The Petrovs guessed his meaning and scrambled between the tables to join him by the front door. He lowered his voice to a stage whisper. "What's in the back end of your café?"

"A banquet room," Emma replied in a small and frightened voice, clasping her hands together. "For wedding receptions, private parties, that sort of thing. What's going on?" Her terrified expression told Amos she'd already guessed.

Don removed his jacket and tossed it on the nearest table. Amos understood—drop anything that could impede freedom of movement—and quickly followed suit. Don unsheathed his combat knife, blade gleaming, and flexed his burly arms. Lukas and Emma stared in wide-eyed silence.

A splintering crash erupted from the back room. Emma gasped, covering her mouth. Lukas moved to shield her behind his body.

That won't be enough. Amos felt sorry for them. *They didn't sign up for this.*

"Get out of here, both of you," he said, not taking his eyes off the rear door. "You can't do anything more. Sheila's gone for the truck. Wait for her outside."

The Petrovs nodded, speechless, and darted out the door.

Another crash emanated from the back room, followed by the unmistakable sound of shattering glass.

Amos swallowed with difficulty. "Think we can hold off a Tracker until Sheila gets here? Two combat knives might not be enough to kill it."

"Kill it?" Don shot him an incredulous look. "Who said anything about killing it? There's more than one way to skin a Hoarder, or a Tracker. All we need to do is hamstring it." He hefted his knife, grinning wickedly.

Amos caught on. He nodded, approving. "If it can't follow us, the Givers will detonate it for failing. I guess hamstringing's not too much to ask."

Don took a deep breath, tightening his grip. "I'll aim high and engage it. You go low and slash away. Hamstring, Achilles, chop it off at the knees for all I care. Then we high-tail it outta here before the Givers put it out of its misery. Ready?"

The crashing in the back room ceased abruptly. A numbing silence descended over the café, and the tension between Amos's shoulder blades worsened.

"Time's up." Don kicked the door open and they rushed into the back room, combat knives poised and ready.

A chaotic scene greeted them.

The back room had been savaged—tables and chairs reduced to kindling, window panes shattered. The exterior door swung in a useless arc from a single surviving hinge. Nothing moved. The stillness was absolute, unearthly.

A Tracker lay sprawled on its back in the middle of the room, arms and legs splayed out, staring blindly at the ceiling. Its mouth hung slackly open, and Amos couldn't put a name to the expression on its face. Shock? Disbelief?

They approached the body cautiously, ready to attack or defend themselves at the slightest provocation.

There was none.

The Tracker was clearly dead, lying in a growing puddle of its own blood. The left side of its head was crushed, as if someone had assaulted the creature with a sledgehammer. Nothing in the back room could account for its savage injuries.

Amos prodded the creature's head with his knife handle, loathe to touch the pallid flesh. The Tracker's head rolled to one side, its remaining eye focused on nothing.

"Scanner's been crushed," Don muttered under his breath as he studied the corpse. "Along with whatever Trackers use for brains. The Givers haven't detonated it. I guess the self-destruct was shorted out by whatever did this."

Amos dropped to one knee, keeping a wary eye on the back door and the alley beyond. "The last time we saw something like this, the killer turned out to be another Tracker. If the Givers *didn't* blow this one up, there could be more in the area."

They were interrupted by the sound of a truck skidding to a stop outside the café. Don jumped to his feet and began gathering pieces of broken furniture, piling them over the Tracker cadaver.

"Our cover's blown, big time," the big man said as he worked. "Bringing the truck into town couldn't be helped, and I'll justify that to Colonel Scott with a clear conscience. But we can't leave a dead Tracker for the townsfolk to find. All hell would break loose. Take a look in that cupboard. There's got to be some lantern fuel around."

Amos dug around in a corner storage unit. He heard the truck's doors open and slam shut. "And a Hoarder truck parked out front won't raise questions?"

Don shot him an irritated look as he tossed the remains of several wooden chairs over the Tracker's carcass.

Amos found what he was looking for. Half-full. He handed the container to Don. "I'll break the news to the Petrovs."

Don nodded as he doused his makeshift pyre with the combustible liquid. "Right behind you."

FORTY-TWO

HIGH ABOVE THE VILLAGE, Connor lowered his binoculars, too stunned to speak. They'd expected to find their newest drones going about their normal business, oblivious to the microtechnology embedded in their bodies.

Instead, they watched a dented truck race recklessly down the steep roadway, skidding to a halt outside a café and throwing its doors open for the shopkeeper and his woman. They didn't hesitate to climb inside. The brazen rendezvous was obviously pre-planned.

"What just happened?" Tony asked, confused and angry. "They were Implanted only two days ago. How could anyone know the drones even exist, let alone find them so quickly?"

"Someone tipped them off?" Connor hazarded a guess. "The Givers use savages as raw material for Trackers. It's not much of a stretch to think they might also supply them with tech to do their dirty work."

Darcy studied the scene, probing, sifting, analyzing. Once he was satisfied, he lowered his binoculars. "Someone has been educating the savages," he said in a sing-song voice. "They've managed to get their dirty fingers on tech that's years beyond their comprehension. They won't live long enough to regret it."

He slid off the roof of the truck and jumped into the passenger seat, pulling out the tablet he'd modified for programming the Implants. His fingers raced over the keys, and a malicious smile creased his face.

Connor hoped he was never on the receiving end of that smile. Darcy was finished in less than a minute.

"I'm accelerating the timeline." He held the tablet aloft. "The savages just drove off with their own executioners."

In the village far below, multiple doors slammed and the driver hastily reversed direction. Dust and gravel spewed from beneath the truck's spinning tires as it raced up the steep hill.

A truck occupied by a pair of Darcy's drones and their would-be rescuers.

Darcy's smile vanished, and he spat after them. "Meddling savages." He raised the tablet and, with a theatrical flourish, activated the Implants.

FORTY-THREE

An hour earlier...

Their trek into the wilderness outside the Enclave seemed to drag on interminably. Connor stared out his window in the rear seat, seeing but not seeing the Old City as it rushed past.

The Cascadia Security guards stationed at the various checkpoints waved them through without incident. Darcy's status as a Councilor guaranteed it. As a precaution, their hunting permits had been meticulously prepared, in the unlikely event they were interrogated by a promotion-hungry zealot.

Darcy brought several of the advanced rifles along, adding credibility to their cover story. The high-tech weapons were donations, awarded by the Givers to members of the Council.

Tony was surprised to learn Darcy hadn't refused the weapons on principle. He didn't know Darcy as well as Connor did. To decline the aliens' generosity could spark unforeseen repercussions, raising suspicion about Darcy's loyalty on a Council that prized their cozy relationship with the Givers.

As far as Darcy was concerned, their use of alien weapons

—even if only to bolster their hunting trip façade—was a delicious slice of poetic justice.

Connor had another use in mind for the alien weaponry. He found himself half-hoping a few savages would dare something outlandish. *I'd love to remind them about their place in the world.*

He stirred uneasily in his seat, aware of his misdirected rage. His contempt for savages was real, but his inner turmoil had nothing to do with them. He toyed absent-mindedly with the locket around his neck. He had no need to open it. His sister's image was burned forever in his mind's eye.

No, he chafed internally for another reason, one that left him conflicted and unsure of himself. Miles of crumbling road sped past as Connor tried to sort out his chaotic thoughts and feelings.

Madison was dead by his foster father's hand. Oh, not literally, of course. Darcy didn't personally wield whatever weapon ended her life, but his decree set the wheels in motion. To preserve their anonymity. For the good of the Enclave.

That didn't change anything. Connor had rescued Madison from the suicide bombing, only for her to be killed the same day at the whim of his foster father.

To correct Connor's idiotic mistake.

Tony shifted gears as they ascended a steep incline. The terrain had changed while Connor was preoccupied. The crumbling remains of the Old City gave way to open fields and rolling hills, supplanted in turn by forest-heavy foothills. Their destination must be close—a fly-speck excuse for a town, nestled in one of the many narrow valleys.

It was time to pay their newest drones a visit.

After the "terrorist attack," Darcy had demanded a meeting

with key figures in their private war against the Givers. The group consensus was to take advantage of the terrorist narrative the Infomedia had fastened on. Sensationalism would work in their favor.

Darcy proposed a coordinated purge, targeting as many collaborators on the Council as possible. The ratings-hungry Infomedia would speculate, inevitably pinning responsibility for the carnage on savages.

Darcy's strategy was two-fold—remove more of the collaborators, and simultaneously deflect any suspicion that Citizens were behind their deaths.

Two hours after the meeting, Darcy led them out of Cascadia on their latest mission.

In addition to the alien weapons, Darcy brought along the targeting tablet he'd invented. The same technology that allowed the Givers to turn savages into Trackers, programming their simple minds to do whatever the aliens demanded, was adapted to create the Implants. The tablet represented another coup—the ability to program drones for specific targets. It was a brilliant example of reverse-engineering.

The dirt road grew narrower and more overgrown. This part of the countryside was obviously not well-travelled. The truck climbed to an advantageous position, high above the primitive village where they'd sourced drones DR-55 and DR-56.

Tony braked to a standstill behind a clump of stunted junipers, dense enough to shield them from prying eyes. Darcy was the first to exit, his feet hitting the ground almost before Tony finished braking.

Connor roused himself from his mental fog and followed, stuffing the locket inside his shirt. The silver chain felt cool against his skin. He closed his door quietly, distracted by his quandary over Madison's death, but not to the point of carelessness. A door slamming could alert the savages below.

Darcy hoisted himself onto the roof of the truck, vying for an ideal vantage point. He had his binoculars out, slung around his neck to free his hands as he scrambled over the cab.

Connor copied him, aiming his binoculars at the village. Tony stood beside him, binoculars in hand, but not in any hurry to use them. The chauffeur seemed to have something else on his mind.

Connor sensed his nervous tension, and wondered if Tony was aware of his transparently obvious angst. He shot a resentful look in the chauffeur's direction.

Were you the hand of Darcy?

"Let it go, kid," Tony said under his breath, as if reading Connor's mind. "You should've been more careful. If Darcy wasn't so well-connected, we wouldn't have access to the video footage. And we'd all be dead if your friend spilled anything to the Peace Wardens."

Connor's stomach twisted. A hot flush of guilt and shame flooded his cheeks. "Are you going to remind me that any loyal Citizen would've turned me in?" He couldn't resist the sarcastic retort, but his voice lacked conviction. *Don't blame Tony for carrying out Darcy's orders. They were cleaning up my mess.*

Tony bristled. "Grow up, Connor." He kept his voice low with visible effort. "A *lot* of people could've made the same connection, but the explosion distracted them. You almost exposed our whole operation. That makes you a liability. You should thank your lucky stars you're Darcy's kid." He clamped his mouth shut, leaving the implied threat unspoken.

Connor bit back a reply, choosing instead to train his binoculars on the village, scanning for anything out of the ordinary.

Darcy's tablet was reliable, even at this distance, but remaining undetected by the locals was a priority.

We don't want to stampede the cattle.

Darcy's muffled exclamation interrupted him.

Connor twisted, looking over his shoulder. Darcy perched atop the cab, his outstretched arm pointing to the left of their position. Connor whirled, binoculars pressed to his eyes, seeking the source of Darcy's interest.

The binoculars were blurry, indistinct. Irritated, he adjusted the focus, zooming in on the forested scene. Beside him, Tony inhaled a sharp breath.

Connor's focus cleared. He spotted a second truck, similar to theirs, rapidly descending the hill. Manufactured in Cascadia Enclave, no doubt—most vehicles in the Old City and beyond were rusted antiques, jointly owned by paranoid and desperate colonies.

The most notable difference was the vehicle's run-down condition. Connor was well-aware savages had no concept of property care, which confirmed the late-model truck had been stolen. A massive dent in the front end testified to a recent collision with something large and heavy. It skidded to a stop in front of the café owned by their newest drones.

His pulse quickened. *That can't be a coincidence.*

Connor zoomed in on the driver, who remained inside the truck. Even from this distance, he could see anxiety on her face. She stared at the café's front door, rigid with tension. He heard Tony mutter under his breath, his words indistinct. He'd apparently come to the same conclusion.

Something was wrong. Very wrong.

The front door burst open. Two figures, faces pale with fear, exited the café, stumbling down the steps in their haste.

Connor recognized them. The shopkeeper and his woman. *Our drones.* They darted for the waiting truck and dove inside.

The driver revved her engine, doors still ajar. She kept a sharp eye on the entrance to the café. *Waiting, but for who?*

Seconds later, he had his answer. An additional pair of figures fled the café, intent on boarding the truck. Smoke began rising from an alley behind the building. The café was burning.

Doors slammed shut, and the driver reversed direction, grinding gears in apparent haste. Dirt and gravel boiled from beneath the truck's tires as it careened down the road and out of the village.

Stunned villagers gathered in the dust-filled road, staring after the departed vehicle. A few gestured to each other in perplexed apprehension. Other pointed to a rising plume of smoke. Pandemonium broke loose, and they rushed to extinguish the flames before the fire spread.

That truck came out of nowhere. Conner gulped, gripped by a sudden chill despite the warm sun. *They stole our drones in full view of the everyone. Are the savages that stupid?*

He lowered his binoculars, stunned.

"What just happened?" Tony asked, confused and angry.

* * *

No ONE NOTICED the silhouette in a window on the second floor of the burning café, staring intently in their direction.

A tiny circle of red light, barely visible through the smoke, zeroed in on their position.

Analyze. Adapt. Enact.

FORTY-FOUR

"Do we go after them?" Tony asked as he started the engine.

Darcy ignored him, stowing the tablet in the glove box. Connor didn't have to be told—Darcy's analytical mind was sifting the variables, mapping out their next moves. His foster father stared straight ahead, as if transfixed on a spot on the horizon. Connor anticipated his response and reached behind the rear seat to retrieve one of the rifles from the cargo area.

Tony revved the engine, hands locked on the steering wheel as he awaited instructions.

Darcy threw him an irritated look. "Yes, of course, follow," he said, waving an impatient hand. "The savages are using advanced tech. I want to know what kind and where they stole it." He glanced at Tony, a humorless smile playing around his lips. "It may not make much difference. Once Implants infuse the bloodstream, drones are predictably ruthless. The savages may suffer an unfortunate accident."

Connor stifled a laugh. *And if any of them survive, we can easily arrange something special.*

"You aren't worried about our drones dying, too?" Tony sounded surprised. "Shouldn't we try to intercept the savages first? It'd save us the trouble of finding another batch of suitable candidates."

"It's an acceptable risk." Darcy shrugged, enumerating items on his fingertips. "Three savages, including the driver, plus two drones—it's a tight fit. I predict a violent struggle, followed by a crash. If the drones survive, they'll continue with their mission as if nothing happened. That's the optimum outcome." He retrieved the tablet from the glove box, and handed it over his shoulder to Connor. "Fire it up. We don't want to get too close, but we don't want to lose them, either."

Connor hunched over the tablet, switching it on and selecting the scan function. The tablet buzzed, and he felt a corresponding vibration in his hands. He squinted at the screen. "We're about ten, maybe twelve miles behind. They're staying on the highway, at least for now."

"Excellent." Darcy settled into his seat, showing no signs of worry. "Standard procedure. Regular updates."

Tony caught Connor's eye in the rearview mirror. "You can track them, too? I thought the tablet was for programming targets and activating Implants." He grimaced and looked away before Connor could reply. "Forget I asked. Of course, we can track them with the same tech."

"One tablet, three functions," Connor said. "Program targets, activate Implants, and trace their whereabouts. Darcy knew what he was doing when he designed it."

"Give credit where credit is due, Connor," Darcy said in a rare show of humility. "A number of our colleagues worked on the project. I wasn't the only one. The Givers install a more complex version in a Tracker's brain, to control and communicate with them. It's diabolical, but it's also brilliant." He shifted in his seat, staring ahead. "We merely simplified the concept. Our Implants are smaller, and targets can be programmed remotely."

"That's to our benefit, too." Connor's enthusiasm overrode his common sense. Darcy didn't like to be interrupted. "If we stay in communication with the drones, the Givers might trace the signal back to us. The tablet allows us to follow them without giving ourselves away."

Darcy's voice was cold and remote. "Keep your eyes where they belong, Connor."

Stung, Connor shut his mouth and focused on the device in his lap. No change. Their quarry was still on the main highway, but their rate of travel … "Looks like they're slowing down."

Darcy straightened abruptly, his face alight with anticipation. "Reduce our speed," he said, aiming an imperious gesture in Tony's direction. "The moment of truth has arrived."

FORTY-FIVE ◉

Tony eased off the accelerator, and the truck's momentum subsided. They emerged from the foothills surrounding the village, and the terrain gave way to a series of undulating ridges and shallow troughs. Stunted trees and untended land framed the highway on either side, while steep ditches, thick with weeds, added an unruly reminder of neglect and abandonment. The Old City lay in the distance, a dark line on the horizon.

Connor double-checked the tablet before saying anything. The screen remained curiously blank. It took only a moment to guess why. "They've stopped, sir. Looks like they hit the ditch. The Implants have gone silent—it's possible our drones didn't survive."

They rounded a curve, and Darcy bolted forward, gesturing emphatically to his right. Twin skid marks drew Connor's attention to the ditch. The roof of a truck was barely visible.

Darcy lowered his window as they closed in. "That's unfortunate. Wasting our drones wasn't my first choice. Ah well, it can't be helped." He leaned back in his seat, and smiled for the first time since the terrorist bombing. "I want to examine any tech the savages have in their possession. If we can repurpose it, we will. Otherwise, we'll destroy it."

"Repurpose savage tech?" Tony laughed derisively. "After we disinfect it, I hope."

The wreckage lay in the ditch to their right. The cabin was mangled, as if a giant had grabbed each end of the truck and twisted in opposite directions.

Tony pulled off the highway and slowed to a halt. They disembarked, keeping a wary eye on the crash site. Dense weeds cloaked the wreckage, half-hidden in the ditch. Connor handed a rifle to Darcy, who aimed it at the wreckage.

Connor circled behind their vehicle and opened the tailgate to retrieve a couple of the advanced weapons—one for Tony, and the other for himself. The chauffeur had said little since they spotted the accident scene.

What's the matter, Tony? Connor smirked to himself. *You've been close enough to smell savages before.*

Connor handed him a rifle, and they approached the wreckage, weapons held ready. Darcy took the lead, a step ahead of them. No movement, no sound from inside the truck.

At Darcy's signal, Connor skidded down the steep embankment, fending off the thorny underbrush, and landed ankle-deep in stagnant water. A rancid odor assaulted his nostrils, and he exhaled quickly, breathing through his mouth.

He raised his weapon and approached the vehicle from the rear. The tailgate hung open, window shattered, but he found no sign of casualties or survivors.

Darcy circled the front of the wreckage, crouching to squint at the shattered windshield. A spiderweb of cracked glass obscured a clear view of the interior, but Connor saw his foster father's scowl. Darcy straightened, aiming his rifle at the sky. *Stand down*, Connor imagined him saying.

Tony squatted on the shoulder of the highway, searching for a glimpse through the side window. Dark-tinted glass, streaked with cracks, frustrated his efforts. He met Darcy's gaze, shaking his head without speaking.

Darcy strode back to join Tony opposite the driver's door. He didn't break stride, sliding down the steep incline, before coming to a jarring stop against the crumpled fender.

Connor placed a cautious hand on the tailgate. Nothing stirred inside. He put his full weight on it, intending to crawl into the cargo area, and almost toppled into the stagnant water when the tailgate gave way.

His abortive actions only succeeded in attracting a swarm of mosquitoes. Connor swatted a handful away from his face and pulled himself into the cargo area for a closer look.

Darcy smashed the driver's window with the butt of his rifle, and stuck his head inside. His eyes met Connor's, and it was clear he was equally baffled.

Streaks of blood were visible on the dashboard, but the truck was empty. Connor stared, trying to make sense of the savages' disappearance. The mosquitoes returned at that moment, aiming a strafing run on the back of his neck and snapping him out of his preoccupation.

What if the savages are circling around?

Connor tumbled out of the cargo area, calling out a warning. He pivoted in a wary circle, weapon cocked, expecting an ambush.

Darcy sprang onto the hood, sliding across it and scrambling up the opposite bank. He unslung his binoculars and scrutinized the fields beyond, rifle cradled in the crook of his arm.

Tony ran to the opposite side of the highway, his binoculars moving in a slow arc as he studied the terrain.

Connor eyed the weeds and thornbushes in the ditch, listening intently. Nothing. Just his pounding heart and the incessant whine of mosquitoes. He lowered his weapon and crawled back into the cargo area.

He squeezed forward, peering over the rear seat, searching for a clue—any clue—to explain what had happened to their drones or the missing savages.

"Anything?" Darcy's voice floated down. "Did they leave any weapons or tech behind?"

Connor crawled into the rear seat, digging his fingers under the seats and gingerly brushing the carpet. "Nothing."

Darcy clumped across the hood, his footsteps heavy on the creased metal. He poked his head in the driver's window, withdrew for a moment, and slid through feet-first. Once inside, he pried the glove box open.

Connor heard his exasperated grunt. "These savages are more cunning than most." He slammed the glovebox shut and turned to look at Connor. "They crashed in a ditch, there's blood all over the dashboard, but they somehow managed to leave nothing behind."

Connor glanced at the cargo area one last time, afraid he might have missed something. "Did they talk our drones into going with them?" He snapped his fingers as a new idea came to mind. "What if their Implants are still ramping up, and the crash had nothing to do with activating them?"

Darcy chuckled and reached for the window frame, a prelude to pulling himself out of the wreckage. "One way or another, they'll feel the wrath of our drones. It's a pity we can't be spectators."

Tony crouched on the shoulder of the highway. He'd heard everything. "What if they've got a tablet of their own?"

Connor crawled over the seats, intent on following Darcy's exit route. His shoes were soaked and he had too many mosquito bites already. He heard Darcy's reply as he scrambled up the embankment. "Impossible. We capped the number of tablets at three, and they're all accounted for. Unless…"

The Givers, sharing tech with savages. Connor's jaw clenched at the idea, until a new angle occurred to him. *Because their Trackers aren't enough!*

His spirits lifted. *Darcy's strategy is working.*

FORTY-SIX ◉

CONNOR CAUGHT UP to Darcy and Tony beside the idling truck. The highway stretched for kilometers in either direction, empty. Darcy held out his rifle as Connor approached, signaling to Tony to surrender his as well. "Stow these, Connor, while I take one last look around."

Without waiting for a reply, he raised his binoculars, scanning the terrain on both sides of the highway.

Connor cradled the weapons in his arms as he circled the truck, stowing them in the cargo area and fastening straps to prevent them from sliding around. He felt the truck lurch to the left—Tony, climbing into the driver's seat, ready to be on his way as soon as Darcy gave the order.

Connor shut the tailgate with a muffled click, and was startled to find Darcy beside him, silent and unmoving. He tensed, instinctively wary. Darcy never did anything without a reason. There was a long pause, an uncharacteristic hesitation on Darcy's part. Tony revved the idling engine, oblivious. Hot exhaust puffed against Connor's legs.

"I'm only going to say this once." Darcy waited for him to nod in the affirmative before continuing. "Everything Tony said is true. Now, pay attention." He leaned in, uncomfortably close, his voice strangely detached. "Your reckless behavior is inexcusable. Do you think I enjoyed ordering Tony to terminate a fellow Citizen? Your friend is collateral damage, yes, but it was *avoidable*. She's dead because of you. Period."

Connor wilted. He stared at his feet, fascinated beyond reason with the muddy condition of his shoes. *No, that will never do. Darcy expects you to look him in the eye.* Connor took a deep breath and looked up.

Darcy waited, allowing what he'd said to sink in. Tension hung in the air between them, swelling to an intolerable level. Darcy was adept at getting his point across. "I've put myself on the line for you, despite your little escapade." His pointed gaze bored into Connor. "When savages murdered your family, I took you into my home, raised you as my very own."

"Yes, sir," Connor mumbled, not trusting himself to say anything more.

Darcy sighed. "You're my right hand. If anything happens to me, I expect you to take up the cause. Our mission isn't over until the Givers are destroyed, and the collaborators punished." He placed a hand on Connor's shoulder. Connor tensed and willed himself not to flinch. "Tony's correct. Only the fact you're my son saved you. There will be no such accommodation in the future."

Whatever else he might have said was drowned out by Tony's frantic shout. They raced around to the driver's door to find him scrambling out of the truck.

Tony held the tablet in one hand, pointing wildly at it. "Another Implant, maybe two hundred yards down the road!" His voice shook with fear. "Our drones are backtracking—they're coming after us now!"

Darcy snatched the tablet out of his hand. "Don't be ridiculous. Unless you've somehow reprogrammed them to target *us*, we're in no danger." His voice trailed off as he studied the screen. He looked up, peering into the distance. "And yet, it appears there's an unaccounted-for Implant, just ahead."

He stalked down the highway, holding the tablet waist-high, like a divining rod. Connor needed no instructions. He ducked behind the truck and retrieved a pair of rifles. He handed one to Tony, who seized it eagerly, and they jogged to catch up to Darcy.

Two hundred yards passed quickly. Darcy dropped to one knee in the middle of the highway, his expression stern and curious. Connor's mouth went dry when he saw what held his attention.

An Implant.

Pinpricks of multicolored light winked across its dark surface, visible through a dark masking of what could only be dried blood and human tissue.

"Don't touch it," Darcy said needlessly.

Did the savages rip it out of one of our drones?

Darby pinched the activated Implant between his thumb and forefinger, careful to avoid touching either end. Connor understood, and Tony's sharp intake of breath told him that he'd figured it out.

"The blood and muscle tissues are dry," Darcy said, studying the Implant with open fascination. "That suggests this wasn't a recent extraction." He flipped the Implant over, exposing its underside. "See this dark strip? It's a magnet. This was attached to something metal."

Tony raised his weapon, pivoting in a manic circle, eyes wide and feverish.

"The savages' truck," Connor heard himself say. "When we activated our drones, the tablet activated this one, too."

"It's definitely one of ours." Darcy sat back on his heels, a grim set to his mouth. "Someone has crossed the line."

FORTY-SEVEN

THEIR RETURN TO CASCADIA was uneventful: the shantytown, Gate Seven, the vehicle lift, and finally arriving at their villa in Oceanview. Darcy was preoccupied and uncommunicative throughout the trip. Connor was still reeling after their discovery of the extra Implant, and thoroughly cowed by Darcy's lecture—and threat—on the highway.

Tony departed for his own home after dropping them off, eager to put the day's events behind him. He swore his family would never know the details.

The lights were dim inside their villa, the perfect counterpart to the somber mood Connor and his foster father brought home with them. Connor reached for the dimmer switch, but froze when he became aware of a stranger's presence in the gathering room.

A tall figure stood just inside their balcony door, backlit by the Enclave's bright lights, hands clasped behind his back as he admired their twentieth-floor view.

He pivoted to face Connor and Darcy as they entered.

They hesitated just inside the front door. Their uninvited guest stood opposite them, cocking his head to one side and studying them with open curiosity.

"Councilor Peterson, the time for a conversation between us is long overdue," he said at last, speaking in a clipped monotone. Connor didn't recognize his voice.

Darcy didn't respond, and the shadowy figure spoke again, his words couched in an odd formality. "I believe your anticipated timeline has been compromised. We must speak."

"*You.*" The loathing in Darcy's voice turned the single syllable into a withering curse. "Why should I listen to anything you say? I know what you are."

"Nevertheless, Councilor." The anonymous figure stepped out of the shadows, unfazed. "The time is upon us." His eyes fastened on Darcy, his expression benign. Connor found his unblinking gaze disconcerting.

Darcy glared, making no attempt to hide his animus. His lips twisted, and he spat out a single word, laced with contempt.

"Mateo."

FORTY-EIGHT ◉

"Mateo?" the name seemed to catch the merchant off-guard. He broke eye contact, looking anywhere but at Garr.

He's scared. Aubrey studied his mannerisms, intrigued. *Isn't that odd? All smiles one moment, and now this.*

"Mateo's shop is near the Enclave." The merchant stole a furtive glance over his shoulder, as if he feared being overheard. His voice dropped to an indistinct mumble, barely discernible. "Next-to-last road before the Gate Seven. Turn right, and it's the second shop on your right."

With that, he waved—too enthusiastically, Aubrey thought —at another shopkeeper across the footpath. He shoved between Garr and Jane, loudly calling his colleague by name, and almost tripping over his own feet in his haste to depart. They chatted briefly, and the second merchant shot Garr a startled look before they ducked into his shop.

"That's what we used to call 'buyer's remorse,'" Garr said, imitating Don's carefree drawl. "He seemed fairly eager to sell us something a minute ago."

"I guess Mateo's reputation isn't what it used to be," Aubrey said, keeping an eye on the shop across the path. There was no sign of either merchant.

"No kidding." Jane jammed her fists into her pockets. "It was the polar opposite the last time we were out here. Mateo was a community leader, helping newcomers settle in and make connections."

It was mid-afternoon in Jericho. Everything appeared to be going well, until Garr mentioned Mateo.

The tension spiked. I felt it. Aubrey tried to keep her shoulders down and arms relaxed. She still had a tendency to tighten up under stress.

Garr craned his neck, peering at Cascadia's monolithic walls over the haphazard roofline of the market. "Make connections," he said absently, repeating Jane's phrase. "Anything to increase their chances of a day-permit into the Enclave. These people live off the Hoarders' crumbs."

"It beats starving, they say." Jane hooked her thumbs into her shoulder straps. "Can we go now? This place gives me the creeps. I know how to find Mateo's shop."

Aubrey stared at her, surprised. *It's not just me. Jane feels it, too. Like we're being watched.*

Garr led the way, but not at his typical ground-eating stride. His pace was casual, as if he were out for an afternoon stroll. Aubrey knew better—he was sizing up their surroundings.

She recalled Jane's less-than-patient training. *You're watching for warning signs, escape routes, and anyone showing too much interest in us.*

She resisted the urge to look over her shoulder in hopes of spotting covert surveillance. *Lots of quick glances, don't stare.*

Her shoulders tensed in spite of herself.

"Check out the crow's nest above the gate," Jane murmured, her lips barely moving. "You can't miss it."

Aubrey glanced up, not tilting her head to look at it directly. The sun was setting to the west, highlighting every detail with a golden glow. The walls appeared seamless, as if cast from a single slab of stone, broken only by Gate Seven and the open balcony above it. A large assortment of weapons protruded, casting elongated shadows.

"That's a lot of firepower." Aubrey kept her eyes on the hard-packed ground as she spoke. *No direct eye contact when making tactical observations. Don't expect a response. Never discuss strategy out in the open.*

"That's an understatement." Garr's reply was nonchalant, as if Aubrey had complimented him on the color of his shirt. "The locals depend on the work permits. They know better than to bite the hand that feeds them. Those weapons are fear-factor overkill."

"Overkill?" Jane kicked sullenly at a stone, sending it skittering ahead. "Not if you think like a Hoarder."

They fell silent. Another cluster of permit workers passed by and between them. The single-lane dirt road was becoming clogged by the heavy amount of foot traffic.

Aubrey sidled closer to Garr. "If a Hoarder truck shows up now..." She swallowed hard, hoping for the best.

He nodded soberly. "A lot of exhausted day-workers will have to switch gears in a hurry."

They turned a corner, at Jane's direction, into a footpath running parallel to the Enclave wall. The dirt was hard-packed from the passage of many feet. Aubrey felt a crawling sensation between her shoulders. Her imagination painted a vivid image of guards training their weapons on them from above. She bit her lip and concentrated on putting one foot ahead of the other. *Hidden in plain sight.*

"We're new arrivals in Jericho, hoping for work," Garr said under his breath. "There's nothing unusual about us asking for directions to Mateo's shop."

"Everyone knows Mateo Reyes! Second shop on the right." Jane's sarcastic mimicry held a cutting edge, even at low volume. "That's all we heard last time. Wonder what caused such a drastic change of heart?"

Garr ducked under the awning outside Mateo's clothing shop. "Let's ask him."

They stepped into the shade under the awning. Mateo's wares hung from several display racks, but they appeared oddly askew. The door to his shop stood slightly ajar, the interior cloaked in shadow. Aubrey skirted a pile of blankets left carelessly on the ground.

The Runners exchanged glances, perplexed. Jane took a deep breath, flexing her hands, and barged inside. Garr followed close on her heels. Aubrey heard their startled exclamations and crowded in behind him.

The interior twilight couldn't conceal the chaotic scene. Mateo's shop had been ransacked, vandalized, all but demolished—display racks splintered, shelves toppled, merchandise spilled in graceless piles on the floor.

The careless arrangement under the awning seemed pristine by comparison. Displays once hanging from the low rafters had been ripped down and piled in a heap by the door. Nothing, it appeared, had escaped the wanton destruction.

Aubrey shed her backpack, allowing it to slide to the floor. Garr pivoted and closed the door. Daylight glimmered feebly through two small windows. Dusk was on its way.

"Here." Jane pounced on a cylindrical object near her foot. She fumbled inside her pack for a moment, and a small spark appeared. Seconds later, a lantern flared, casting odd shadows on her face.

Aubrey found her voice. "What happened, and why hasn't Mateo cleaned this mess up?"

"Maybe he can't," Garr replied grimly. "He may have been the target." He pulled the curtains tight over both windows. Jane turned the lantern up and skirted past a broken display to place it in the middle of the shop.

Aubrey found a small office, tucked into the front corner of the shop. She peeked cautiously past the threshold and, emboldened, slipped inside.

There wasn't much to see.

An overturned table in one corner, it contents scattered haphazardly around the room. A pair of wooden chairs, one tossed on top of the inverted table. An open cashbox in the opposite corner, trailing a meager number of coins across the floor.

Violence had visited the spartan office, as well.

But no sign of Mateo.

FORTY-NINE

Aubrey gave the office a final once-over, and returned to the main room. Jane prodded warily at a tangled pile of blankets, and Garr tugged a hanging rug aside, revealing another door at the rear of the shop. His knife appeared in his hand and he gave the room a cursory scan.

"Living quarters." Garr said tersely, resheathing his weapon. "Also trashed. Aubrey, keep an eye on the door. Jane, you're with me. Whoever did this was looking for something. I want to know what and why."

Jane snatched up the lantern, and they disappeared behind the hanging rug.

Aubrey repressed a shiver as twilight reclaimed the interior of the shop. She returned to front door and cracked it open, but her view of the footpath was limited by the displays under the awning. She decided to step outside.

The early-evening air had chilled after the sun's departure, but her line of sight was an improvement. Aubrey crossed her arms, looking from side to side, alert for ... what, exactly?

Mateo's shop had been ransacked, yet nothing appeared to have been stolen. She puzzled over why none of the desperate locals had claimed his deserted and obviously unguarded space. *There's something else going on. There has to be.*

A hulking figure passed the shop twice before Aubrey noticed. The guy was huge, nearly the same size as Don. Even the way he walked reminded Aubrey of the big man. The stranger wasn't in a hurry, ambling casually down the beaten path.

Instinct guided her. She crouched behind a pile of blankets, making herself as small as possible. A security guard? Did that explain why Mateo's shop hadn't been looted or repossessed during his absence?

Jane's voice grew louder behind her. "What a dump." Aubrey glanced over her shoulder, relieved to see she had lowered the lantern's glow. "This is the most primitive Hub I've ever seen, and I thought Eastside was bleak."

"Mateo has to survive in Cascadia's shadow..." Garr's voice trailed off. Aubrey heard a muted whisper, and the lantern was abruptly extinguished.

She hunkered low behind the blanket pile, spellbound as the obvious sentry passed by a third time. He paused at the intersection adjacent to Gate Seven and pivoted to resume his patrol. She caught a brief glimpse of the faint red light around his left eye.

The Soul-less, here?

Aubrey ducked her head, praying that the massive Tracker wouldn't notice her. She pulled her jacket hood forward, trying to blend in with the blankets. She felt Garr and Jane's presence behind her as they crept outside.

Stealth mode. Aubrey recognized the protocol. *They saw I'd gone to ground.* Jane's tutoring was paying off.

Garr tapped her shoulder, his voice the barest of whispers. "What is it?"

"Tracker." Aubrey mouthed the word, pantomiming a quick circle around her eye.

Their grim faces told her—they understood.

"No sign of Mateo," Jane murmured close to her ear. "No footprints, no messages, but on the other hand, no bloodstains. He could still be alive, somewhere."

Aubrey's heart dropped.

Mateo Reyes, whoever or whatever he might be, was missing. His meticulously cared-for shop had been ransacked, the threat of violence very clear.

And one of the Soul-less was patrolling the footpath outside his shop.

FIFTY ◎

THE RUNNERS CREPT back inside Mateo's shop and crouched on either side of the door while the Tracker was at the furthest point of its patrol. The Tracker completed another sentry run, betraying no indication it was aware of their presence. So far, so good.

"Now what do we do?" Aubrey whispered. The butterflies in her stomach refused to settle. She tried her best to keep her voice neutral. "It's a safe bet everyone in Jericho knows Mateo's shop has been vandalized. We can't stay here indefinitely, pretending we're shopping."

"Don't forget that other merchant we met." Jane crouched opposite Aubrey, avoiding a direct line-of-sight through the door. "He couldn't get away fast enough when we mentioned Mateo, but he didn't bother warning us." She scowled. "I'd love to go back and ask him why."

Garr dropped to one knee beside her. "It's almost dark, but that may not increase our chances. I'll bet the Givers included night vision in a Tracker's upgrades."

Aubrey thrust out her hand, shushing them. The Tracker made another pass in front of the shop.

She waited until she felt certain the Tracker was far enough away not to overhear. "Never thought I'd miss the sewers, but right now, nothing would make me happier than an underground escape route."

A idea popped into her mind, triggered by her half-hearted joke. She crawled past her companions to the tiny office and eased the door open, beckoning them to follow.

"Are you crazy?" Jane balked. "Jericho is a ghetto next to Hoarderville. There's nothing under this shop but dirt."

Aubrey rapped her knuckles on the wooden floorboards. The sound was muffled but solid. No basement. No secret escape route. She didn't let that discourage her. She crept into the office, tapping guardedly as she went.

Garr joined her a moment later. Jane crowded in behind him, pausing to relight the lantern. The flickering glow, even at its lowest setting, provided sufficient light.

Aubrey pointed to the corner. "See? Trashed, just like the rest of the shop, except for one spot. No debris, not even a scrap piece of paper."

Garr knelt to examine the floorboards. He unsheathed his knife, working the point into a crack between two boards. His efforts were thwarted at first, but he managed to pry up a small section of the floor, revealing a dark hole about a yard across. Garr propped the section of flooring against the office wall, careful to muffle any betraying noise.

"Well, well, well," Jane said, eyebrows raised. "What's Mateo got buried under his floorboards?" She handed Garr the lantern, and knelt beside Aubrey.

Garr lowered the lantern into the hole, leaning over for a

better view. "Hard to say." He glanced up. "It goes down about six feet or so, and then it appears to widen out."

"You mean it *is* a tunnel? Where to?" Jane craned her neck to look over his shoulder. "Look—there's rungs built into it."

Garr set the lantern on the floor and swung his legs into the hole. "Only one way to find out." He climbed down the make-shift ladder, pausing after a couple of rungs to extend a hand. "I'll take that lantern, if you don't mind."

Jane lowered the lantern within reach, and Garr continued his descent, awkwardly one-handed. The lantern flared bright-er as he reached the bottom, and he took a quick step to his right, disappearing from view. His voice wafted up to them. "Come on in, the water's fine."

Jane fairly flew down the ladder, and Aubrey followed, de-scending hand-over-hand on the wooden rungs.

Aubrey found a second tunnel at the bottom of the shaft, doubling back under Mateo's shop. The tunnel was roughly spherical, equal in height to her waist. She dropped to her hands and knees and crawled after her companions.

Garr shone the lantern around the earth-walled chamber. It wasn't large, perhaps the same size as the office, but they could stand upright. The spartan furnishings consisted of a wood-en table against one wall and an equally ascetic barstool. An assortment of unfamiliar objects were scattered in haphazard fashion on the table.

"Mateo did a thorough job." Garr held the lantern high, admiring the compact space. "See the braces supporting the ceiling? This wasn't built overnight."

He lowered the lantern. The objects on the rough-hewn ta-ble cast odd shadows on the walls. Predominate among them were various bits of microtechnology and assorted craftsman's tools. Garr picked up a piece of tech, studying it with a practiced eye. "Just bits and pieces," he said, returning it to the table. "No telling what Mateo's up to. Not unless we question him in person."

Aubrey's stomach sank. *The more we learn, the more questions we have about Mateo. That shouldn't be a shock. He was —or is—one of the Soul-less.*

"This is a dead end." Jane ran a finger over one of the tools. She snatched her hand away, rubbing her palm against her thigh. "We still need to find a way out. We've been down here too long already."

Garr nodded absently. "There's nothing more to learn here." He turned his back on the microtechnology strewn across the table, lantern in hand, and strode back to the circular portal. "Let's go."

He ducked out of the small workroom, plunging it into murky twilight. Aubrey and Jane followed on his heels, grateful to find him holding the lantern above them to aid their return climb.

Aubrey scrambled up the ladder in Jane's wake. Garr replaced the flooring over the hole.

Jane disappeared into the main room, to return moments later, her pack already buckled on. "It's gone." She gestured outside, edging toward the door. "The Tracker. It's not patrolling anymore. Let's move before it comes back."

She led the way into the main room. Aubrey shrugged into her pack. Garr eased the door open, pack held in one hand as he peered cautiously outside. Satisfied, he half-turned. "If anyone asks, we're just a bunch of disillusioned job-seekers. We came all this way, but nothing turned out like we hoped it would. So, we're taking our broken dreams and moving on."

Aubrey nodded. It was a plausible alibi, hopefully enough

to satisfy anyone they might encounter. *And it's not far from the truth.*

She pulled her hood up and tucked her hair inside. *No Mateo, and more questions than answers.*

FIFTY-ONE ◉

THE TRACKER EXECUTED its assigned sentry duty with tireless efficiency, stalking resolutely along the footpaths in the impoverished shantytown.

The bio-forms returning from the Enclave gave it a wide berth. The red glow around its left eye ensured that. The Tracker welcomed the solitude, as well as the lack of distractions.

The Quest burned within, but the Givers had issued specific parameters for this assignment. The Tracker was incapable of the emotion once known as *exasperation*, yet their directive was as troubling as it was puzzling.

It could detected no Implants within range. There was no logic to this pointless exercise, except ... the Givers were not to be questioned, only obeyed.

A click echoed in its processor. New data from the Givers. The necessity for the patrol was over. Its sentry duty was complete. The Tracker turned its back on the nondescript row of shops and stalked away, abandoning the shantytown. Nothing mattered but the Quest.

The Givers were generous but they were not to be denied.

It had traveled perhaps five miles cross-country when a new click sounded in its processor. The determined pace the Tracker had maintained slowed as it assimilated the new data.

Analyze. Adapt. Enact.

No. Inaccurate. This was not new data. This was ... something else. Fear erupted, blocking out rational thought.

Fear was all it had left.

The explosion flared white-hot in the early-evening dusk, but there was no one present to witness it. Scavengers gathered to feast on what was left.

FIFTY-TWO ◉

"THERE'S NOT MUCH ELSE to tell." Aubrey winced as Doc exerted pressure on the tender spots in her forearm. "The most useful part of the mission was Jane pounding her training into me. Aside from that, you could sum it up: went to the Enclave, didn't find Mateo, turned around and came home. Colonel Scott was *not* happy."

Doc sighed and shifted her attention to Aubrey's hand. "Short summaries are becoming the new normal." Her mouth twisted as if she'd bitten into something sour. "Tracy deceived me. Then she escaped. Took an Implant with her." She paused, shaking her head. "I'm guessing she stole it to impress the Givers, maybe get back into their good books. We'll probably never know, unless the Givers show up here unannounced."

Aubrey jerked her hand away. "The Givers, here? Please tell me you're exaggerating."

Doc wiped her hands on a small towel. "Tracy knows Eastside's location. She concealed the true extent of her recovery, *and* we know she was listening to our conversations." She sighed in frustration and tossed her towel on the worktable. "She's a walking encyclopedia of intel where we're concerned. The perfect gift for the Givers, even without the stolen Implant."

"What's going to happen?"

Doc waved a weary hand at an assortment of packs just inside the infirmary door, each filled to the brim. Very few items remained on the worktable. "Remember when I told you we're always ready to leave at a moment's notice? Well, as soon as Garr gets back from the dropbox, he'll give us our timeline. And it won't be *if*, it'll be *when*. Mark my words."

"Don't beat yourself up, Doc." Aubrey leaned forward, concerned. "Tracy fooled us all. We underestimated how fanatical she was about the Givers. And those two 'guards' left a lot to be desired. You said so, yourself. Maybe we should turn *them* over to Jane for retraining."

She smiled as she finished, hoping to lighten the mood.

"Only if I can watch," Doc replied with a dark smile. She resumed packing. "Speaking of Jane," she said, changing the subject, "it sounds like the two of you are learning to coexist peacefully. Or am I too optimistic?"

"Never say never, Doc." Aubrey laughed. "On the other hand, don't hold your breath." She flexed her aching fingers. *Battle scars. I'm a survivor.*

"I was hoping for more than a ceasefire," Doc said lightly, "but progress is progress."

"Don't get too excited, Doc, but Jane *did* tell me a bit about the Runner she killed." Aubrey watched for her reaction. "Is it true? She shot her own brother?"

"Yes." Doc tugged sharply on the pack's drawstring, harder than necessary. "It was self-defense, kill or be killed. Davey was

Jane's only living relative. Her mother died a few years earlier, and her father deserted the family ages ago. Jane doesn't remember him. Davey was all ..." Doc caught her breath.

Aubrey felt her cheeks burn. *Heartless, Aubs. Nicely done.*

The door opened before she could apologize. Garr entered, his hands balled inside his jacket pockets. Judging by the look on his face, he was under a great deal of strain.

We're evacuating. Aubrey's heart skipped a beat. *Doc wasn't kidding. Tracy could lead a whole army of Trackers straight to Eastside.*

"Nothing new in the dropbox." Garr came straight to the point. "We left a message to warn the other Hubs about Mateo, and to steer clear of this location. Eastside's been attacked before, so we know Trackers are familiar with it. I advised Uncle John to shut down for at least a week. He'll come up with a plausible excuse. That should protect his staff."

Doc nodded, her expression haunted. "Wise precaution."

Garr ran a hand along the gurney frame, halting when his fingers came into contact with Tracy's empty restraints. He took a deep breath, and issued his orders much like the colonel of old. "Evacuation protocol. Thirty minutes. Doc, I see you've prepped already. Give Aubrey a hand. Don't forget extra trail rations."

Everything's falling apart. A hollow dread filled Aubrey's gut, draining her energy. *We couldn't find Mateo, we lost Tracy, and now we have to evacuate. It's like Eastside is cursed.*

"Where is Jane, by the way?" Doc found an empty pack and handed it to Aubrey. "This one's for you. Pack your gear and meet me in the mess hall. Bring blankets. We don't know how long we'll be between Hubs."

"Jane's in the mess hall already," Garr replied. "I sent her to do the same. Gear and rations. I also gave her permission to bring her Glock—after I told her where I'd hidden it." In better times, his comment might have been amusing.

Aubrey said nothing, not trusting herself to speak. She opened her pack and gazed forlornly at the empty interior. The idea of abandoning Eastside was more demoralizing than she'd expected. *Thirty minutes. Probably waiting until Don, Sheila and Amos return. And then we evacuate.*

Footsteps sounded in the corridor outside the infirmary.

The door, half-ajar, swung fully open with a bang, rebounding off the wall. Aubrey dropped her pack, Garr's eyes widened, and everyone pivoted to stare at the figure in the doorway.

It wasn't Jane.

FIFTY-THREE ◉

EASTSIDE'S MESS HALL FELT cold and empty. Jane stuffed as many rations as she could fit into her backpack and fastened the buckles. She leaned against the counter, surveying the room one last time.

It had never been much of a home. There was only so much one could expect from concrete, dust, and tension, but it was all she'd known for almost three years. She eyed the vacant chairs around the table, picturing her fellow Runners' faces.

Everyone has a favorite chair. We do our best to carve out a tiny piece of normal. For all the good it does.

Her fingertips brushed over a solid lump in her pocket, and she pulled out her grandfather's handgun. Her most treasured —and hated—possession. She steeled herself and inspected the Glock, hoping for at least a modicum of objectivity.

She couldn't find any.

Jagged memories wrapped around the Glock like a choking vine. She'd lost count of the number of the times she'd stared into a mirror, mouthing the word *self-defense*.

It didn't matter. Nothing changed.

Garr—what an idiot. Her thoughts turned dark and angry. It felt good to direct her loathing at someone else. *I should've refused to train Country Girl.*

She examined the gun out of habit, admiring and repelled by its metallic beauty. Her lethal protection, and executioner of the only person who mattered to her.

Gah! How could you do this to me, Garr? One mention of Davey, and all the old feelings are back.

Her hand shook. She stared at the handgun, loathing it, and loathing herself for her inability to part with it. She wished, not for the first time, she'd thrown it into the sewer when she'd had the chance.

She stuffed the Glock into her pocket, snatched her pack off the floor with her other hand, and stormed out of the mess hall without a backward glance.

Eastside Hub had never been much of a home. She had no intention of it becoming her grave.

FIFTY-FOUR

GARR THREW HIMSELF forward, shielding Doc and Aubrey behind his body. Aubrey edged up beside him, trembling in shock. She couldn't see what Doc Simon was doing, but at least they were screening her from attack.

Combat knives won't be enough…

Tracy stood motionless in the infirmary doorway, left arm bent sharply at the elbow. She held her clenched fist against her chest as if her life depended on it.

Garr motioned to Aubrey and Doc with his hand. *Stay put.* He advanced slowly, moving with exaggerated care, his hands open and palm up.

Tracy cocked her head to one side, eyeing him with an odd expression. Aubrey tried to identify the look on her face. *Confusion … like she's never seen Garr before.*

Tracy struck without warning, taking three lightning-fast steps into the infirmary and shoving him violently out of her way. Caught off-guard by her unexpected attack, Garr reeled back, slamming hard against the gurney.

He grabbed for the gurney rail and levered himself upright. His face was pale, and he cupped a hand over his ribs, gasping for breath. Tracy ignored him.

"Doc Simon." Tracy spoke for the first time, her voice clear and strong. She extended her left arm and opened her fist. "For you."

The stolen Implant lay in her palm.

Aubrey held her breath. Tracy stood only three feet away, the diminutive piece of alien technology cupped in her palm.

"For you." Tracy took another step, eyes fixed on Doc. She held the Implant out for emphasis, jaw muscles working as she forced the words out. "Doc Simon. I am. Sorry."

Garr clung to the gurney for support. His hand rested on the hilt of his knife, but he hadn't drawn it. Aubrey held her position, shielding Doc. Her heart thudded in her ears.

Doc excused herself past Aubrey and calmly approached Tracy. She halted an arm's length away, and gently took the Implant from her palm. "Thank you, Tracy."

Tracy dropped her outstretched arm, shaking her head. Aubrey stared, dumbfounded, as she broke into a smile. A genuine, warm, *human* smile.

"No, Doc," she said, her words deliberate and slow. Her smile widened. "Megan. My name."

FIFTY-FIVE ⊙

"WHAT'S THE PLAN?" Amos twisted in the passenger seat to catch Don's eye. "We can't risk the checkpoint, not with extra passengers. Our permits won't match."

Emma sat between her husband and Don, looking slightly ill as the truck careened down the road. Lukas sat directly behind Amos, clutching his wife's hand.

Don snorted. "I wouldn't risk that checkpoint, even if we had a fresh set of permits. Besides, we've put off ditching this truck too long already."

Sheila downshifted as they ascended a steep incline. "There's a tunnel access near the outskirts of the Old City. Let's get as close as possible before we abandon the truck."

They crested the ridge that marked the remote valley's outer boundary. Sheila looked relieved as they descended the steep slope. Rolling terrain spread out before them, the paved highway—such as it was—visible in the distance. She nudged the accelerator, increasing speed.

Amos settled into his seat, momentarily stymied by the

pack on the floor between his feet. He bent over, shoving it aside for more leg room. He flipped the pack open, checking on its contents.

"How much longer?" Emma's anxious voice rose from the rear seat. "When can we get our Implants removed? Does your Hub have a medic? I feel sick."

Sheila answered in her most reassuring tone of voice. "Yes, her name is Doc Simon. Don't worry, the first thing she'll do is take care of your Implants."

She reduced speed as they reached the bottom of the hill. The gravel road gave way to a paved highway, and their tires bucked as they merged onto the blacktop. Sheila accelerated, dodging around frequent potholes. Amos hoped Emma's motion sickness wouldn't get worse.

Lukas spoke up behind him. "You managed to find us, and so did that Tracker, but you never explained how the Hoarders knew we existed in the first place." Suspicion hardened his voice. "They had no reason to target us."

"Maybe, maybe not." Don leaned forward, looking past Emma to answer him. "Our only concern is staying ahead of Trackers until Doc can remove your Implants. No one knows how or why the Hoarders choose their victims."

Emma slouched between them, arms crossed, a petulant look marring her face. "We don't deserve this," she said sullenly. "We've done nothing to the Hoarders. We've never even met one. Lukas is right—someone told them where to find us."

Amos understood the source of their resentment. *Finding out you've been Implanted is hard. Add a Tracker to the mix, and Don setting fire to their café—who could blame them?*

A violent outburst in the rear seat caught Amos unaware, and his chair rocked forward. Lukas slammed his shoulder into his seat a second time. Amos braced himself against the dashboard, his head ringing.

"*Enough.*" Don's voice erupted, a bear's roar inside the cab of the truck. The word reverberated, loud and punishing. He reached for Lukas.

"This is your doing." Lukas cuffed his arm away, jabbing an accusing finger at him. His rage was incendiary. "We're not a threat to anyone. You led that Tracker straight to us!"

Emma bolted upright, pounding her fist on Don's shoulder. "You told us we have Implants." Her voice rose in an angry crescendo. "There's no mark on our bodies, no proof. Just your words—and I don't believe you anymore."

"Amos," Sheila whispered, so softly he nearly missed it. He tore his eyes away from the escalating confrontation. Sheila pointed with her chin to the floor at his feet.

Amos's heart skipped a beat. A telltale glow radiated from the open flap of her pack.

The scanner was still on. Highest intensity.

FIFTY-SIX ◎

A TRUCK IDLED next to the highway, the Old City a dark smudge in the distance. The off-road vehicle was sturdy, its design ideal for navigating rugged terrain. Dark-tinted windows mirrored the latest trends favored by Citizens of the Enclave. The added anonymity, even if unintentional, was a welcome feature.

The fugitives would soon arrive. It was only a matter of time. Patience. Diligence.

The windshield reflected the glow of the Tracker's scanning eye, faint but noticeable. The scanner's intensity was at its lowest level. That would change as the fugitives drew closer. Only patience and diligence were required.

Everything was proceeding as anticipated.

* * *

AMOS REACHED inside the pack, his movements nonchalant, stealthy. The glowing scanner was at its peak. He saw the confirming data on the attached reader—activated Implants. The Petrovs' aggressive outburst took on a more sinister cast.

Amos pushed the scanner aside, intent on the other items

Sheila had thought to include. Two prods. Charged and ready, she'd said. He seized one, switching it on with his thumb, careful to shield what he was doing from view.

The animosity in the rear seat intensified, washing over him like a wave. Sheila took her foot off the accelerator, and their momentum began to subside. She kept her eyes glued to the road ahead, her grip on the steering wheel iron-tight.

"Stop!" Lukas lunged between the seats, clawing wildly at Sheila's arm. Amos, still hunched over the backpack, found himself pinned under his weight.

The truck lurched to one side. Sheila wrestled for control as she tried to fend Lukas off. Amos heard, as much as he sensed, Don's attempt to intervene behind him. He had no way of knowing what Emma was up to, but it was clear she was somehow interfering with Don.

He yanked the prod out of the pack, twisting to grapple with Lukas. The weaving truck made it difficult to keep his balance, and he pushed back in a desperate effort to free himself.

Lukas wrestled with Sheila, kicking his legs for leverage as he wedged himself further into the front seat. Lukas's elbow caught Amos in the side of the head, and he almost dropped the prod. He heard Don's angry cry, but he couldn't see what Emma had done.

The truck lurched sharply to the left. Their situation was deteriorating—fast. Amos's mind raced, weighing variables.

He braced his left arm against the dashboard, pushing back as hard as he could. Sight unseen, he jammed the prod under his arm, desperate to connect with Lukas's ribs.

He was rewarded by a piercing cry—the prod's effect was anything but gentle—and Lukas's full weight landed on him, limp and heavy.

His sudden collapse dragged Sheila's arm down, sending the truck careening in a different direction. Tires squealed on the pavement, giving way to spitting gravel.

Amos braced himself for the inevitable.

FIFTY-SEVEN ⊙

THE FUGITIVES' DELAY was cause for alarm. The time calculated from their point of departure had more than elapsed. Yet there was no sign of their stolen vehicle. Patience. Diligence.

No. Inaccurate data—*incomplete* data.

Investigation required. The delay was not anticipated. An unpredicted factor, a random element, had been added to the equation.

Analyze. Adapt. Enact.

The truck shot forward, engine roaring and tires protesting against the pavement.

* * *

BRAKES SQUEALED and the truck lurched sharply, skidding off the highway before plunging into the ditch. Sheila struggled to control the steering wheel, hampered by Lukas's weight, but managed to keep them upright. The truck ricocheted from one side of the ditch to the other, and the sound of buckling metal filled Amos's ears.

Their manic slalom came to a sudden halt. The windshield

had been reduced to a spiderweb of cracked glass. The engine emitted a final, convulsive shudder and died.

An eerie silence filled the cab.

Amos groaned as he tested his arms and legs. Nothing seemed to be broken. He spied the prod on the floor, by his feet, and gave silent thanks he hadn't inadvertently shocked himself. He licked his lips, tasting blood.

Sheila slumped in the driver's seat, her face a bloody mess. She looked dazed, but not seriously injured. Lukas lay awkwardly between them, limp and unconscious. Amos breathed a sigh of relief.

He heard a sudden rustling behind him. Emma.

Her Implant's active. Amos lunged for the prod, heart racing. He flicked the power on and tried to reach over Lukas, whose limp body suddenly became a maddening barricade. Amos struggled with his free hand to move him aside.

Don shook his head, groggy and unfocused. Emma erupted in a whirlwind of frantic energy. She wriggled over the back seat, into the cargo area.

Amos tried to force his door open, but it jammed against the side of the ditch. He thrust his right arm through the narrow opening, mindful of the active prod in his hand, and squeezed through the doorframe. It was a tight fit. The ditch was deep and narrow, filled with thorny vegetation and the reek of stagnant water, thick and pungent. He fended off the barbed foliage, enduring bloody scratches as he won free.

There was a flurry of motion inside the wreckage.

Emma kicked violently against the tailgate. She was stronger than she appeared, and the barrier gave way. She ducked out of the truck and, undeterred by the thorns, scrambled with surprising agility up the steep embankment.

Tires screeched on the highway, followed by the sound of a door opening. A helpful passerby? Amos instinctively doubted the odds of that.

He circled behind the wreckage, sloshing through ankle-deep water. A cloud of mosquitos rose to engulf him in furious retribution. He scaled the ditch, awkwardly one-handed, and reached the highway, chest heaving from exertion.

A second truck blocked his way—engine idling, driver's door flung open. He darted around it, his muddy shoes sliding on loose gravel, and skidded to an abrupt halt.

The driver, feet firmly planted shoulder-width apart, held Emma by the throat. She thrashed in a futile attempt to free herself, her eyes strangely vacant. Her captor said nothing.

Amos stared in disbelief, one hand braced against the truck for support. Don clambered out of the ditch behind him. Amos heard his sharp intake of breath, followed by a rasp of leather as he unsheathed his knife.

The driver turned to look at him, stoic and expressionless. The circle of red light around his left eye came as no surprise. "Good welcome, Amos." He extended his free hand, palm up. "Your prod, if I may?"

Mateo.

FIFTY-EIGHT ◉

AMOS AND SHEILA LOADED Emma's unconscious body into the truck. Don and Mateo returned to the crash site, to pry a mangled door open and bring the unconscious Lukas out. The grating sound of a door forced open carried loud and clear from the ditch. Amos winced at the noise.

Sheila set her pack on the tailgate. She'd had the presence of mind to bring it along when she climbed out of the ditch. She took a seat on the tailgate and dabbed at the cut on her forehead with a linen cloth. "At least I didn't break my nose again," she said wryly, checking the cloth for fresh bloodstains. "I hope Don knows what he's doing."

Amos concurred, uneasy. Don had raised a single finger to his lips—*say nothing*—while Mateo subdued Emma with the prod. "I had a hard time *not* asking the obvious. If the real Mateo died two years ago …"

"I know." Sheila placed the cloth beside her and wiped her hands on her pants, frowning at the bloodstains and streaks of dried mud. "I had the same thought. Lucky for us, Don's thinking two steps ahead. Our truck's a write-off. We need Mateo's help, but if we spill what we know, or suspect…"

Amos glanced at her pack, alarmed by a new discovery. A faint light glowed through the canvas. "We deactivated their Implants. Why's the scanner still showing red?"

Sheila stifled an exclamation, knocking the bloody rag to the ground. She seized her pack, fumbling with the buckle as she ripped the flap open. Her eyes widened and she backed away, looking wildly in all directions. Her reaction was all the answer Amos needed.

He whirled as he heard Don approaching. The big man carried Lukas, unconscious, slung over one shoulder. "Trouble, Don—we've got another Implant."

Mateo appeared behind Don. His scanning eye blazed, almost as if it might burn through his skin. He held a pair of pliers aloft, not speaking.

Amos caught his breath as he spied the winking lights.

"This was attached to your vehicle chassis," Mateo said in his detached instructor's voice. He rotated the pliers, examining the Implant from all angles. "A Tracker on its inaugural Quest could trace you with no effort at all." The red light around his eye winked out. The Implant's flickering lights danced in a random pattern.

Mateo spun on his heel and climbed into the driver's seat, slamming his door shut. The invitation—and the need for haste —was unmistakable.

Amos and Don deposited Lukas beside his wife. They looked as if they were enjoying a deep and dreamless asleep. *They still need surgery to remove their Implants.*

Don shut the tailgate and they climbed into the rear seat, Don in his preferred position behind the driver.

Mateo sat motionless behind the wheel, as stoic as ever. He held the blinking Implant in one hand, insulated from his own flesh by the pliers.

Interesting. Amos noticed how gingerly Mateo handled the pliers. *What effect would an Implant have on a Tracker?*

Mateo kept his eyes on the road and held the pliers over his shoulder. "Take this for me, Amos, if you don't mind."

Amos took the pliers, fighting nausea. The hair-thin filaments were invisible to the eye, but he knew they were diligently at work, secreting poison from either end of the device. He caught Don's dark scowl out of the corner of his eye.

"We should prod it," Don said gruffly. "That might throw off whoever planted it on our truck. They could be tracking us right now, for all we know."

"They are." Mateo shifted into gear and reversed direction in a wide turn. "Don, I must say I'm disappointed. You continue to default to an emotional reaction. You could be an excellent strategist, if you put your mind to it."

Don opened his mouth, but apparently thought better of it. Amos nodded his silent approval. *Don't let him get under your skin. He owes us a lot of answers.*

Mateo accelerated sharply and Amos tightened his grip on the pliers, grimly determined to keep the venomous tech secure. They didn't travel far—roughly two hundred yards, he guessed—before Mateo reduced speed. He pressed a button, and the window beside Amos slid open.

"Drop the Implant here," Mateo said, not looking at him. Amos leaned out of the window, holding the Implant as far away as possible, and let go.

Mateo nodded, looking pleased. "An activated Implant on a remote highway will spark lively debate among your pursuers.

I predict they will squander precious time by their attempts to explain it."

The window closed and Mateo accelerated sharply. Amos twisted in his seat to view the road behind, but saw no signs of pursuit. The rolling terrain thwarted his line of sight, but he took comfort in knowing their pursuers would have the same disadvantage.

"What now?" Sheila raised her voice over the road noise. "We can't risk the checkpoint. Not looking like this." Her face was a mask of dried blood. The nasty slash on her forehead had stopped oozing, but hiding her injuries was impossible.

Amos winced as he examined his ripped shirtsleeves and the bloody scratches underneath. *Even a rookie security guard would be suspicious.*

Mateo's calm monotone intruded on his thoughts. "Our newest companions still have Implants requiring extraction. Active or dormant, Trackers will sense their presence." He fastened his unblinking gaze on Sheila. "You have alternate routes to Eastside Hub, do you not? I would be pleased to provide transportation, if advised of its exact location."

Careful, Sheila. Amos wished for some subtle way of warning her without Mateo noticing. *He's fishing for intel.*

Sheila lowered her visor, grimacing at her reflection in the vanity mirror. "That's not a bad idea, Mateo." Amos relaxed. She was stalling. "But then we'd have to physically carry them the rest of the way."

"Good point." Don leaned forward in his seat. "I'd like to think I'm in reasonably good shape, but Lukas and Emma are deadweight. Pardon the expression."

He shot Amos a quick glance, his brow furrowed. Don had his suspicions, too.

Amos glanced over his shoulder at the cargo area. Nothing had changed. Lukas and Emma slept on, breathing shallowly. His pulse quickened as he spotted something he didn't expect, tucked just behind the rear seat.

The butt end of a rifle, one of the advanced Hoarder weapons, stored within easy reach. He resisted the urge to grab it, gazing with feigned nonchalance at the passing terrain.

He hoped Mateo's enhancements didn't include the ability to hear his pounding heart.

FIFTY-NINE

"I'm not sure Lukas and Emma are in any condition to hike an alternate route," Sheila said, heaving a convincing sigh. "They've just been on the receiving end of a solid electric jolt. They'll be groggy when they wake up."

"I believe I can be of help," Mateo said smoothly. The miles sped by, bringing the outskirts of the Old City closer. "Eastside isn't the only Hub with the required medical staff. If there's no compelling reason to insist on your location, allow me to transport them elsewhere."

"A different Hub?" Don winked at Amos, feigning innocence. "You don't mean a certain shop by Gate Seven, I hope."

Two can play at the intel-gathering game. Amos hid a smile. *Why should Mateo have all the fun?*

Mateo tilted his head to one side.

Silence filled the cab, broken only by the sound of tires whining on pavement. "You have a saying, I believe, 'what you don't know, you can't reveal.' I'm surprised you continue to allow emotion to override rational thought."

Don crossed his arms, his expression darkening. "I'm *really* beginning to dislike this guy," he muttered under his breath.

Quoting our own protocols to avoid Don's question. Amos was impressed in spite of himself. *Smooth, Mateo, very smooth.*

He kept his hands low behind Sheila's seat, pantomiming a sign for a gun, and pointed at the cargo area with his thumb. His gesture was subtle, but Don caught on instantly. The big man raised an eyebrow and one corner of his mouth twitched upward. *And now Don hatches a new strategy.*

The Old City, and the checkpoint, were fast approaching. Three or four miles remained until they'd be forced to part ways. Don leaned forward, drawing Sheila's attention to some vague spot ahead. "Isn't that our exit, just ahead?"

Sheila squinted, feigning recognition as she played along. "Right you are, big guy. The dead tree, just before the next curve." She pointed to her fictional landmark. "If you'll drop us off there, we can cover the remaining distance on foot."

Mateo nodded, taking his foot off the accelerator and easing the vehicle to the edge of the highway. "Diligence and avoiding detection are two sides of the same coin. I'm pleased to have been of some minor assistance."

I'll bet you are. Amos kept his expression studiously neutral. He caught Don's attention, pointing at himself with one finger. *Let me do it. The gun behind us.*

Don coughed into his hand, covering his slight nod.

They slowed to a halt next to Sheila's dead tree. A shallow gully hid them from prying eyes in either direction.

Sheila opened her door and slid to the ground. Don leaned forward between the seats, addressing Mateo and blocking his view of Amos in the rearview mirror. "Thanks for the lift, Mateo. We owe you one."

Amos unlatched his door and casually reached behind the seat with his other arm. He seized the rifle without looking, kicking his door open simultaneously. He launched himself out of the vehicle, spinning around to aim the weapon through the passenger window at Mateo.

Don made an equally hasty exit on the opposite side, slamming his door to underline their triumph.

"Out." Amos accented his terse order with the Hoarder rifle. He'd never held one before, but his instincts guided him. He circled in front of the truck, keeping the unfamiliar weapon trained on Mateo.

Don pulled his knife, standing a healthy distance beyond the truck. Sheila positioned herself by the tailgate, keeping a wary eye on their unconscious passengers.

Mateo's face gave nothing away. His placid demeanor seemed unshakable. He disembarked from the truck and closed the door, as if nothing unexpected had occurred. He fastened an unblinking gaze on Amos, arms loose at his sides.

"Before you start spouting any new riddles, let's cut to the chase." Don's baritone drawl was at odds with his steely glare. He hefted his knife, reinforcing the implied threat. "Aren't you dead?"

Mateo gave him a curious look. "A question, in turn inferring another question, all based on unproven assumptions. Do you consider such a query any less obscure than my 'riddles,' as you call them?"

"Is that supposed to be a joke?" Amos took a step closer, raising his weapon. "Would you like to hear my 'unproven assumption'? I think you killed the real Mateo, and took his place so you could feed us bad intel."

Mateo glanced at him and then quickly away. "You see, Don?

This is the result of your example. Your emotional thinking patterns have spread to your colleagues, as well." He shook his head, looking disappointed.

"Answer the question." Don flexed his grip on his knife. "Never mind our *assumptions*. You want us to leave Lukas and Emma in your tender care, but you can't—or won't—give us a straight answer. Just so it's been said, that doesn't inspire trust." He raised his knife, squinting along its finely-honed blade. "Let's try it again, without the double-talk. Mateo Reyes is dead and buried, isn't he?"

Mateo remained motionless for what seemed an eternity, studying Don with an inscrutable expression. "You are correct," he said at last. "Mateo is dead."

Amos heard Sheila gasp behind him. His finger tightened on the trigger. *A straight answer, for once.*

"And you are also in error," Mateo's gaze shifted to include Amos and Sheila. "Death can take many forms. Burial was not an option."

Without warning, he stood at rigid attention, his scanning eye flaring an ominous red. Amos stepped in between them, shielding Don and giving himself a point-blank shot at the cryptic shopkeeper.

"Trackers live, and die, at the whim of the Givers," Mateo said in the same emotionless voice he'd used during their tour. "That is a death you cannot understand. I'm no longer who I once was, but I am Mateo Reyes. More important, I am the Jericho Hub at Gate Seven—a conduit of information."

"You've given us no reason to trust you." Sheila raised her voice, hovering by the tailgate. "This could be another one of your tricks: shock us enough and get a free pass. You're a *Tracker*—how do we know the Givers aren't controlling you?"

Mateo pivoted to stare at her, swiveling at the hips without moving his feet. The unusual movement underlined the drastic changes he'd undergone at the hands of the Givers. He studied her without comment, and turned to face Don.

"I appeal to your rational mind." He lifted his chin, looking Don in the eye. "You overcame your visceral reaction at the café and set an effective fire to cover your tracks. Your fire also destroyed any evidence of the Tracker's presence." He bowed his head in a show of respect. "I commend you."

"The dead Tracker." Don caught his breath. "The Givers couldn't force it to self-destruct because its head was crushed. That was you, wasn't it?"

Mateo lifted his chin. His scanner faded, restoring his human appearance. "You are caught between two very different adversaries. The ones who activated the Implants in our sleeping guests aren't the same as those who hid the third Implant beneath your vehicle."

Don eyed him with open skepticism.

"I intervened at the café," Mateo said, barely pausing, "and intercepted you at the crash scene before the other 'Hoarders,' as you call them, arrived." He cocked his head to one side. "Think about it rationally. My actions provide ample evidence of my intentions. There's another colloquial saying you're also quite fond of, 'I've got your back.'"

Amos heard Sheila scoff behind him.

Mateo shifted his footing, extending one hand to Amos. "This pointless exercise in paranoia and suspicion is a waste of valuable time." His voice turned abruptly strident. "Lukas and Emma will awaken soon, and those who activated their Implants are closing in. My weapon, Amos, if you please."

Don lowered his knife, although his burly hand continued

to flex around the handle. Sheila said nothing, but her face betrayed her suspicions. Amos's finger tightened on the trigger. *We can't afford to get this one wrong.*

Don took a deep breath and sheathed his knife. "Give Mateo his weapon, Amos. The Petrovs need medical attention, and we've got a long hike ahead of us. And if there's Hoarders on our trail..."

Amos balked, but reluctantly upended the Hoarder weapon. He approached Mateo and placed it in his outstretched hand. Neither one broke eye contact as the exchange took place. Mateo tucked the weapon under his arm, the barrel pointed at the ground.

Think whatever you want. Amos held Mateo's gaze as he backed away. *I'm not turning my back on him.*

* * *

THE RUNNERS MELTED into the wooded fields adjacent to the highway. Mateo waited until they had disappeared between the trees. Patience. Diligence.

Once they were safely out of sight, he hefted the advanced weapon from its non-combative position, gazing with interest at the firing mechanism.

He reached into his pocket, withdrew the missing power pack, and attached it to the weapon. The targeting mechanism beeped once, and a small green light, indicating a full charge, winked back at him. Satisfied, he deactivated the weapon and climbed into the truck.

He'd counted on Amos's ignorance of advanced weaponry to work in his favor, and his gamble had paid off. None of the Runners realized that the weapon was useless without a power source.

Mateo didn't allow himself to gloat—such an emotion was

foreign to him—but a sensation that could be labeled *triumph* flickered somewhere within.

Mateo placed the weapon on the seat beside him, restarted the engine and merged onto the highway. The vehicle accelerated smoothly, tires bouncing and grumbling on the uneven surface.

Lukas and Emma Petrov were his bargaining chips. They were the key.

He hoped Darcy would be pleased.

SIXTY ⊙

THE TRAVELATOR HUMMED beneath the Connor's feet as it transported a steady stream of Citizens around the commercial district. The downtown core of Cascadia was vibrant and crowded on weekends. Retail shops catered to a vast array of consumer wants and needs. Theaters and concert venues boasted long line-ups of chatty patrons. Restaurants and cafés buzzed with animated conversations and camaraderie.

All blissfully ignorant about the Givers. The idea left a sour taste in Connor's mouth. *Or how our Council sold us out for the illusion of power and prestige.*

He stepped off the travelator near a cluster of unfamiliar eateries and threaded his way between the patio tables to the outer rim railing. His mood was dark, and he welcomed his anonymous solitude, lost in the crowd.

Directly opposite, across the chasm overlooking the traffic level, lay the ruins of Mojo's Coffee Cartel, as well as several layers of infrastructure immediately below it. Three lanes of traffic remained closed while repairs were under way.

Connor leaned on the rail, giving free rein to his conflicted emotions. Mojo's had already removed its iconic signage and shuttered the café. He wondered if the owners would rebrand, and whether he'd ever want to go back. He didn't think he could. Too many people died in the explosion. Including Reagan.

But not Madison. Her death came later.

His grip tightened on the rail until his knuckles turned white. He'd spent the previous sleepless night replaying the events from that day. No matter how hard he tried, he couldn't make peace with the idea that he should've let Madison die in the fiery aftermath of the bombing.

The more he tried, the greater his guilt.

At least he hadn't been forced to watch her fall to her death. To see her look of horror and betrayal after he deliberately let go of her hand. He felt sick to stomach—it didn't matter. Madison was dead and it was his fault.

Maybe Darcy's right. I'm a liability.

His foster father was in a foul mood during the return trip. Two valuable drones lost. Stolen—by *savages*, no less. The tablet possessed a limited range. Darcy couldn't reprogram the drones to their original targets, and the chances of finding them were virtually nil. A write-off.

Darcy ranted and railed over the lost assets for most of the trip. Connor reminded him that the savages were probably dead, a fitting reward for their thievery, which did little to placate him.

The stolen tech could be easily remanufactured, but they needed another pair of drone candidates. Perhaps more. They were on a schedule and Darcy resented any delay. Despite the increasing risks, another hunting trip had to be arranged.

Connor shivered, still shaken by the discovery that the

Givers were aiding savages, providing them with tech years beyond their comprehension. The Givers used savages as raw material for Trackers—common knowledge inside the Enclave—but Connor couldn't believe the aliens would stoop to *equipping* them.

Darcy stole the Givers' technology to create Implants, deftly using the aliens' own science against them. Collecting savages to Implant just was common sense—it was the only thing they were good for.

This was different.

Educate savages? Darcy gave full vent to his fury as they neared the shantytown. *We've worked too long and too hard to secure our borders. They can't have tech of any kind, period. The next thing you know, they'll be on our streets, as if they have a right to be there.*

Tony foolishly attempted to calm him. Connor knew better. Tony's every suggestion, no matter now reasonable, was shot down by Darcy's volcanic rage. To find Mateo waiting for them in their villa only made things worse.

Connor knew it was in his best interests to stay out of Darcy's way after his confrontation with the duplicitous Tracker. Connor had been pointedly excluded—sent to his room, of all things—and after Mateo's exit, Darcy exploded.

Whenever his foster father was in one of his rages, it was best to give him a wide berth until the storm passed. Connor learned that lesson years ago.

He decided to spend some time in the cultural district, absorbing the reassuring ambiance of the Museum. He needed space to think, and to surround himself with people unconnected to his clandestine activities.

Now he leaned on the outer rim rail, surveying the wreckage of his favorite café. Repair-bots swarmed over the substructure, their repair efforts swift and sure.

The pedestrian level would be functional within a few days —the travelators, within a week. The Council's commitment to the Citizens of the Enclave would allow nothing less than the quickest possible return to normal. Mojo's Coffee Cartel would be replaced by another gathering spot, tailored to the same demographic, similar in design—but not *too* similar, at the risk of appearing tone-deaf.

Connor pushed away from the rail with more force than he intended, startling customers at the nearest table. He had to keep moving, before his dark imagination overwhelmed him. He boarded the nearest travelator, losing himself in the crowd as it whisked him downtown. He avoided eye contact, wanting only to be left alone.

The cavernous lobby of the Museum felt like the welcome of a life-long friend. He'd been coming here since childhood, even before losing his family. The larger-than-life displays of society's past were a consistent source of wonder and awe.

The history displays were also reassuring, in their own way. The barbarity of humanity's past served as a poignant reminder why the Enclaves had been constructed in the first place, and why they were so fiercely protected.

Connor wandered aimlessly among the exhibits, including some familiar mainstays, interspersed with a variety of new displays. His feet led him, out of long habit, to the military wing. No matter how many times he visited, his fascination with conflict and its resolution remained strong.

"Connor?" He turned as he realized someone had called his name. A girl, flanked by two males. He vaguely recognized them from university, although he couldn't recall their names.

They were Reagan's friends. Or had been.

They know me about as well as I know them. He took some comfort from that. *I can keep this short without looking rude.*

"Did you hear what happened?" The girl spoke first, her voice hushed. "A terrorist attack took out Mojo's Coffee Cartel. It's all over the Infomedia."

Great. Connor stifled a grimace. *I came here to forget.* "Yeah, I saw it on the Infomedia," he lied, his expression neutral. *Not too neutral. I can't act like it doesn't affect me.* "I was home, studying. Lucky me, I guess."

He hoped Tara Lindholm had done a thorough job of deleting the video footage.

"Reagan said he was going to Mojo's." One of the guys, the taller one, was eager to share what he knew. "He and Madison were planning to hang out after a movie or something. I haven't heard from him since. I tried calling his family this morning, but no answer. Turns out, he was one of the victims. Can you believe it?"

Connor felt a sharp pain. Survivor guilt?

The girl elbowed her tall companion in the ribs. "Reagan and Connor were friends." She placed a sympathetic hand on Connor's arm. "I'm so sorry for your loss. Everyone's in shock. I mean … terrorist attacks *here*, inside Cascadia?"

"Sorry," the tall guy mumbled, looking awkward. "I knew you had some of the same classes, but I didn't know …"

Connor realized he should say something. "It's okay," he said, disappointed by how lame he sounded. *Keep it simple. Complex lies are a trap.* "I was going to meet them at Mojo's, but I got so busy studying that it must've slipped my mind."

And the video evidence has been erased.

"A lot of people are talking," the shorter guy said. He was

nervous, fidgeting absent-mindedly with his eyeglasses. "Even with all the surveillance inside the Enclave, and checkpoints at the gates, terrorists are *still* finding the soft spots. Maybe it's time to cancel the temporary worker permits. You know, keep the rabble outside."

"Are you volunteering to work in maintenance?" His tall companion appeared ready for a debate. "Savages are necessary for the low-level jobs. What we *really* need is a better screening process. Some people are saying we should allow the best-quali-fied workers to live long-term on the maintenance level. At least there'd be less in-and-out traffic."

Connor welcomed the diversion from talking about Rea-gan and Madison. "I don't want savages inside Cascadia any longer than absolutely necessary," he replied, meaning every word. "If we let them live on the maintenance level, they'll even-tually demand access to the rest of the Enclave." He caught him-self, shaking his head in real anger. *Don't say too much.* "They need to mind their place. Outside, where they belong."

"I'm with Connor," Shorty said, looking defensive and ad-justing his glasses for the umpteenth time. "I'd be willing to work maintenance—not all the time, just every now and then—if it meant our borders were more secure."

"Not me." The girl shuddered, making a show of holding her nose. "It's disgusting down there. We need tighter security, that's all. In this day and age, there's no excuse for the kind of violence we saw last night."

"Last night?" Connor repeated, alarmed. "What are you talking about?"

SIXTY-ONE ◉

THE GIRL'S TWO COMPANIONS stole furtive glances around the Museum, as if they feared being overheard.

"Two more political assassinations," Shorty replied, his nasal voice betraying his ambition, as if sharing new information was a contest and he was determined to win. "A military commander and a councilor."

"*Two* councilors," the taller one interrupted with a lofty and self-important air. "One was a military commander, earlier in his career, but they're both councilors. Or, they were." He lowered his voice to a conspiratorial whisper. "The Council's called for an emergency session today. Location undisclosed, strictly need-to-know. Something's up, no doubt about it."

The girl shivered again. "I don't blame them for keeping it secret. Terrorists seem to infiltrate Cascadia whenever they feel like it—it's scary. The threat from savages is worse than ever. No one feels safe anymore."

Connor's couldn't believe what he was hearing. *Two* dead councilors, including a former military commander?

Darcy didn't mention additional targets. *Must be another cell on its own mission. We lost two drones, but at least some of theirs got through.*

He couldn't wait to ask Darcy which Councilors—collaborators—had been eliminated. *Good riddance, traitors.*

He realized he'd become lost in his own thoughts. "I hadn't heard about the assassinations," he said, answering Shorty's comment. "After the attack at Mojo's, I couldn't listen to the Infomedia. I turned it off." *Keep the lies simple.*

The girl nodded, looking at him with sad eyes. "It must be so hard, losing your friends like that." Her expression abruptly changed from empathy to anger. "*Savages,*" she spat. "Council should send the Peace Wardens on a purge—crush their ugly ghetto and teach them some respect."

"Crush the day-labor pool?" The tall know-it-all was quick with his rebuttal, arching his eyebrows to accentuate his wise opinion. Connor felt a flash of annoyance. "Cascadia needs savages as maintenance workers, after all."

"There's more where they come from," she shot back, her eyes furious. "They'd rebuild Parasite City in a matter of days, and a new batch of smelly barbarians will line up at the gates, begging for work. Those people breed like rabbits."

"Here's the Infomedia segment," Shorty interrupted, offering his tablet to Connor.

The screen was awash with footage from one of the trendy Infomedia channels, the one favored by the university crowd for its cultural content. Shorty adjusted his glasses. "They're saying there may be a pattern to the attacks."

A pattern? Connor's heart skipped a beat. His companions crowded around, watching footage they'd probably seen multiple times already. *Relax. You do the same thing.*

Specific details about the assassinations were sketchy. The Council was tight-lipped, stonewalling speculation over how or why two of their colleagues died.

What the report made clear, emphasized repeatedly during the short segment, was the presumed identity of the assassins. Savages, depraved barbarians from the rabble encamped outside the Enclave. A panel of Infomedia experts squawked and debated over the best solution. The majority seemed in favor of closing the gates permanently, while conceding the need for alternate cheap labor.

The report answered the most important question in Connor's mind. He recognized the names of the deceased. He'd never met either one, but Darcy had included them on his list.

At least it wasn't random. He felt a morbid satisfaction about that. *The collaborators are disappearing, one by traitorous one. Our strategy—Darcy's strategy—is working.*

"They'd have to be idiots to shut the gates permanently." Know-it-all actually sniffed in disdain.

Connor was fast losing patience with him. *This is just a theoretical exercise to you, isn't it? Savages would gut you without a second thought. The collaborators betrayed all of us. They deserve whatever they get.*

What he said out loud was much more restrained. "Wow, I had no idea." He handed the tablet back. Shorty stowed it in his messenger bag, a popular item among university students.

Reagan had had one. Connor heard a mental echo of Madison teasing him about it. *They're so retro. Possibly pre-Enclave.* Connor shoved the memory away. Thinking about Reagan or Madison was dangerous.

"I'm so sorry for your loss," the girl repeated in a formal tone. Her flash of self-righteous anger had dissipated, and she looked at him with sympathy. Connor realized her words were a prelude to leaving, and was secretly relieved. The superficial trio exhausted him.

Her friends mumbled similar condolences, as if they knew Madison or Reagan as well as Connor did, which he doubted, and went their way. They disappeared and were absorbed quickly by the crowds in the Museum.

Connor glanced at the warfare exhibit behind him. There was no point entering. His interest had been eclipsed by news of the collaborators' deaths.

Council has called an emergency session. Darcy was probably already there, working his charm among coworkers and allies. An invaluable opportunity to evaluate the impact of the assassinations. Darcy was in his element there.

Connor smiled to himself, gazing at the exhibit without seeing it. *That's why he's special. None of his fellow Councilors suspect a thing. That gives Darcy access—a blank check of intel.*

Connor exited the Museum, jogging down the front stairs, his steps light and eager as he located the correct travelator. He wanted to be home by the time Darcy returned. He couldn't wait to hear Darcy's report, and what their next steps would be.

Anticipation filled him, banishing all thoughts of Reagan and Madison. *We're winning. The Givers and their human stooges are on the run.*

His excitement grew as the travelator whisked him away from the cultural district, bound for Oceanview and home.

He even forgot Darcy's threat.

SIXTY-TWO ◉

"HE TOLD US to wait here," Tony said, adamant. "You should know, even better than me, that when Darcy gives an order, he expects it to be followed. To the letter. So, we stay put."

They sat in Darcy's truck, parked at street level in front of one of the high-rise towers in the financial district. The cluster of skyscrapers was a testament to the wealth and stability of the Enclave. Their soaring architecture turned them into Cascadian monuments.

Connor was in his usual spot in the rear seat. Tony slouched behind the steering wheel, subservient and dutiful, like a proper chauffeur. Connor was excited and impatient. Tony seemed depressed. He kept his gaze fixed on the front entrance, as if he expected a harbinger of the apocalypse to wander through the revolving doors.

A "top-secret" Council meeting, and the best they can come up with is an office tower in the financial district? Conner wasn't impressed. *Councilors are coporate CEOs. This is the first place anyone would think to look for them.*

A flurry of motion erupted. The revolving doors spun vigorously, and several councilors made a quick exit. The first few made a beeline for their waiting vehicles. Traffic volume was moderate for this time of day, and none of their late-model vehicles stood out, but a group of councilors fleeing an office tower didn't fit Connor's definition of "top secret."

Tony snorted in derision when Connor said so out loud.

"Councilors have no stomach for hands-on violence," he said sourly. "We're the ones fighting a secret war against the Givers, not them. They're used to business lunches and cocktail parties."

"That's a toxic opinion of our esteemed Council," Connor replied, grinning as he anticipated Darcy's report. "Lucky you've got your window shut—with all the surveillance in the financial district, it would be child's play to overhear you."

Tony's jaw clenched, but he didn't take the bait. More councilors appeared, their paces ranging from a brisk walk to a mild sprint. "We should always be careful," he said. "The last thing we need is getting caught by a surveillance operator who's good at lip-reading." He started the engine. "Here comes Darcy."

Connor had already spotted Darcy's self-assured stride. He always appeared confident, unhurried and unworried. It was all part of his personal brand, which earned him respect.

And access to intel. Darcy knows how to win allies and sway potential enemies.

Darcy climbed into his seat, nodding at Tony as he closed his door. Tony shifted into gear and pulled away from the curb, guiding them to the nearest vehicle lift. The lifts were near full capacity, shoppers mingling with business people heading home from the office. The line-ups would expand into near-gridlock during the afternoon commute.

Darcy said nothing as they descended to the traffic level. Connor fidgeted, barely containing his curiosity.

The lift settled into position with a slight shudder. Gates split open, green lights flashed, and Tony accelerated smoothly, merging into the traffic level, to join a large number of vehicles leaving the downtown core. At his first opportunity, Tony maneuvered their truck close to the outermost lanes, beneath the shadow cast by the pedestrian level.

"An interesting series of developments," Darcy said, his voice remote, with none of the gloating tone Connor was used to hearing after Council meetings. "Our drones have made an impression. But it was only a matter of time—we all knew this —before someone noticed a pattern to the targets."

Connor unbuckled his seatbelt, scooting forward. Darcy's usual bravado was conspicuously absent. He watched in consternation as Darcy planted his elbow on the doorframe, raising a hand to mask the lower half of his face.

Connor hunched forward, directing his gaze at the console between the seats. "You think the Givers are spying on us? Here, on the vehicle level?"

"Take nothing for granted," Darcy said behind his hand, his voice as neutral as his facial expression. "Between the success of our drones, and the Givers' clever deployment of their exploding Tracker, the public outcry for security has reached the Council's sympathetic ears. They've voted to adopt an aggressive expansion of surveillance throughout Cascadia."

Tony lowered his sun visor, as if he thought it would be enough to mask his identity. "More operators reviewing the digital feed?" His lips barely moved and his voice was all but inaudible. "Or more surveillance cameras around the Enclave in general?"

"Both." Darcy's terse reply confirmed Connor's suspicion. "We knew this would eventually happen. The collaborators are terrified by the prospect of losing their so-called 'status.' Paranoia is the inevitable by-product. They're on the lookout for any potential threats."

"That's not all, is it?" Connor kept his voice down, eyes focused on the console. There was more to the story. He sensed it. "How sensitive is the new surveillance equipment?"

"Let me put it this way." Darcy paused to take a deep breath. "We'll do a complete sweep of our villa the moment we get home." He glanced over his shoulder. "Where were you this afternoon, Connor? You were absent when the Council called its special meeting."

"The Museum," Connor replied without hesitation. "And before that, watching the repair-bots reconstructing what's left of Mojo's."

Darcy straightened. He was in strategic thinking mode. Connor hid a sigh of relief. *That's the Darcy I know.*

"Not the café," Darcy said decisively. "It could suggest an unhealthy interest in the events of that day. You went to the Museum, period. We'll observe the usual protocols."

"Yes, sir," Connor and Tony murmured, giving the routine response to his invocation of standard procedures.

Connor rehearsed what was expected of him. *Once we hit the garage, talk about nothing but the Museum. Same goes for the elevator, and the hall. Then, sweep the villa for hidden tech.*

A tension headache blossomed at the base of his skull. He sat back in his seat, massaging his neck.

Now it's our turn to be paranoid.

SIXTY-THREE ◎

THEY MADE A GOOD SHOW OF IT after exiting the traffic level. Tony maneuvered the truck into their assigned space in the parking garage, sandwiched beneath their high-rise apartment building and above the traffic level.

Tony proved to be adept at small talk, asking Connor benign questions about the Museum. Connor hid his surprise. If anyone was eavesdropping in the elevator, they'd collect twenty floors' worth of historical trivia, and nothing more.

Their villa was locked and secure. Connor keyed in his personal code, and the door hissed open. He hesitated, frozen by an intangible sense of warning. Darcy stalked over the threshold, halting just inside. At his signal, Connor and Tony followed him inside and fanned out across the gathering room, alert for anything out of the ordinary.

Darcy spotted the anomaly first. The door to the balcony was wide open—Connor knew he'd closed it before they left. A solitary figure lounged outside, admiring the panoramic view as if he didn't have a care in the world.

Mateo pivoted and, with an unhurried, fluid pace, joined them in the gathering room. His gaze flitted from Connor to Tony before settling on Darcy. The patio door closed with a soft *whoosh* behind him.

"Good welcome, Councilor Peterson. And to your worthy colleagues, the same." He bowed slightly from the neck, the rest of his body at rigid attention, hands clasped behind his back. "We may speak freely. I have accounted for the hidden surveillance devices, and placed them in a fruit bowl on your mantle, should you wish to examine them later." His eyes fastened on Darcy. "I trust you've reconsidered your earlier rejection of my proposal?"

Tony and Connor spread out, one on either side of Darcy, and advanced toward Mateo. Connor braced himself. Trackers were justifiably feared for their enhanced physical strength.

He can't stop us all.

"You *knew*." Darcy's words stopped them in their tracks. He spoke softly, but the underlying menace was razor-sharp. "Yet you said nothing. What game are you playing, Reyes?"

Mateo cocked his head to one side, his expression indecipherable. Connor couldn't resist—the tension was unbearable. "What does he know, Darcy? What haven't you told us?"

Darcy took a belligerent step forward. "Go ahead, *Tracker*. Tell the truth for once, if you're even capable of it."

Mateo regarded him for a long moment, not blinking. "As you wish, Councilor." He addressed them all, but his gaze remained on Darcy. "The Givers, with the Council's full support—and the Enclave's grateful appreciation—have announced a new initiative. One which will provide the level of safety and security needed to preempt any future terrorist attacks."

Darcy glared. "The *whole* story, Tracker."

Mateo's expression didn't change, but Connor was sure he detected a mocking tone in his voice. "In the coming days and weeks, every Citizen will receive a subcutaneous identification device. The right forearm, if I'm not mistaken." He paused, looking from Connor to Tony and back to Darcy. "Citizens will enjoy the benefit of having, at all times, their exact location known to your security and peace-keeping forces. If renegade Citizens are behind the terrorist attacks, it will be a simple matter to track them down. And then, of course, eliminate the threat they pose to the peace and prosperity of Cascadia."

Connor stared in dawning horror, mouth agape.

Darcy spoke first—he'd apparently learned about the plan during the Council meeting. "In other words, whenever anyone leaves Cascadia for 'recreational purposes,' the Council—and the Givers—will be able to track their every move. They're also enhancing border security. Any suspicious activity will be dealt with immediately. With lethal force, if necessary."

Bile rose in Connor's throat. "We can't hunt for new drones." He swallowed convulsively. "The Givers have cut us off."

Tony could only stare, deflated and speechless.

"Are you prepared to listen now, Councilor?" Mateo tilted his head toward the opposite shoulder. "I'm afraid your remaining alternatives are few. But, if you prefer, I can wait until you arrive at the same conclusion for yourself."

"Where are they?" Darcy lurched toward him, fists clenched in rage. "What have you done with the drones you stole?"

Mateo didn't flinch. His steady gaze was unnerving. "I assume you are referring to Lukas and Emma Petrov. They are under my care, at a location known only to me."

"I don't care about their *names*." Darcy was livid. Connor had seen his temper explode before, but this was darker, more malevolent. "Here, in Cascadia, we give names to our children and our pets. Drones DR-55 and DR-56 are property—*my* property—and I order you to return them."

"I repeat, their location will remain known only by me," Mateo replied. "Rest assured, Councilor, I shall not waver in this. You wouldn't listen before, but you will listen now. The four of us have another journey ahead, one which we must take before—if you'll excuse the ironic comparison—you and your companions are outfitted with implants of your own."

Flecks of spittle showed in the corners of Darcy's mouth. "You expect us to partner with *savages?*"

Connor stared in horror as his words sank in. *The savages who stole our drones?*

Tony's mouth hung open. It was obvious how he felt.

"You have a legendary ability to devise alternate strategies," Mateo replied, with no trace of mockery. "Can you concoct one now? Time, as they say, waits for no one."

Darcy snarled at him. His loathing was palpable, but it was clear he was at a loss.

Mateo's shocking proposal goaded Connor into speaking without permission. "You mean the savages we saw yesterday, the ones who ran off with our drones. *You let them go?* The Givers are using them as pawns to thwart our cause. They're the enemy, twice over."

Mateo's eyes widened. He seemed surprised by Connor's outburst. "I don't share your viewpoint, young man. When have any of your drones returned alive? The Runners rescued the Petrovs from certain death. In addition, I remind you, others of my kind regularly eviscerate them. Harvest, we call it."

Tony found his voice at last. "We don't know how to contact the savages. Even if we were that desperate . . ."

His voice trailed off as his own words caught him.

That's just it. Connor found the idea appalling but inescapable. *As of now, we're desperate.*

Mateo unclasped his hands, ducking his chin in slight bow. He appeared smugly satisfied. "I propose visiting a Hub where I believe the individuals you mentioned may be found." He gestured to the door, his invitation plain. "Are you familiar with the Old City's Mission district?"

SIXTY-FOUR ◉

"MOVE, AND I'LL KILL YOU." Jane stood just outside the infirmary, framed in the doorway, feet planted shoulder-width apart. She glared with deadly resolve, aiming her Glock at the back of Megan's head. No one had heard her stealthy approach, least of all Megan.

"Hold your fire," Garr said tersely, one hand half-raised in a cautionary gesture. "It was her decision to come back. I want to know why."

"I don't care." Jane resolutely held her position, eyes boring into her target. "Deep down, she's still a Tracker. There's a good reason Country Girl calls them *soul-less*."

Megan cautiously raised her hands—shoulder high, palms out—and pivoted in a slow circle, her motions fluid, steady. Her awkward smile faded, and she studied Jane with a dispassionate eye, expressionless.

Jane didn't flinch under her unrelenting stare. She shifted her weight from one foot to the other, but her grip on the Glock didn't waver.

Garr tried to catch her attention. "Jane..."

Megan exploded into action, launching herself at Jane with the speed and ferocity of a cobra. Her right hand shot out, snatching the Glock out of her hand. Jane recoiled, eyes wide with shock, and retreated a step or two. Megan coolly flipped the Glock and aimed at Jane, heart center.

Time slowed to a crawl. Megan studied Jane, her expression a mix of curiosity and appraisal, as if analyzing a series of calculations. Her grip on the Glock was rock-solid, unyielding.

Jane met her gaze without flinching, standing motionless in the doorway as if rooted to the concrete floor. She swallowed once, hard, but said nothing.

Snake Lady doesn't beg. Aubrey held her breath, looking back and forth between a defiant Jane and the impassive Megan. She stole a glance at Garr, but his expression was unreadable. Doc looked stricken. Aubrey had never felt so powerless.

Megan broke the impasse, casually upending the Glock and retreating a step. She broke eye contact with Jane, equally nonchalant, and pivoted to address Doc Simon.

"Take this." She extended her arm, weapon cradled indifferently in her palm. "Only you." The expression on her face was unfamiliar—confident, self-assured, in control.

Aubrey wondered what had happened to her. *She seems like... a new version of herself.*

Doc took the Glock from her, calm and unhurried, and, without turning to look, placed it on the worktable behind her. "Thank you, Megan. You've remembered your name?"

"What about the Givers?" Jane's question was a direct challenge. She seemed to have recovered from the shock of being forcibly disarmed. "Tracy, Megan—what difference does it make? You stole the Implant. A gift for the Givers, right?"

"That's my question, too," Aubrey said abruptly, balking at the shushing gesture Garr aimed at Jane. "And let's not forget —she attacked her guards, and now we're supposed to welcome her back as if nothing happened?"

"Yes, Doc," Megan replied, ignoring Aubrey's outburst. "Megan. My name."

Her ability to speak seemed to have improved, which only made Aubrey more suspicious.

"Stop underestimating her, Doc." Jane was fast losing her temper. "She's still part-Tracker, and you don't know what she's capable of—none of us do."

Megan pivoted to confront her. Jane stopped short, but didn't draw back. Megan's lips moved, soundlessly at first, before she managed to force out short sentences.

"Yes. Implant—gift for the Givers. But no more." She reached up and tapped two fingers on her forehead. Her phrases were choppy and disjointed, but understandable. "No more voices. No Givers. I am Megan."

"How is that possible?" Aubrey looked past Tracy—*Megan* —to Doc Simon, hopeful but cautious. "Can a Tracker actually break free of the Givers' mind-control?" She decided to leave her real question unvoiced.

How can we tell if she's dangerous?

"It's possible." Garr's quiet voice drew their attention. He motioned for Jane to step away from Megan. Aubrey understood his subtle direction.

Gun or no gun, Jane's as unpredictable as Megan.

Garr leaned on the gurney, his steady gaze on Megan. "That's why we went to the Enclave in the first place. One other Tracker has managed to break free of the Givers."

"We can't be sure of that." Jane straightened her shoulders, her expression defiant. "All we found was an empty shop, random bits of tech, and a Tracker on patrol. There was no sign of Mateo."

No one anticipated Megan's reaction. She whirled and took a half step toward Jane. Jane recoiled warily, one hand half-raised in self-defense.

"Mateo." Megan's voice was eager and alive. A wide smile split her face. "Come back. Implant to Doc." She reached up and tapped her forehead, nodding vigorously. Her next words sent a chill down Aubrey's spine.

"Mateo. Said go back."

SIXTY-FIVE ◉

THEY SLEPT OVERNIGHT in the forest. It was Don's idea, and neither Sheila nor Amos argued. *Mateo was fishing for Eastside's location. The legit leader of Jericho Hub would already know.*

They awoke early the next morning, cold and cramped. The eastern sky lightened with dawn's approach as they picked their way through the forest. Just under an hour after they crossed the perimeter of the Old City, Amos spotted a tunnel access. They left the sun-warmed streets behind, and descended into the damp chill of the subterranean maze.

The artificial dusk made it difficult to keep track of time. The dampness and noxious odors were familiar, if under-appreciated, signs they were heading in the right direction.

Amos drew shallow breaths through his mouth, ignoring the stale odor. They dodged around sporadic puddles where condensation dripped from overhead pipes. They jogged when they could, but the intermittent lighting forced them, more than once, to slow to a snail's pace.

"I don't trust Mateo," Amos said flatly. His voice raised

a faint echo. "We're supposed to believe he's the real Mateo Reyes, only in Tracker form? There's no way of proving it. Every time he gives us an answer—when we can drag one out of him—he expects us to take his word for it."

Sheila wiped her forehead on her sleeve. "I don't think we 'forced' Mateo to say anything. I get the impression he says exactly what he intends to, nothing more and nothing less."

"He's definitely got a talent for talking out of both sides of his mouth," Don replied, scowling. "Then again, he *did* take care of that Tracker at the Petrov's café. We planned on hamstringing it and letting the Givers finish it off. Mateo never gave them the chance."

"And he got us out of harm's way after we crashed the truck." Amos grimaced, reluctant to let Mateo off the hook. "Maybe it's *because* he's helpful, and then plays mental games. He's evasive. That gets on my nerves."

They slowed as a familiar junction appeared out of the murk. To the untrained eye, there was nothing to differentiate it from any number of others they'd passed. Don pointed to an overhead pipe.

Amos spotted a ragged notch carved into the pipe's crusted surface, a hands-breadth above the door.

Sheila uttered a low laugh. "Garr's been trailblazing, I see."

Don coughed politely into his hand. "It's possible he had some expert help." He tested the door. It responded grudgingly, and he lowered his shoulder and put his weight into it. The hinges shrilled a rusty protest and surrendered.

Sheila followed him through the door and gave a small cheer. "Ladder to the stars," she said, grasping one of the rungs. She turned to grin at Amos. "Or, one level higher than raw sewage, at least. Every level helps."

"Eastside Hub level, you mean," he replied, surprised at the way his spirits lifted. "Feels like forever."

Don wrestled the door shut, sealing off the odors from the main passageway. "Time's wasting. Up y'all go."

Sheila scrambled up the ladder. Amos followed, feeling every bruise from the previous day's accident. No matter.

Don waited until Amos pulled himself out of the ladder well before climbing. He wore a goofy grin by the time he reached the next level. "Familiar territory, friends and neighbors," he said as he got his bearings. "Home, sweet Hub, dead ahead."

Sheila tapped him on the shoulder. "No, *that* way, big guy," she said, pointing.

Don shrugged good-naturedly and they set off at a trot, trusting her sense of direction. Amos felt a surge of energy at the thought of their Hub's proximity. A short tunnel and greasy staircase later, he caught sight of a glowing lantern, beckoning to them from the infirmary. A solitary figure waited, silhouetted in the doorway.

"Hot coffee, a dry bed, and no more field rations," he said to no one in particular.

Sheila laughed. "Amen to that."

SIXTY-SIX ◉

JANE LINGERED BY the infirmary door, arms crossed, keeping a wary eye trained on Megan. Aubrey couldn't blame her. The former Tracker's speech impediment was clearly at odds with her physical prowess, and reconciling the two was a challenge.

Jane's attention wandered to the worktable—for the third time, at least—but Garr's decision wasn't open to debate. The Glock was to be stored in the infirmary, under Doc's supervision, until further notice.

"Could I have a moment, Megan?" Doc guided her away from the door—and Jane—for a perfunctory visual examination. "Any aches, pains, or bruises?"

Megan shook her head, hesitated, and appeared to reconsider. She opened her hand, palm up, and Aubrey saw a series of overlapping cuts on her palm.

Doc took Megan's hand in her own to inspect it. "These aren't deep, but let's not risk an infection." She deftly wrapped a strip of linen around Megan's hand. "The Implant, am I right? You must have a strong grip."

Megan nodded, her expression mildly sheepish.

Aubrey found her reaction intriguing. *It seemed normal, natural, almost ... human.* She opened her mouth to comment but, remembering Doc's protective nature, decided against it.

A sharp noise diverted her attention to the infirmary door. Jane pivoted to block the entrance, both hands braced against the doorframe. Something had caught her attention. Approaching footsteps—Aubrey could hear them now, as well.

Jane lowered her arms, relaxing noticeably. "It's Don and the others," she called over her shoulder. She stepped aside to allow him to enter.

Don's booming voice filled the room. "Did anyone miss us?"

"Maybe." Jane eyed his rumpled clothing. "Looks like you slept in a ditch."

"More or less," he replied cheerfully. "Nothing that a fresh pot of coffee can't cure."

Sheila crowded in behind him, closely followed by Amos. The infirmary suddenly felt claustrophobic. Aubrey retreated behind the gurney to stand next to Garr.

"Uh-oh." Sheila pointed to the packs Doc had arranged by the door. "Looks like an evacuation protocol. What did we miss, and do I have time to pack?"

"A lot, and we'll wait," Garr replied. All eyes turned to him. "I'll keep the debrief short. Jane, Aubrey, and I made it to Cascadia, but couldn't locate Mateo. His shop had been ransacked by persons unknown. We also found an underground lab of sorts, directly below the shop. Mateo's experimenting with tech of some kind, but for what purpose, we can't be sure."

"Don't forget the Tracker patrol," Jane said sourly. "For a guy who claims to be a 'simple merchant,' Mateo sure attracts a lot of attention."

Garr nodded. "We slipped past the patrol and hiked back to Eastside." He gestured to Doc Simon. "You're better qualified to report on the rest. The floor is yours, Doc."

Doc tucked her hands into her coat pockets. "Where to begin, where to begin?" She placed a protective hand on Megan's shoulder. "First things, first. Allow me to introduce Megan, our resident enigma. She overpowered her guards, stole an Implant, and set off to find the Givers. That's why Garr ordered the evacuation. Now that she's back, maybe it's no longer necessary."

"I'd still like some fresh coffee," Don said, studying Megan with interest. "Stop me if I'm hallucinating, Doc, but didn't you name her Tracy?"

"I did indeed, but I've since been corrected." Doc shrugged. "We were focused on the evacuation protocol, and she suddenly appears, hands me the stolen Implant, and identifies herself as Megan. And—before anyone asks—no, she doesn't remember her last name."

"And she met Mateo," Aubrey interrupted. *That* got everyone's attention. "Returning the Implant was his idea, she says."

Megan nodded once but said nothing, apparently content with her non-speaking role.

Gathering intel? Aubrey banished her suspicions. *Don't get paranoid, Aubs.*

"We ran into Mateo yesterday," Sheila said, glancing at Don and Amos. They added nothing to her cryptic statement. "We've got lots to debrief, too."

"Not here, Sheila," Doc interrupted, taking charge. "This is an infirmary, not a conference boardroom. You look famished. Why don't we adjourn to the mess hall? Debrief over a meal—doctor's orders."

"I like the way you think," Amos said, a rare grin lighting

his face. "Make sure you're sitting down before Sheila fills you in. You'll be glad you did—trust me."

They filed out of the infirmary, Don leading the way, Garr at his side. Jane brought up the rear, still keeping a close eye on Megan.

It took a moment for Aubrey's eyes to adjust in the unlit corridor. The door to the mess hall was open, allowing the warm glow of a lantern to spill out onto the concrete floor. She focused on that.

Jane's voice rang out as they reached the mess hall. "Wait up—I doused the lantern before …"

Her shrill warning arrived too late. Don and Garr stepped inside and were lost to sight. Their startled exclamations brought their Hub-mates crowding in behind them.

A trio of lanterns burned brightly, filling the mess hall with a warm glow. The amber-tinged radiance served to spotlight a solitary figure, seated at the far end of the table.

"Good welcome." Mateo inclined his head in their direction. He seemed genuinely pleased. "As Don is fond of saying, did anyone miss me?"

SIXTY-SEVEN ◉

"LETTING MATEO OUT of our sight was a mistake," Tony said as they rode the vehicle lift, descending through the lower levels of the Enclave. "We should've insisted he come with us, if you ask me."

No one's asking you. Connor bit back a sharp retort. *You're Darcy's chauffeur. Learn your place.* His bitterness boiled over, scalding hot. He gave it full rein. *You executed Madison. Darcy blames me, but I blame you.*

Darcy hadn't spoken since leaving their villa. He stared out the passenger window, seemingly fascinated by the utilitarian design of the vehicle lift. Tony's pompous comment infringed on his reverie, and he erupted, his voice sharp as a bullwhip. "*Protocol.* Don't you know where we are?"

Tony's grip tightened on the steering wheel, and he averted his eyes, staring straight ahead through the windshield.

Nothing more was said.

They descended past another level and Connor tensed. The checkpoint for Gate Seven wasn't far off.

The vehicle lift shuddered to a clanking halt, and the gates split vertically, retracting into the floor and ceiling. Gate Seven loomed large, the only legitimate hurdle between them and the wilderness. Line-ups were seldom long, but theirs was the only truck queuing up to leave the Enclave today.

"Behold the effect of fear," Darcy said as they neared the checkpoint. Cascadia Security guards closed in, rifles held ready as their sergeant stepped up to Tony's window. "This may be our last excursion for some time. Enjoy it while you can."

He fell silent as Tony rolled his window down, and they parroted their way through the usual questions and answers.

Connor affected a bored expression, staring out of his window, not deigning to look in the sergeant's direction. He focused on the enormous metal pillars, tracing the pattern of rivets that held each one together. *Funny what you notice when it may be your last trip.*

They cleared the checkpoint in less than two minutes. Even now, faced with tightening security, Darcy's position on the Council guaranteed them preferential treatment.

Connor's mood darkened. *That'll change soon.*

Gate Seven slammed shut behind them, raising a cloud of dust. Tony accelerated, mindful of the constant threat of attack. The aura of brooding desperation in Parasite City hit Connor harder than usual. Their future appeared equally bleak.

"I can't believe we're going to work with *savages*," Tony said, in a whiny voice that Connor found irritating. The chauffeur steered their vehicle over muddy ruts and rain-filled potholes, remnants left behind by an overnight thunderstorm.

"We don't have much choice," Connor replied, with no attempt to hide his disgust. "The collaborators have driven us to a new low—partnering with savages." He resisted the urge to spit, mainly because his window was closed as a safeguard against airborne toxins from the filthy ghetto.

Darcy's continued silence made Connor uneasy. It wasn't like his foster father to be distant at times like this.

There's never been a "time like this" before. Connor shifted uncomfortably in his seat. *No right-thinking Citizen of the Enclave wants anything to do with the savages, let alone form an alliance with them.*

Tony stole repeated glances at Darcy. Connor smirked, reading him easily. The chauffeur was bursting with questions, but afraid of provoking his employer's ire. When it came to instilling respect, Darcy was second to none.

Their tires spat mud and small stones as they passed the final row of run-down shacks and skidded out of Parasite City. Tony shifted gears, making up for lost time. Their journey through the Old City wouldn't take long. Connor secretly hoped the destination Mateo had specified didn't lead directly into a trap set by the thieves who'd stolen their drones.

Darcy roused himself from his internal reverie, twisting sideways in his seat. "Allying ourselves with the savages—I'll admit it wasn't my first choice, but it's the key to Cascadian freedom," he said, surprising Connor with his obvious enthusiasm. "The collaborators on the Council think they've cut us off, but overconfidence is their Achilles' heel. They'll drop their guard at the worst possible moment. Mateo's about to hand us a strategic advantage."

Appalled, Connor spoke before thinking. "You *want* us to partner with savages—and Mateo?"

A chilling silence greeted his outburst, and he knew he'd said the wrong thing.

Darcy's enthusiasm vanished as if it had never existed. He

turned to glare at Connor, his voice ice-cold and cutting. "Don't be so naïve. It makes no difference what he *wants*. What matters is what Mateo's giving us, even if he doesn't realize it."

He's been strategizing since before we left Cascadia. Connor shrank into his seat.

Darcy gestured at the Old City with a derisive laugh. "Mateo thinks he can wave his magic wand and forge an alliance between Citizens and savages? He's delusional." He glanced at Tony, then over his shoulder at Connor, his expression eager and alive. "It won't be long before we're forced to abandon our 'hunting' trips. That changes *nothing*. We'll still have a steady, guaranteed supply of fresh drones."

Connor held his breath, hoping Tony wasn't so stupid that he'd interrupt by asking the obvious question.

"This is a minor delay, nothing more." Darcy leaned back, his leather chair creaking. "Thanks to Mateo, hunting trips will no longer be needed. The savages will *voluntarily* enter Cascadia, under the illusion that they've come to 'assist' us." He shook his head, chuckling at their good fortune. "And then we'll make drones out of them."

SIXTY-EIGHT ◉

THE MESS HALL felt lopsided. Amos, Don, Jane, Garr, Aubrey, Doc, and Megan clustered in a tight knot just inside the door, opposite the lone figure seated casually at the far end of the table.

"Good welcome," Mateo repeated when no one responded to his greeting. "I can see why family reunions are so highly prized. Don, Sheila, Amos—you must be hungry after your journey." He gestured at the nicked and scarred cupboards. "Help yourselves to some trail rations."

"Lost my appetite," Don replied, scowling at him. "Looks like you made pretty good time after you dropped us off. That wasn't even twenty-four hours ago."

Garr cut in front of Don and advanced, stopping just short of the table. "You abandoned your Hub in a hurry." His voice snapped with authority, the challenge clear. "And a Tracker was patrolling in front of your shop. What tipped the Hoarders off?"

Jane added a taunt of her own. "We found that hole you dug under your floor, and scraps of tech you left behind. You're getting sloppy, oh great Hub-master Reyes."

Mateo folded his hands and rested them on the table. He cocked his head to one side, his unblinking gaze fixed on Garr.

Why does he do that? Amos's temper flared. *He acts more lizard than human.* He caught himself, stifling a sardonic laugh. *Of course. He's not human—he's a Tracker.*

"Colonel Scott, I'm pleased to make your acquaintance." Mateo seemed unfazed by their accusations. "I see now where Don learned to react emotionally, rather than rationally. He's made great strides to overcome this handicap after I pointed it out. You would do well to learn from his example." He leaned back in his seat, continuing before anyone could respond. "If I may be permitted a moment of immodesty, I'm equally pleased none of you detected my strategy in gathering you today."

"You planned this gathering?" Garr's piercing eyes bored into Mateo's. "I find that highly unlikely."

"Then let us review." Mateo turned his unblinking gaze to Don. "You're aware that I deactivated the Tracker at the café, and also discovered the magnetized Implant under your vehicle. I invite you to expand upon your excellent track record. Put your powers of deduction to work, and tell us *why* Garr's team found my shop in such a lamentable condition."

Don didn't hesitate. "You spotted the Tracker patrol and realized the good folks of Hoarderville were getting suspicious. So, you trashed your shop to throw them off your scent, and also as a warning for us, if we returned."

Mateo didn't smile, but he seemed pleased. "And the technology that I 'forgot' in my makeshift catacomb?"

Jane pounced on the question. "You knew we'd search the shop. You *wanted* us to find the tunnel, and the tech." She sucked in a sharp breath. "You didn't want us wasting our time hanging around Jericho. You wanted us back here. Why?"

Garr interjected. "And our other resident Tracker? What part does Megan play in your game plan?"

For the first time, Mateo hesitated, stealing a glance at Megan. She stood just inside the door, shoulder to shoulder with Aubrey. Her posture was relaxed and confident, a marked contrast to Aubrey's pins-and-needles stance.

Mateo studied his fellow Tracker for a long moment. "Megan is a random element," he said at last. "Our encounter was a fortunate coincidence. It was her intention to offer the Implant to the Givers, perhaps to regain their favor."

"You talked her out of it," Aubrey interrupted, looking back and forth at the two Trackers, so alike and yet not. "You have some other use for her—for us."

"My first impulse was to kill her." Mateo leaned back in his seat, not quite answering Aubrey's question, Amos noticed. "Just imagine—a chance encounter with an unknown Tracker, one who could betray the news of my continued existence to the Givers." He shot Don a knowing look. "Closer observation, and deductive reasoning, showed me she was not what she initially appeared to be. A fortunate discovery. It wasn't necessary to terminate her."

Doc Simon stepped between Garr and Don and approached Mateo, waving her hand in the general direction of the table. "Do you mind? I'm tired of standing."

Mateo gestured with an open hand to a chair on his right. Doc seated herself, showing no indication of being intimidated by him.

Emboldened by her example, the rest of the Runners arranged themselves around the table.

Except Megan. Amos made a mental note. Follow up later.

"She tells us her name is Megan." Doc Simon folded her

hands on the table and got straight to the point. "Was that your clever idea, or did she remember her real name?"

Mateo raised his eyebrows. "I fail to see the relevance. If you're asking whether I've had previous dealings with her, the answer is no. She was well on her way to rediscovering her former identity before we met. I merely suggested that she return the Implant. The decision to comply was hers."

Garr cleared his throat. Aside from Megan, who hovered just inside the door, he was the only one who hadn't taken a seat around the table. Amos recognized his strategy—observe, analyze, gather intel. Now, the colonel was ready to wade in.

"You called Megan a random element," Garr said, grasping the back of his chair and flexing his hands. "We can talk about her later. I want to circle back to something you said earlier." He jabbed a finger at Mateo. "You claim that you set up this gathering, but that makes no sense. We live here—gathering us isn't a problem. I want to know *why* you want us here, and why now?"

"Well done, Colonel Scott. I'm impressed." Mateo stood, beaming at him. "You are correct. I've convened this gathering for a specific purpose. However, our circle is not yet complete." He lifted his chin. "I've also invited three Citizens from Cascadia. They will arrive shortly. I've instructed them to wait in your mechanical shop until we can join them. 'No man's land,' I believe is the traditional military phrase."

It was as if all the oxygen was instantly siphoned from the mess hall. Around the table, eyebrows raised, mouths dropped open, and eyes widened as the full impact of Mateo's benign announcement sank in.

Then, predictably, their reactions boiled over.

"Hoarders—*here?*" Don whipped out his knife, pointing it at Mateo, heart-center. "Have you lost your mind?"

Sheila shoved back from the table and jumped to her feet. Her chair tumbled loudly to the floor behind her. "You gave our location to Hoarders? They know *where to find us*?"

Amos had never seen her so shaken. He thought she might attack Mateo before Don had the chance to.

SIXTY-NINE

AUBREY BACKED AWAY, stopping only when she brought up short against the wall. She covered her mouth with her scarred hand, her breath escaping in sharp, rapid gasps. Amos watched as she pivoted on her heel and bolted from the mess hall.

Jane stood shoulder to shoulder beside Don, ashen-faced and clutching her combat knife in white-knuckled desperation. Amos joined them in two swift strides. His knife rasped out of its sheath, as clear a threat as anything he might have said.

Only Doc and Garr remained where they were.

Doc settled back in her seat, studying Mateo with a shrewd expression. Garr stood at attention behind his chair. His fists clenched and unclenched, but he didn't draw his weapon.

Mateo returned his gaze, lifting his chin to view Garr from an odd angle. "Colonel, if memory serves, you sent your companions to Jericho Hub with a specific objective in mind. You want to know how to infiltrate what Don refers to as 'Hoarderville.' Frankly, that's impossible without assistance from *inside* Cascadia. I'm offering to facilitate this." He glanced around the table, addressing each of them. "Again, emotionalism has clouded your judgment, Colonel Scott, as well as that of your companions."

"We've seen what Hoarders are capable of." Amos hefted his knife, his voice ragged. "Hunting us for sport, using us for Implants, turning innocent people into Trackers."

He couldn't finish. His chest constricted, and his face felt hot. Out of the corner of his eye, he saw Doc bolt forward in her chair, a flash of alarm creasing her face.

Jane snarled at Mateo, her eyes burning with undisguised hostility. "You want a *list*? Stephen, Sarah, Thomas, Davey . . ." Her voice cracked on the last name. She swallowed hard, fighting back tears. "Those are just the names we know. I don't care if the Givers started it—the Hoarders are just as guilty. They'll Implant *children* if it suits them." She swung her knife, her meaning plain. "Hoarders are only good for one thing."

Garr waited them out, allowing the first spike of shock and outrage to wane. "I won't argue with you, Mateo. If we're going to thwart the Hoarders' plans, we've got to get inside Cascadia." His voice was quiet and measured, but there was fire in his eyes. "You mentioned 'dissidents,' who might help us, even if it meant betraying the Enclave. Is that who we're about to meet?"

Mateo opened his mouth but hesitated before replying.

Tension flared, setting fire to Amos's nerves.

"Yes and no, Colonel," Mateo said at last. "Yes, you must ally yourselves with these Citizens, but no, they aren't dissidents. In fact, their leader, a member of Cascadia's ruling Council, is the one who invented Implants in the first place."

Jane staggered, horror etched on her face. Her knife slipped from her grasp and clattered to the floor. She swayed, pale and off-balance, as if she was about to faint.

Amos instinctively caught her arm to steady her. His mind reeled. *This isn't happening. This can't be happening…*

"They're *on their way?*" Don edged closer, his polished blade glinting in the lantern's warm glow.

Mateo didn't reply to his implied threat, but the muscles in his arms rippled. Amos stiffened, remembering who they were dealing with. A Tracker, in possession of all the enhancements the Givers could provide.

Garr's voice, quiet but authoritative, cut through the emotional whirlwind. "Like it or not, Mateo's right—this is bigger than all of us. We need access into the Enclave. That means we need to dig deep and put our feelings aside." He circled the mess hall, pausing to make eye contact with each of his companions. "I'm going to accompany Mateo. I'd rather have all of you with me, but I'll go alone if I have to."

He completed his circuit, resting a hand on the back of Doc's chair. She returned his gaze, her mouth forming a hard line.

Garr nodded at her and wheeled to face the group. "Let's just say it—there will never be a 'good time' to meet Hoarders face-to-face. Keep in mind what's at stake. We can't get inside Cascadia without help."

Amos managed to find his voice. "You're taking Mateo at his word?" He couldn't look at the smug Tracker. "I don't trust him. None of us do."

"Risk versus reward," Garr replied evenly. "I'm not minimizing the risk, but this may be our best chance. Who's with me?"

A long, strained silence followed. One by one, heads nodded in affirmation. Jane stooped to retrieve her combat knife and jammed it into its sheath. She crossed her arms, defiant but determined. Amos caught the glance she aimed at him and stowed his weapon.

Aubrey reappeared in the door, her face ashen. She'd heard Garr's challenge. "I'm in."

In the end, the decision was unanimous. They would follow Colonel Scott.

Garr nodded, his solemn expression an acknowledgement of the outlandish assignment they'd agreed to shoulder. The moment passed, and he issued his orders.

"Doc, you'll stay here with Megan. The rest of you, disarm." He placed his knife on the table. "I mean it. Meeting the Hoarders will be hard enough. Let's not tempt ourselves."

After a moment's hesitation, they acquiesced with obvious reluctance, and unbuckled their weapons.

Mateo spoke up in the grim silence. "Perhaps you're familiar with another wise old adage, 'the enemy of my enemy is my friend'?"

That was as far as he got.

Don slammed his sheathed knife on the table, the sharp *crack* painfully loud. "If you're collecting folk wisdom, try adding this one—'read the room.' The enemy of my enemy is still my enemy, as far as I'm concerned." He took a deep breath, glancing at Garr. "But I might accept him as a temporary ally, at least until the Givers are gone."

Mateo ducked his head in a slight bow.

Don turned his back on him and addressed his fellow Runners. "Okay, you heard the colonel. Let's get this over with."

SEVENTY

Doc busied herself in the infirmary, emptying the packs and sorting their contents on her worktable. She put Megan to work, removing the restraints from the gurney.

Doc had never been comfortable confining a patient, and now that the restraints were no longer necessary, she was glad to be rid of them.

Megan tackled her assignment without comment.

"The most outrageous thing you've ever asked them to do," Doc muttered under her breath, shaking her head in disbelief. "Garr, you've pushed them to their limits before, but this time, you may be asking too much."

"Doc?" Megan appeared beside her, carefully arranging the detached restraints into a neat stack.

"Oh, don't mind me, Megan." Doc straightened, grimacing at her stiff spine. She couldn't recall the last time she'd felt such grim foreboding. "Just talking to myself. Old army medics can be a little eccentric that way ..."

Her voice trailed off.

Megan wasn't paying attention. She seemed preoccupied with the items Doc had piled on the worktable.

"Megan, is something troubling you?"

The former Tracker pointed at the neat piles, her expression puzzled. She struggled to put her thought into words, but managed to force her lips and tongue to cooperate. "Gun. No gun … Doc, gun is gone."

Doc rummaged through the piles, searching with growing panic. The handgun—Jane's Glock—was missing. Someone had taken it, defying Colonel Scott's order to disarm.

And then, stricken, she realized whom. "Aubrey." Her heart sank. "Oh no, Aubrey, no …"

SEVENTY-ONE ◉

Tony paced another stress-fueled lap around the circumference of the spartan mechanical shop. He seemed incapable of relaxing. Connor couldn't blame him. The same restless energy gnawed at him, as well.

Mateo had promised to return, savages in tow, but was taking much longer than expected. The protracted delay grated on their nerves, heaping another layer of tension on their outlandish situation.

For Tony, pacing seemed to help.

Connor toyed absent-mindedly with his locket, slipping the small token back and forth on the chain around his neck. He wondered what his sister would say, if she knew they were about to form an alliance with her murderers.

"This place is a dump." Tony finished another lap, his fifth so far. "Are you sure this is the location Mateo meant?"

"This is the place." Darcy leaned against a cinderblock wall. He appeared confident, eager. "We could hardly expect Mateo to give us the exact location of their base, this so-called 'hub.'

The Eastside Mission is nearby, and is somehow connected to their network. That could prove useful in the future."

Connor glanced around the room, unimpressed. The decrepit shop was consistent with the general decay of the Old City. A pair of lanterns burned on either side of the room, creating a shifting pattern of light and shadow. Darkness cloaked the far end of the shop.

Two doors allowed access from the street—the larger a rolling garage door, and a single conventional door to the left. A metal crossbar secured the garage door, limiting the savages to a single point of entry.

"What's on your mind, Connor?"

Connor looked up, startled. *Darcy doesn't miss a thing.* He licked his lips before answering. "We've never been in this part of the Old City before. I knew the buildings would be run-down, but it's even worse than I expected. I don't know how people can live here."

Tony snorted. "*People* don't live here, just savages. The first thing I noticed was the hostility. Maybe I'll drive over a few of them next time, just for good measure. Teach the savages a lesson about respect."

Darcy laughed. "That's not a bad idea, Tony. They expect it from us, and I, for one, hate to disappoint them." His laughter faded. "But not today. It's vital these savages trust us. We need to deploy more drones as quickly as possible. Play nice."

Connor hung his head. Their situation was as ridiculous as it was humiliating. "I'll do my best, sir, but it won't be easy. I'd rather tranquilize the savages and smuggle them into Cascadia while they're unconscious. We could Implant the whole batch and turn them loose. The collaborators would never know what hit them."

"Enough." Darcy's patience had worn thin. Connor knew the signs. Conversation over. "The Givers didn't leave us much choice. For the good of the Enclave, we're forced to strike a deal with the scum of the earth. So be it. Once they're Implanted, we'll never see them again anyway."

Tony was on his next lap. "Oh yeah, this isn't a long-term partnership. We just need them to 'volunteer.'" He pantomimed wiping his hands clean of something distasteful. "After that, it's nothing a hot shower can't cure."

Connor glanced at the dirty windows. Even through the grime, it was clear the sun had all but set. The crumbling relic of the Old City would soon be blanketed in darkness.

Hard on the heels of his casual observation, a possible explanation for Mateo's delay surfaced. *They're waiting until it's dark. We're gambling they'll come willingly. What if the savages have other ideas?* A chill ran down his spine.

Darcy abruptly pushed away from the wall. He faced the door, shoulders squared, his face alight with anticipation.

Connor froze, listening intently, and heard the same noise. Outside, on the street, someone fumbled with the door fastening. He scrambled to his feet, tucking the locket inside his shirt for safekeeping.

Darcy winked, gesturing for Connor and Tony to stand on either side of him. His expression was eager, his eyes bright—a predator poised to strike. "Show time," he said with a grin.

Connor nodded. They'd follow his lead.

The door swung open.

SEVENTY-TWO ◉

Splitting up was Colonel Scott's idea. He singled Amos out, along with Jane, to accompany Mateo. Garr's team—Don, Sheila, and Aubrey—would arrive from a different direction.

Amos understood his reasoning. Smaller groups drew less attention. Their recent encounters with Trackers in the Mission district added weight to the need for caution.

"Safety in numbers" means nothing to a Tracker.

Amos, Jane, and Mateo trekked the tunnels for just over a half hour before it was prudent to ascend to street level. Amos gave the all-clear signal, and they doubled back, taking a circuitous route to the mechanical shop where the Hoarders—Citizens—waited.

He flanked Mateo on the right. Jane mirrored his action to the Tracker's left. Amos felt naked without a weapon, even though he knew a combat knife was nothing compared to the advanced weaponry the Hoarders had at their disposal. Garr's insistence on disarming made sense, but that did little to soothe his nerves.

If Mateo's information was accurate, they were about to meet the Hoarder responsible for inventing the Implants. If so, Amos wasn't sure he could resist tearing the inventor's throat out with his bare hands. He traced the scar under his ribs, and his memories led him down a dark path.

Jane was in an equally foul mood. Jaw clenched and lips pressed together, she stole furtive glances down the dark alleys, as if daring the shadows to fight. Her hatred of Hoarders and Implants was different than his, but just as malignant. Revenge would be a strong temptation for either one of them.

"Who are these 'dissidents' you keep telling us about?" Jane spoke for the first time since they'd left the tunnel. "I thought you meant Hoarders—*these* Hoarders—but you told Garr these aren't them."

"I'm impressed by your ability to detect nuance," Mateo replied. His compliment sounded sincere, but Amos wasn't convinced. "In fact, I commend your entire unit for your progress in evaluative skills."

"You wanted us to think it was these Hoarders," Amos interrupted. *I'm sick of your evasiveness.* "You've got another plan up your sleeve. You've been manipulating us all along."

Mateo didn't break stride. They were less than a block from their destination. "I've also intervened on your behalf. It's not unreasonable to suggest that you, Don, and Sheila owe me your lives. Ah, we have arrived." He paused, resting his hand on the doorknob. "I remind you—the Citizens need your help as much as you need theirs. Perhaps more. It would be wise, as Colonel Scott said, to remember who the real enemy is."

Any lingering questions went unasked. Mateo twisted the doorknob and stepped inside the dilapidated building.

Adrenaline spiked through Amos's veins. He felt a tremor

in his hand, muscles instinctively tensing around a weapon he wasn't carrying. He exchanged glances with Jane. She took a deep breath, exhaling slowly.

Together, they squeezed through the open doorway.

SEVENTY-THREE

AUBREY REMINDED HERSELF to relax every four or five steps. Her instinctive habit of hunching her shoulders was a symptom of heightened anxiety, or so Doc said. Aubrey suspected Don's uncharacteristic silence and Sheila's pinched expression came from the same source. Only Garr seemed untroubled.

They rounded a corner at the third intersection, circling the block to rendezvous with the others at the mechanical shop. Amos's team had utilized a different strategy, taking advantage of the tunnels to circumnavigate the neighborhood. Garr gave them a head-start, but Aubrey guessed her team was no more than two minutes behind.

Garr led the way across a deserted intersection as the sun slipped below the horizon, cloaking the street in an ominous twilight. The mechanical shop was located eight blocks from the dropbox, another faceless façade in a district filled with abandoned and boarded-up buildings.

Hidden in plain sight.

Aubrey placed a protective hand over the lump in her

303

jacket pocket. She'd fled the mess hall in visceral, unthinking terror after Garr agreed to meet with the Hoarders, and took refuge in the room she shared with Sheila and Jane.

She huddled on her mattress, knees hugged to her chest. Her thoughts ran wild, but began to coalesce as her heartbeat slowed.

A vivid memory surfaced—Doc Simon placing Jane's Glock on the worktable after Megan surrendered it. Aubrey seized on the memory, crawled off her mattress, and tip-toed down the corridor to the infirmary. Meeting the Hoarders wasn't an option. It was now her mission.

Aubrey kept pace with Don's longer strides, mentally refining her strategy. She shoved her sleeves up, snugging the cuffs above her elbows. She wanted the Hoarders to see her scars. To acknowledge their crimes.

She would bide her time, until she was certain which one was responsible for the Implants. One Hoarder, at minimum, would not return from this meeting.

She had no intention of sharing her plan with her fellow Runners. They were her friends, especially Doc Simon. They extended sympathy and support, but none of them were able to comprehend the horror she'd experienced after learning that she had an Implant. An insidious piece of alien technology, surgically hidden under her ribcage, reducing her to a human time bomb, to be detonated at the whim of a sadistic Hoarder.

Garr slowed as they crossed a final intersection. Diffused light beckoned from a grimy window a half-block ahead.

Aubrey rehearsed the names of the dead. Sarah and Thomas Cooper, Stephen Bradshaw, Sullivan Quinn, Kellen O'Reilly, the anonymous Runners they'd found dead in the streets, the young boy they'd rescued, Jane's brother Davey…

In a few minutes, she would avenge them all.

She added Amos Morgan's name to the list, as well as her own. They'd also been marked for death, unwilling pawns in another's game. *We got lucky.*

The guilty Hoarder will pay.

SEVENTY-FOUR

CONNOR THOUGHT he was prepared to meet the savages face-to-face, but their brazen entrance was more disturbing than he could have imagined. A pair of them stood little more than ten feet away, flanking the creature known as Mateo Reyes.

The scene felt contrived, unreal, a nightmare.

Mateo entered the mechanical shop first, inclining his head in a benign acknowledgement of their presence. As he'd promised, the savages were empty-handed. Their facial expressions, on the other hand, were anything but deferential.

Connor's blood boiled at their deliberate posture of disrespect. The savages had the audacity to look him in the eye—to look them all in the eye—as if they were equals.

His hands balled into fists. *The arrogance.* He glanced at Darcy. His foster father stood motionless, eyes bright with restless intent. Connor recoiled. He'd seen that look before.

"Good welcome, esteemed Citizens." Mateo spoke first, his voice as neutral as if he were buying a drink in a local café. "May I present Jane Avery." He gestured first to the hard-faced female on his left, and then at the hostile male to his right. "And this is Amos Morgan."

Connor thought he recognized the one called Amos. He looked a lot like one of the thieves who'd stolen drones DR-55 and DR-56.

"You made excellent time," Darcy replied lightly. He didn't bother to introduce Connor or Tony. Mateo already knew who they were, and it would be degrading to introduce them to the savages.

You'll all be drones before you know it. Connor controlled his animosity with an effort. *Then you can "help" us remove the traitors on the Council.*

"Only two?" Tony inserted himself into the conversation, suspicion underscoring his words. "Where are the others?"

The question was barely out of his mouth before the door opened a second time.

SEVENTY-FIVE ◉

DON STEPPED IN FRONT OF GARR, opening the door and entering first. Aubrey didn't need Jane's coaching to know why. *If the worst happens, he'll shield the colonel.* She squeezed in behind Garr, with Sheila bringing up the rear and easing the door shut behind them.

The interior lighting was muted. A pair of lanterns burned at half-strength on opposite sides of the room, their meager glow overlapping to create a rough clearing in the middle of the mechanical shop.

Mateo stood at stiff attention, silhouetted near the edge of the lamp-lit area. Amos and Jane mirrored his stance, rigid with tension. And eight or ten feet beyond...

Aubrey knew she was staring, but she couldn't help herself. Seeing the Hoarders was like a kick in the stomach.

These are no ordinary Hoarders. One of them is the monster who invented the Implants. She couldn't tear her eyes away. She read the contempt on their faces, sensed their condescension and naked hostility, which they made no effort to conceal.

The Hoarder to her right was the eldest, his mane of dark hair, sprinkled with gray, tied back in a ponytail. He looked belligerent, sullen, as if spoiling for a fight. He reminded Aubrey of a playground bully—all bluster and ego.

To her left was a much younger Hoarder, probably a year or two younger than her. His blond hair was stylishly cropped and his lips curled into a sneer when he saw them. His arrogant expression evaporated when he caught sight of Aubrey's scars.

Yeah, buddy, take a good look. You did this, trying to turn me into one of your killing machines.

She glared back at him, relishing the triumphant moment when she realized she'd caught him staring. He averted his eyes, clearly rattled, and pretended to concentrate on Mateo.

Her gaze settled on the last Hoarder. He was roughly Garr's age, give or take a few years, and carried himself with the pompous entitlement of a typical Hoarder. His pale eyes were bright, oddly feverish in their intensity.

Aubrey was fascinated and repelled. *It's him.* The monster. The devil incarnate, inventor of Implants.

The true Soul-less.

Aubrey's hand hovered near her jacket pocket. She felt dizzy, breathing hard between her clenched teeth. *The Givers turn us into Trackers, but you Implant children.*

She recited her internal litany of his victims, steeling herself for the final confrontation.

SEVENTY-SIX ◉

CONNOR TRIED TO AVOID staring as four additional savages crowded into the mechanical shop. The first to enter was a giant figure, well-muscled and fierce-looking. He didn't appear very bright. *Probably best-suited for manual labor.*

The other male carried himself with an infuriating level of insolence, eyeing Darcy with a menacing glare. *He spotted Darcy right away. Watch him like a hawk—he's the leader.*

Connor almost succeeded in ignoring the females, but the deformed arm of one caught his eye. Her facial features, despite the dirt, betrayed her youthfulness. Probably not much older than him.

Like her companions, she was clothed in the coarse attire typical for the rabble outside the Enclave. Her jacket sleeves were bunched above her elbows, revealing an ugly swath of scar tissue running from her hand to where her arm disappeared into her sleeve.

The scarred woman's eyes darted wildly from Connor to Tony to Darcy, her expression feral, almost rabid.

All of the savages were filthy and unkempt. *Tony's not kidding. We're going to need a shower after this.*

"Councilor, this is Colonel Garrison Scott." Mateo gestured to the savage standing beside him. "Garr, this is Darcy Peterson, a respected member of Cascadia Enclave's ruling Council. He is the one of whom I spoke."

The scarred girl flinched at his words, her attention now riveted on Darcy.

Connor stared, wide-eyed, from the savages to his foster father, aghast at the undisguised insult. Was Mateo actually suggesting the savages address Darcy *by name*?

Tony took an aggressive step forward. He appeared more than ready to protest Mateo's insolent introduction.

Darcy flung out a hand, without looking, to restrain Tony's impetuous move. He fixed his attention on the one called Garr. Mateo had just, intentionally or not, confirmed his identity as leader of the savages.

Garr returned Darcy's look, neither one breaking eye contact. Darcy was in his element, staring down a lesser opponent. Establishing dominance.

None of the savages missed Tony's combative stance, or Darcy's authoritative gesture holding him in place. They clustered around their leader, sizing Darcy up. It wasn't hard for Connor to read the dull hatred on their faces.

A twinge of dread ran down his spine. *Animals are always the most dangerous when they're cornered.* Mateo, flanked by a pack of six savages, stood between them and the only exit.

He repressed a shiver.

The tense stand-off—Connor wasn't sure if it lasted a few seconds or much longer—was broken by Darcy. "I'm impressed, Mateo. You're as good as your word. On behalf of the

Cascadia Enclave, we are grateful for new allies in our fight against the Givers."

Good move, Darcy. Connor applauded mentally, taking a deep breath and trying to appear calm. *Focus on our common mission. Lull the savages into acquiescence.*

Mateo bowed his head slightly. "They are as necessary to your plans, Councilor Peterson, as you are to theirs. The Givers, as you say, are the common enemy." He raised his head to look Darcy square in the eye. "There's a wise old saying, 'the whole is greater than the sum of its parts.' Neither of you can hope to prevail without the other."

It was the truth, but Connor resented him saying it within earshot of the savages. *We can't show any sign of weakness. They have to acknowledge that we're in charge.*

If Tony had the same thought, he kept it to himself.

"I *am* puzzled by one thing," Darcy said, ignoring Mateo's speech. He paused, frowning as if the thought had just occurred to him. Connor knew better. Nothing was unplanned when it came to his foster father's negotiating skills.

Darcy didn't disappoint. "My drones, DR-55 and DR-56? It appears you've neglected to bring them along."

Mateo cocked his head to one side, as if pondering. "I fail to see why you insist on referring to Lukas and Emma as if they were your property," he replied. "As I've made clear, Councilor, the Petrovs will remain under my protection."

The savages recoiled, backing away from Mateo as if confronted by a poisonous snake. Their reaction confirmed Connor's earlier suspicions.

These are the savages who stole our drones.

Darcy's predatory glint hardened to needle sharpness. He erupted, lunging forward a step, every muscle taut with fury.

"Those are *my drones.*" His face contorted in fury and his voice rose in a maniacal crescendo. Flecks of spittle showed at the corners of his mouth. "Nobody plays games with me. Remember your place, *Tracker.*"

The savages reacted with terrifying intensity. The hard-faced girl beside Mateo actually bared her teeth and snarled at them. Dread gnawed at Connor's stomach.

They really are animals.

A flurry of motion answered Darcy's outburst. One savage forced her way to the front of the group. It was the young girl, the one with the scars. She shoved in front of Mateo, her arm raised shoulder-high, pointing at Darcy.

She's got a gun. Connor could only stare, paralyzed.

The scarred girl raised her other hand, bracing the weapon. She was breathing hard, teeth bared like a rabid animal, her face flushed as dark as the ugly scars on her arm.

No one moved—even the savages seemed frozen in shock. It was impossible for her to miss at such close range.

She aimed straight at Darcy.

SEVENTY-SEVEN

In the end, it was Darcy's furious outburst that spurred her into action. Aubrey ripped the Glock out of her pocket, shoving her way between her companions to confront the Hoarders.

She took careful aim, the Glock's unfamiliar weight pulling against her wrist. *I've got one chance at this.*

The Hoarders flanking Darcy appeared genuinely fearful, their earlier arrogance wiped from their faces. But not Darcy. He eyed her with a sly grin, as if she was nothing more than an amusing annoyance. He held his hands out, palm up.

"Are you going to shoot me, little girl?" He had the audacity to laugh at her. "You and your friends will never get inside Cascadia that way."

"Thomas, Sarah, Stephen, Sully, Kellen!" Aubrey found her voice, giving full vent to her pent-up fury. "Slaughtered by Trackers, because of what *you* did to me."

"Me, personally?" Darcy smirked and raised his hands in mock surrender. "I'm not the only one manufacturing drones, young lady. And Trackers were around long before we realized what the Givers were up to." He gave her a patronizing look and lowered his hands. "Were you aware that Trackers were originally designed as bodyguards for the Givers? No? Well, I can't say I'm surprised, given the appalling level of ignorance outside Cascadia." His grin faded, giving way to a quizzical expression. "On the other hand, now that I think about it, you *do* look a little familiar. Perhaps we've met before. Do you have an Implant, by any chance?"

His smile returned, but there was no humor in it. He was taunting her, Aubrey knew, daring her to pull the trigger.

"Lower your weapon, Aubrey." Garr's voice came from behind her, low and steady. "I don't like this any more than you do, but we need this alliance."

Sheila echoed the same sentiment. "Listen to Garr, Aubs."

"Do it, Aubrey," Amos hissed, his face twisted in fury. "He invented the Implants. He's ground zero. If it weren't for him, none of this would've happened."

Don growled under his breath. He sounded torn.

Jane appeared next to her, standing shoulder to shoulder. "If you can't do it, Aubrey, give me the gun." Her voice was thick with loathing. She held her hand out, her blazing eyes only for Darcy. "I owe him."

"It's okay, Jane." Aubrey glared at Darcy, refusing to break eye contact. "I've got this." She stiffened her arm, finger tightening on the trigger. She took a deep breath, held it, aiming …

"Aubrey, *please*," Sheila pleaded.

A sudden whirlwind erupted behind them. The door burst violently open, slamming against the wall like a gunshot. Before Aubrey could pull the trigger, an unseen assailant pounced on her. A vise-like claw, strong and merciless, clamped around her hand, crushing her fingers against the Glock.

Aubrey cried out, powerless to prevent her attacker from prying the gun out of her grip. She fell to her knees, cradling her throbbing hand against her chest. Her fingers spasmed uncontrollably, and she wondered if they were broken. She looked up, her face twisted in pain and fury.

Megan stood over her, clutching the Glock and aiming it at the ceiling girders overhead. She had a strange expression on her face—one Aubrey had never seen before—earnest, pleading, almost begging.

"Aub, no." Megan worked hard to force the words out. "We need—them." She took a deep breath, her tortured voice clearing. "We need them."

"The dissidents have spoken." Mateo's solemn proclamation fell into a stunned silence. He moved to stand beside Megan, one hand resting on her shoulder. He glanced around the room, catching everyone in his gaze, Runner and Hoarder alike. "This alliance must survive. The Givers are your common enemy. Only together can you defeat them. The dissidents have spoken."

Aubrey knelt on the rough concrete, cradling her hand. She turned in desperation to Garr, Don—anyone who could make sense of it all. "I don't think I can do this. Not with them, not with *him*. He put Implants in *children* ..."

No one answered or returned her pleading look. They were captivated, spellbound, by something behind her. Garr's face was tense and wary, as was Don's. Sheila radiated alarm, and Amos looked shellshocked. Even Jane retreated an involuntary step, staring in wide-eyed astonishment.

Aubrey heard a choked cry from one of the Hoarders, followed by the scrape of boots on concrete. She twisted around on her knees to confront the loathsome trio.

Darcy's leering arrogance was gone, replaced by blank-eyed

shock and disbelief. Aubrey stared, uncomprehending, as he stumbled back, retreating to the outer perimeter of the lantern-defined clearing. He was shaken, speechless, raising his hands as if warding off the unthinkable.

The gray-haired Hoarder appeared perplexed and demoralized by Darcy's reaction. *He has no idea what's going on.*

It was the young Hoarder—the blond kid—whose voice she'd heard. Contrary to Darcy's retreat, he took two awkward steps forward, extending a shaky hand. A silver chain dangled between his trembling fingers. His face turned pale as he stared at something cradled in his palm.

What's wrong with him?

The blond Hoarder raised his eyes, horror and disbelief etched on his face. His lips moved, but no sound escaped. He gulped a quivering breath and tried again, managing to choke out a single, anguished word.

"Megan?"

# # #

AFTERWORD ◉

TIJUANA IS A FASCINATING city on the border between the United States of Mexico and the United States of America. I've been there numerous times, volunteering with a non-profit organization that builds houses for the less-fortunate in *las colonias*.

The people we met were warm and welcoming. Mexican culture is hospitable to the core and they were gracious about my fumbling attempts at *español*.

"You're trying, and we appreciate it," one friend said. "But yeah, you need to work on your *pronunciación*."

Crossing the border back into California was never a problem. The lineups were long, but the Customs and Border Patrol guards were gruff yet professional. The same was true of their Mexican Army counterparts.

As an outsider, I was intrigued by the border city culture. The economic disparity was obvious. But it was the casual assumptions people carried, on both sides of the wall, that got me thinking.

Every country is filled with amazing, good-hearted people.

And every country also produces its share of self-absorbed idiots. I've learned, as a general rule, to never judge a country by either (a) its politicians, or (b) its tourists.

When I sat down to write *Dissident*, I knew the Runners needed to find a way inside the Enclave by book's end. I was also aware that if the only viewpoints were those of Amos, Aubrey, and the Runners, we would forever view Cascadia through the lens of, as Don calls it, "Hoarderville."

And so, a new POV character, Connor Sinclair, was born. As a Citizen/Hoarder, Connor gives us an insider's view of the Cascadia Enclave—and their opinion of Runners—guided by his own unique set of prejudices and stereotypes.

If there's a metaphor at work in *Dissident*, it's simply that we need to learn how to work together for the common good.

Or, to word it in reverse—our prejudices, stereotypes, and partisan divides are as much the enemy as any crisis our nations have faced or will face. If we can learn anything from the precarious alliance between Hoarders and Runners, it's to recover the ability to listen beyond our cultural echo chambers.

Of course, in the case of characters like Darcy Peterson, all bets are off. Some people are so blinded by...

Whoops, I'm getting ahead of myself. That portion of the story will have to wait until *Scorpion*.

On a side note, Tracy/Megan was never supposed to live past the first chapter or two. I'd written, in bold letters at the top of my first draft outline, "Don't do the 'recovering her humanity' schtick." I was afraid it was an overused plot device, and I didn't want to fall into that trap.

Megan didn't agree. We arm-wrestled. She won.

Mateo Reyes was supposed to be a one-scene character. His primary (only?) purpose was to take Amos and Don on his "guided tour," and show them how seriously the guards took their jobs and how much firepower they had at their disposal.

I also didn't realize Mateo was a Tracker at first. He hid it from me until the final paragraph of the first draft's opening scene. Characters are often like that. They have minds of their own and aren't above arguing with the author attempting to tell their story.

Mateo wreaked havoc on my outline, but I've forgiven him. One beta reader liked him so much, she named a cat after him. Another developed a soft spot for an unexpected character. "I *like* Connor. I'm rooting for him in the next book!"

Characters can also be shrewd negotiators. Not only will they take the story arc in unforeseen directions, they're also savvy enough to bolster their bargaining position by endearing themselves to readers.

"You *do* realize the voices are all yours, right?" Wendy asks, looking concerned when I complain about characters digging their heels in and refusing to budge.

Time slows to a standstill, like molasses left on a Canadian porch in January. "Well, yeah, obviously," I reply, shrugging casually. "Why do you ask?"

"Just checking," she says, but I feel her eyes following me as I exit the kitchen.

Until next time, drive friendly.
Deven

ABOUT THE AUTHOR

DEVEN KANE PLAYS a mean bass and loves to tell stories. He writes dystopian sci-fi thrillers and urban fantasy, which he describes as "supernatural thrillers set on another world."

"Speculative fiction allows me to explore human nature, interpersonal conflicts, the desire to rise above our circumstances, and the obstacles holding us back," he says.

"Settings can change—Earth's near future, the past, or an alien culture on another world—but the most engaging stories are about our personal interactions. The good, the bad, the ugly, and our need to transcend."

His novels include the dystopian *Tracker Trilogy*, the urban fantasy *Darkwood*, and the *Treehawke Saga*.

Deven and Wendy live in western Canada under the benevolent supervision of a bemused Husky named Dakota.

Visit Deven online @ devenkane.com.

TRACKER
BOOK 1

"An imaginative world, an array of
diverse, well-rounded characters, and
a pleasantly unpredictable plot."

FEAR THE HARVEST

Before the Trackers, survival was easy

A generation ago, Earth's wealthiest citizens—the Hoarders—seized control of the planet's resources, retreated into their fortified Enclaves, and left the rest of the population to fend for itself.

Now, the Hoarders have begun randomly Implanting people with a new kind of microtechnology, capable of converting their unsuspecting hosts into violent and deadly automatons.

They also created Trackers, a stealth unit of mechanically and chemically enhanced creatures fanatically devoted to hunting down and killing anyone unlucky enough to have an Implant.

Amos Morgan and Aubrey Carter, together with a small band of fellow Runners, must unravel the mystery, racing against time before the Trackers discover them.

And before their own Implants change them into ...
Something else.

SCORPION

TRACKER BOOK 3

"Kane keeps you guessing – a crisp and
satisfying conclusion to the trilogy!"

FEAR THE HARVEST

Where Trackers
fear to tread

Time is running out for Amos Morgan and Aubrey Carter. Their uneasy alliance with a cadre of renegade Hoarders—vital to gaining access into the Enclave—teeters on a razor's edge. Years of suspicion and prejudice, on both sides, wars against their need to present a united front.

The dissidents, Mateo and Megan, claim to hold the key, but can anyone be sure whose side they're on?

Life inside the Cascadia Enclave is fast deteriorating into chaos, covertly manipulated by the shadowy Givers and their power-hungry Hoarder accomplices. In a matter of days—or less—the Givers are poised to unleash an army of Trackers on Cascadia's unsuspecting populace.

Earth's fate hangs in the balance, leaving the Runners with one last, desperate option … dance with the Scorpion.

SNEAK PREVIEW

WHERE TRACKERS FEAR TO TREAD

ONE

A GUST OF COOL WIND rustled the leaves under Amos Morgan's feet, a subtle reminder of the impending change of season. Towering evergreens, like sentinels on patrol, kept watch over the rocky hillside. Silence cloaked the idyllic scene, broken at sporadic intervals by an occasional birdcall.

Amos stood over his brother's unmarked grave, hands shoved into his pockets. He was peripherally aware of the wind, the creaking of needle-laden pines, and the infrequent cry of birds. Sunlight filtered through the branches overhead, spilling in uneven patterns across his shoulders. He took a deep breath of cool autumn air—inhale, exhale, inhale, exhale—a steady rhythm that should have had a calming effect.

Peace proved elusive. Tension radiated in its place, revealing itself in his clenched fists, the tingling alarm knotted between his shoulder blades, and an accompanying headache.

I hate this place. The hollow sensation in his gut threatened to overwhelm him. *It's like a dark magnet, dragging me to return.*

Amos glanced over his shoulder, up the steep incline, to the cave. His personal bunker in the wilderness. Moss-covered stones framed the low entrance, overshadowed by tough pine trees above, growing tall and driving roots into cracks and crevices.

Dried leaves and pine needles from countless seasons carpeted the ground. Dozens of similar outcroppings littered the forested hillside, each a minor variation on the others.

His cave was unique.

Amos squared his shoulders, turned his back on the grave, and faced the shadowy cave entrance. The last place he'd seen his brother alive. He steeled himself against resurgent guilt.

Fourteen years ago, he'd left Trey here—seriously wounded after a Hoarder shot him—in order to seek help. And because Amos, twelve years old at the time, was afraid the Hoarders might discover their hiding place.

During his absence, Hoarders found the cave and ended Trey's life. Amos returned, with the promised help, to find his brother's lifeless body a few meters outside the cave.

Amos the coward goes on living, and we buried what was left of Trey in an unmarked grave.

The blame wasn't his. Amos understood that, intellectually. The real killers, who pursued the teenaged brothers, shooting at them for sport—as if they were wild animals—were the so-called "Citizens of the Enclave." Hoarders…

Amos lurched into motion, forcing himself to climb the steep hillside. He hadn't come back to grieve his brother's death, or reminisce about hiding his Implant in the underground burrow. He crouched, peering inside the cave.

It always comes back to the Hoarders.

Hoarders murdered Trey. Hoarders deployed Trackers to hunt down and kill anyone unlucky enough to have an Implant. Like Amos and Aubrey.

He squeezed his eyes shut, as if the simple action was sufficient to hold his memories at bay. He'd like nothing more than to forget they'd met that trio of Hoarders yesterday.

Hoarders that Mateo insisted they partner with against the alien Givers. Hoarders who freely, proudly, admitted to inventing the cursed Implants.

And their leader, Darcy, taunting Aubrey, insinuating he was responsible for her Implant.

And mine, too? He couldn't fathom how Mateo—let alone Colonel Scott—could expect them to work with *any* Hoarder. Especially Darcy Peterson.

Amos crawled into the cave, rolling over on his back to stare at the stone overhead.

Returning here is—let's face it—pretty dysfunctional. His lips curved into a wry smile. Doc Simon would probably send him to a therapist, if their Hub network had access to one. *This cave is where it all started for me. I need space to think.*

He was stalling, and he knew it. Yes, meeting the Hoarders had triggered memories of Trey's murder and his own Implant. Just recalling the hellish meeting wiped the smile from Amos's face.

He was tempted to ignore it, refuse to confront the trauma, but he'd sought refuge in the cave for that very reason.

Yes, to sort things out. But even more, to solve a life-and-death riddle—an ambush by an entire squadron of Trackers.

Someone had betrayed their location. But who?

TWO ⊙

Muster Chateau was damp and cold. Aubrey Carter wrapped a threadbare blanket around her shoulders. She sat on the concrete floor, cross-legged, leaning against a cinderblock wall.

She massaged her scarred hand, shivering from a chill she couldn't seem to shake. Her hand ached. Megan's physical enhancements didn't function as originally designed, but she retained a punishing remnant of her Tracker grip.

I'm lucky she didn't break my hand.

"Here, eat this. You need to keep your strength up." Don's gruff voice interrupted her musing. He dropped a handful of dried trail rations into her outstretched palm. Salted meat and some kind of leathery fruit. "It's Sheila's gourmet best. I'll send her chef's compliments on your behalf."

Aubrey smiled and gratefully accepted the rations. *His jokes aren't as funny as he thinks they are, but I love that he tries to keep our morale up.*

"Go easy, though." Jane ran a hand through her dark hair, in a futile attempt to loosen the tangled knots. "Those rations won't last much longer. When we stocked the Chateau, we never expected to stay more than one night."

Megan sat a meter to Aubrey's right, chewing mechanically on a chunk of fruit. Her facial expression was hard to decipher, partially obscured by an eyepatch over her ruined eye socket. She continued to be an enigma. A former Tracker, who once pursued Aubrey with murderous intent and, in a twist of fate no one could have predicted, was now part of Eastside Hub.

The Hoarder kid—the blond one—recognized her. Aubrey recalled his look of shock and disbelief. *Good news or bad? Whose side is Megan on?*

Jane's acerbic voice cut her paranoid musings short. "Let me look at your arm, Don. You're soaking through the bandages again. We need to get the bleeding under control."

For once, Don didn't argue. He upended his metal rod, his most recently-acquired weapon of choice. The rod was two meters in length, well over Aubrey's height, and raised a faint echo as he set it down. He seated himself next to Aubrey, his massive bulk dwarfing her.

They'd lingered in the Chateau for a night and a day already. Wisdom dictated they bide their time before returning to Eastside. No one balked when Don insisted on caution. They had no way of knowing if their Hub had been compromised. Not after the Tracker ambush.

"We make for the Eastside tonight," Don said as Jane loosened his blood-stained bandages. Doc Simon needed to treat the gash on his forearm, soon. "I don't think anyone, or any *thing*, followed us, but we're not taking any chances. Let's hope Eastside's still secure."

"Deja vu, all over again" Jane replied wryly as she bandaged his arm. "Trackers ambushed the Mission last spring, too. They didn't find the subbasement, but they were closer than they knew. Too close."

"True enough," Don replied, exaggerating his drawl. "But I don't want to lose another night's sleep in this stink-hole."

"Thanks a lot, Don." Aubrey laughed, wrinkling her nose. "I forgot about the smell until you reminded me." Her humor faded. "Garr warned Uncle John to shut Eastside down for a few days." She hoped the Mission's manager had responded in time. "If Trackers are scouting the area, there shouldn't be anything to give Eastside away."

Don winced as Jane tightened the fresh bandage with a deft tug. "Plan for the worst and assume nothing. Megan, can you can tell if other Trackers are nearby?"

Megan shook her head, still chewing. She swallowed with difficulty before replying.

"No more voices," she said in her halting way, tapping two fingers against the side of her head. "No more Givers." She ducked her head and resumed eating.

Conversation over.

Aubrey studied her covertly, unsure of her own feelings. A few months ago, Megan had been just another nameless Tracker, obsessed with killing a young boy for his Implant. At their first encounter, Aubrey was sure she was about to die, along with the boy. She jammed an electric prod into Megan's scanning eye in a final, desperate act of self-defense.

The energy surge flattened Megan like a bolt of lightning, and Garr insisted they bring the crippled Tracker back to Eastside. Doc's diagnosis was dire at the time: she predicted Megan's wounds would prove fatal within a matter of days.

But she survived and, through her, they learned of the real power behind the Hoarders—alien beings who called themselves

"Givers." In an unanticipated reversal, the damage caused by the prod triggered Megan's halting and incomplete journey toward recovering her humanity.

Once a mindless killing machine, now an ally. Sort of. Aubrey massaged her scarred forearm, concealed under her blanket. *I don't regret what I did. Because self-defense… and protecting the boy.*

"That'll have to do for now." Jane twisted an improvised sling over Don's shoulder to support his injured arm. "You need Doc Simon's tender care. We're good to go, whenever you want to give the word."

"The word, my friend, is given," he replied with a facetious grin. "You know, I've always wanted to say that. Why should Garr have all the fun?"

Jane scoffed and handed him the metal rod. "Garr *never* said anything like that, even when he was still the colonel." She paused, her eyes haunted. "I lost sight of everyone after the attack. Do you think they managed to get away? We can't be the only survivors."

"We're not." Don exuded carefree confidence. "Amos will go to ground and lay low. Once we confirm Eastside's secure, I know exactly where to find him."

"What about Garr?" Aubrey got to her feet, pulling the blanket tighter. "Everything happened so fast, I couldn't see what happened to him."

Don chuckled, his baritone voice reassuringly warm in the chilly room. "He had Sheila by his side, and she's a force to be reckoned with. They'll have each other's back." He paused, suddenly pensive. "I hate to admit it, but Mateo deserves a bit of credit. He's a slippery fish, but he used his Tracker-ness *against* the other red-eyes, not for them."

"Trackers—for us?" Megan's tortured voice caught Aubrey by surprise. "Or for them?" The eye patch and surrounding scar tissue made her expression difficult to read, but Megan's surviving eye held a pleading look. Aubrey couldn't tell if she was asking a question or trying to warn them.

Don broke the silence, flexing his hand around the metal rod. "Were we the targets, or the Hoarders? Excellent question, Megan."

"And who gave our position away?" Jane got to her feet, dusting her hands on her pants. "That's what I want to know."

THREE ◉

CONNOR USUALLY FOUND the bright lights of Cascadia comforting, but they offered no solace tonight. He heard a musical kaleidoscope in the distance, radiating from an assortment of venues and concert halls, beckoning to potential patrons and ticket-holders with the promise of an evening's entertainment and distraction.

Connor enjoyed a commanding view from the twentieth-floor balcony of the villa he shared with Darcy Peterson, his foster father. Here, in the Enclave's historic Oceanview, he normally found a sense of security and peace, a welcome respite from their secret war against the alien Givers.

Peace was decidedly absent tonight. The events of the past few days all but guaranteed it. Connor's hands shook as memories paraded through his mind, a laundry list of disaster. The implausible meeting arranged by Mateo and his band of so-called "Runners." Darcy's near-execution by a deranged savage—the girl with the disfigured arm. The sneak attack by a squadron of Trackers.

All eclipsed by a bombshell revelation ...

Connor's gaze fastened on the locket and chain he held. He turned his back on the brightly-lit commercial district and leaned against the balcony rail, opening the locket for the umpteenth time to stare in disbelief at the image inside.

His sister, Megan Sinclair.

Five years ago, the Cascadia Enclave Peace Wardens had informed Connor, after a painstaking investigation, that his parents and sister had been murdered by savages while on a family hunting trip. Cascadia's Infomedia outlets responded to the shocking news by stoking a prolonged and incendiary debate via nonstop public commentary.

The tragedy became the rallying point for a draconian overhaul of border security. Citizens of the Enclave, shocked and justifiably outraged by the savages' barbarism, voted unanimously to adopt the Council's proposed crackdown.

The Sinclair family legacy. Until yesterday.

Despite her disfiguring scars, and the patch covering one eye, Connor recognized her. The image inside his locket confirmed it. His sister was alive ... and held hostage by Mateo and his pack of savages.

"Connor? Did you hear what I said?"

Darcy's voice was sharper than usual. Connor, startled by his stealthy approach, clutched the locket in his fist, panicked by the prospect of dropping it off the balcony. He pivoted to face his foster father, his expression harder than he realized.

Darcy's mouth was open, about to issue orders. He caught sight of the silver chain dangling between Connor's fingers, and his lips tightened against his teeth. He stood motionless for several moments before speaking again.

"I've called for Tony," he said in a neutral tone of voice,

but his eyes blazed, hot and feverish. "We have a great deal of work ahead of us, and very little time in which to do it. I need you to—"

"Megan's alive," Connor interrupted, his voice low and grating. "The savages are holding her hostage."

Darcy closed his mouth. His expression was opaque, unreadable. "Yes," he said at last. "It appears so."

"That's it?" Connor's fist tightened on the locket.

Darcy placed a hand on his shoulder. Connor stiffened, unsure how to respond. Physical contact with Darcy was usually shrouded with an aura of menace. "I'm as shocked as you are, Connor. The Peace Warden's report said there were no survivors. There was so little left of the bodies—you know how the savages are. No one could have known she was still alive."

"They *tortured* her, Darcy," Connor said harshly. "You saw what they did to her. She didn't even recognize me ..." His voice broke and his eyes burned with unshed tears.

"They'll be punished, Connor, I swear to you." Darcy's grip turned into a claw, matching the ice in his eyes. "I can't imagine how traumatic it must have been for Megan, forced to watch the savages butcher your parents. It might have been more merciful if they'd killed her, as well. Holding her hostage all these years, abusing her to the point where she does their bidding ..." He paused for a heartbeat. "Or Mateo's."

Connor stared, stunned.

Darcy dropped his grip. "The savages we met last night, every last one of them, will be converted into drones—weapons against the aliens. Or we'll program them to target the collaborators on the Council." His eyes blazed with the fervor of his cause. And revenge. "If any of the savages survive, it won't be for long. Once Cascadia is under human-only control again, we won't need them. One way or another, the savages will atone for their brutality."

"It's all they're good for, anyway." Connor wiped his eyes with an impatient hand, a cold hatred settling into his chest. "They're animals, nothing more." He paused, eyeing his foster father. "And Mateo—what happens to him?"

Darcy smiled, an expression Connor found more chilling than his fits of rage. "Mateo Reyes is *mine*. Once we've dealt with the Givers, I'll teach that Judas Tracker some respect. It'll be the last lesson he learns."

The doorbell chimed. Connor followed Darcy into their gathering room. The door opened to admit Tony, their chauffeur and most recent recruit. He halted just inside the door, fiddling with his cap as if unsure of his welcome.

"I waited in the parkade." Tony spread his hands in a helpless, aimless gesture. "Cargo's loaded, thirty minutes ago—"

"No matter," Darcy said, cutting him off with a preemptive gesture. Tony was a decent chauffeur, but not the quickest thinker. Connor found him increasingly abrasive. "We were having a father-son conversation, but now that you're ready, we should be on our way."

Their trek down the hall was executed in absolute silence, as was an elevator descent to the parking garage. The Cascadia Security Monitoring Division, always vigilant against a possible incursion by savages, had been recently granted expanded powers by the ruling Council.

Connor had trouble curtailing his cynicism over the collaborators' blatant power grab.

Under the pretext of "internal security," the Givers and their human stooges had fast-tracked an increase of surveillance inside the Enclave. Darcy and his followers were too savvy to let casual words slip in an elevator—an obvious surveillance trap. Once inside their vehicle, engine running and windows closed, they dared to speak freely. Even so, they kept their voices low. Darcy leaned an elbow on the doorframe, cupping his chin on his hand to shield his face from exterior cameras.

"Clinic is prepped and ready," Tony mumbled into his collar, his words difficult to decipher. "Medical team standing by."

Connor edged forward in his traditional spot, the rear seat, directly behind his foster father. He would never presume to sit up front. "I'm trying to wrap my head around that Tracker ambush last night. How did they know where to find us?"

"Mateo Reyes," Darcy replied instantly, no hint of doubt in his voice. "It's impossible to pinpoint where his loyalties lie— always has been. I've long suspected he was playing one side against the other. It was only *after* the ambush that I deciphered the game he's playing." He paused, clearly enjoying the drama, holding his listeners in spellbound thrall.

Tony spoke first, his husky voice betraying the struggle between wariness and reckless curiosity. "Game? What kind of game are you talking about?"

Darcy rewarded him with an icy silence. Connor knew, without asking, that the chauffeur's over-eager query stole some of Darcy's thunder. Darcy tolerated nothing that cheated him from a moment of triumphant revelation.

They cleared the exit ramp and entered the express lanes on the traffic level before he spoke again.

"Mateo serves the Givers," he said with a knowing smile. "His plan was to lure us all, savages *and* Citizens, to the same location. A Tracker squadron could then easily slaughter us in a single, surgical strike. *Outside* the Enclave. The average Citizen would never hear a word about it."

Connor felt his blood boil at Mateo's treachery, but he kept his mouth shut. Speaking out of turn was Tony's domain.

Darcy leaned back in his leather chair. "Mateo's playing the Judas card on both sides of the fence. He's the ultimate collaborator, even lower than his kin on the Council." He turned to catch Connor's eye. "That's why, when the time comes, I'll deal with him. I want to see the look on his smug Tracker face when he realizes he didn't fool me. And then he'll die."

"And them?" Tony jerked a thumb over his shoulder, his attention riveted on the road. "What if they survive, or figure out what you've done to them?"

Now you've done it. Connor smirked. *Never, ever second-guess Darcy's strategy.*

"They won't, on either count," Darcy replied, his voice as frosty as the glare he threw at his chauffeur. The ensuing silence was more threatening than anything else he might have added. Tony caught on, and focused on driving.

Connor glanced into the cargo area behind him, reaching over the back of the seat to peel back a corner of the tarp. A pair of bodies lay side by side, breathing shallowly, tranquilized. Two of the so-called Runners, en route to Darcy's off-the-books clinic, and Implant surgery.

Connor studied their faces. The savages' leader, the one introduced by Mateo as Garr. And a woman, late-twenties, tall, athletic, long dark hair. He couldn't recall her name.

It didn't matter. Before night's end, they'd simply be drones DR-57 and DR-58.

For the good of the Enclave.

Where Trackers
fear to tread